The Scarecrow's Secret

An Alton Oaks Mystery

by

Megan Rivers

For information, email **Cozy Cat Press**, cozycatpress@aol.com or visit our website at: www.cozycatpress.com

ISBN: 978-1-946063-66-3

Printed in the United States of America

1 2 3 4 5 6 7 8 9 10

To Michigan Grandma (and her family) for being my
Alton Oaks away from home.

PROLOGUE

September 27, 2016
Dear Jackson,

I don't know where you are these days, but I figure if I send this to your parent's house, it'll eventually get to you. I owe you an explanation. Everyone tells me I should call you or answer your texts, but I'm not ready. I might never be ready. But here it goes.

Five months ago.

I still think back to that nothing-special morning when I rolled out of our empty bed, not knowing that it'd be the last time, not knowing where you were (again). Not knowing that twenty-four hours later, I'd be across the country wondering what the hell happened to us... to my life. Five months ago.

It was a rough day as a teacher. It was the kind of day where I couldn't help no matter how hard I tried. The I.C.E. came to the school, only this time they deported one of my students' family. That student's family was just taken from them. Suddenly, they had no home, no future. It was so rough to watch every other student shocked, surprised, and scared. Were they next? Would they have parents when they returned home that day? Would they be at school tomorrow? But this isn't about them.

All I wanted was to come home to your arms, for you to stroke the hair away from my face and tell me the things I needed to hear in order to have faith in humanity again. You know, how things used to be with us... in the beginning.

I knew you'd be at your studio, working towards your dreams, and I was okay with that. I supported you. But imagine how my heart swelled when I found the door to our apartment unlocked and your canvas bag was lying in the front hall! Knowing you were somewhere in our apartment already made me feel better.

Of course the bedroom door was closed—you were napping, right? You had been out all night. I urged myself not to go in right away; to give you a few more moments of peace. I actually went into the kitchen and made a snack before I crawled into bed with you, to shut out the world in your arms. Before I could steal a moment of simply us in my chaotic world.

I was at the kitchen table, leafing through the pile of mail, with half of an orange wedge in my mouth when I heard her voice. My heart stopped. How many times had I heard her flirtatious schoolgirl giggle or her moaning in ecstasy through the thin wall between our apartments? Only... only this time, she was a lot closer.

I didn't expect any of it and I don't know why. Denial, maybe. Naivety, more likely. But how many times did she come over, asking for a random object while looking over my shoulder? How often did you two walk upstairs from the mailbox together? Why didn't I see it coming?

I hate thinking about how slowly I got up and walked to the bedroom door. How my hand hesitated on the handle and my heart beat twice as fast. I hate how neither of you noticed me when I finally did open the door—too busy in the twisted sheets, moaning in the muted light from the roman shades I'd put in the window for you. How you didn't even have the decency to move our wedding photo from the dresser beside you.

What I hated the most, though, was that you chased after her. After I slammed the bedroom door and tried to justify what I saw, pacing in the living room and holding my head in disbelief. The scene kept replaying in slow motion, no matter how much I tried to tell myself I was dreaming—it wasn't real!—there had to be an explanation! You eventually came out dressed only in your cargo shorts.

I hated how I noticed how flushed your face was and how your collarbone glistened with beads of sweat when you asked what I was doing home already. How your blue eyes looked scared and concerned as you stumbled over your words—a mixture of apologies and "it's not what it seems."

And when Jessica—our neighbor in the next apartment who I made cookies for at Christmas, despite how much she interrupted our time together—when she tip-toed out behind you, as if putting her shirt in front of her face would help your case—you left my heartbroken side without a thought and followed her out our apartment door.

I watched your back—the way it curved from your shoulder blades and down to the waist band of your jockey shorts that peeked out from beneath your cargoes; the four birthmarks on your shoulder that I used to trace softly with my finger those lazy Sunday mornings—I watched it all leave our apartment, following the trail of her long blonde hair.

That's when it all changed... my whole life. I stared at that white interior, stuck in the moment. You left me. You really did it; you left me behind. I stared at those three scratches in the back of the door—the ones we made moving our new bed inside the day we signed the lease. You clearly and definitively made your choice and I had to make mine.

And I wanted to escape.

Do you know how much of my life in Albuquerque was spent waiting and hoping for you? How many nights I spent worrying if you'd come home or when you'd answer my text messages? How much time I spent blaming myself, putting myself down, drowning in self-doubt? All the things I didn't see before—your evasiveness, your purposeful distance, your out-of-the-room phone calls—filled the apartment around me, squeezing me, suffocating me. You checked out of our marriage a long time ago, didn't you?

Not me. That's what probably hurt the most. It was the twist of the knife; the salt in the wound. Because until the moment I watched you follow Jessica out the door, I still pictured us growing old together.

But not anymore.

Honestly, Jackson, I don't know where to go from here.

I guess the first step would be to actually talk, but the thought of hearing your side—truth or lies—hurts. I don't know if I'll ever get past it in order to hear your side—and all the while not wanting to run away screaming as your voice fills my ears and your eyes pierce my innocence; my naivety.

I want to yell at you.

I want an explanation from you.

And yet, I never want to see you again.

Dammit, Jackson! Was that you I heard in her bedroom on the nights I slept alone in our bed? When I fed her cat when she was out of town, were you with her instead of visiting your parents? Did you spend all those nights with her instead of me, using your work as an excuse? Did I really fall for it all?

Why in the hell wasn't I good enough for you? Why wasn't I worth it? Why didn't you have the decency to talk to me, to tell me? Why did I have to find out in our bed?

I just can't do this anymore, Jackson. Not now.

I'll be in touch, when I'm ready. When I figure out

what I want to do.

        —   *Charlotte*

I read the letter for what had to be the fiftieth time that night. A fly had squeezed through the screen of my bedroom window and hovered around the desk lamp. It buzzed an unsuccessful lullaby as I stuffed the letter into the addressed envelope. I had been taking it out and stuffing it back in indecisively for two hours now as night was slowly disintegrating into dawn.

Fall was in the breeze. Summer was coming to an end. In the early morning, just as the sun was rising, there was a chill in the bottom layer of air. For that hour or so, you could smell the crispness of fall instead of the humidity of summer. I took a deep breath as I stepped out onto the porch that morning. The sky started showing hints of light as the flies buzzed around the porch light and bats dove against the backdrop of dawn. I pulled my blue flannel shirt tighter around me, hearing the paper of the envelope crinkle in the chest pocket while I descended the stairs.

The crickets were still strumming as the birds began to wake and sing. My gym shoes kicked up the dirt of Oak Street, leaving a grimy layer of dust on my goose bump covered legs. There was an upstairs light on in Jake's house which flooded into the yard below. I had no doubt that he was getting ready for work.

Three months ago he told me to do something about Jackson before I snapped. He had kept his distance since.

He didn't know I struggled each day with putting my feelings into words. How many sleepless nights did I spend writing and rewriting letters? How many times did I find Jackson's number in my contact list and freeze in panic before I could call him? He didn't know I walked three other letters to the mailbox before, but didn't have the courage to mail them. Not even Sadie knew that.

It was this walk that was half the battle. The thirty minute trek into town was full of doubts and what-ifs, and maybe-I's, and too many whys. Meaningless sentences, darling proclamations, embarrassing cusses, red-faced memories, and I'm-not-good-enough ideas left a bloody battlefield in my head until I broke down in tears, tore up the letter, and told myself that I could bear this burden a little bit longer. I could confront Jackson another time... when I was stronger, healed, loved.

My breath came out in a shutter and before grief could hold me back and buckle my knees, I began to run. I imagined kicking up the dirt behind me on Oak Street, putting a barrier between that shadowy world and me. I focused on how my throat burned and my heart throbbed with life; that my legs felt strong, full of purpose. I trusted them to get me to where I needed to be.

My battered gym shoes slapped against the pavement now and my flannel shirt felt more like the cape of a superhero. I stopped only when I ran into the blue metal mailbox on the corner of Oak & Main. With my clammy hands grasping either side of the mailbox, I left myself breathe heavily. A thick breeze tucked my knotted hair behind my shoulders, my overgrown bangs sweeping across my vision.

Standing here, in this familiar spot, I once again found myself frozen. The horizon was dark in front of me. As I turned back east, where the Alton House stood somewhere in the distance, the first rays of sunshine were breaking through the clouds. The crisp scent of autumn tickled my nose and I took a deep cleansing breath of it once more. This corner—usually busy and loud in our small town—was quiet, hushed.

The letter seemed to gain weight sitting in my breast pocket, and I wondered if this wasn't going to be *the* trip—that I'd find myself walking another letter to this mailbox in a week and that maybe I should mail that one.

Just turn around, I told myself. *You're not ready. Go back home.*

A large gust of wind chased the leaves that already fell in the September air. Above me, the branches of the nearest oak tree were already spewing small, green acorns. Change. It was coming.

Today is *the day,* I told myself. It had been five months and six days since I left my husband and something needed to change.

I pulled open the mailbox and slipped the envelope out of the pocket from my shirt. With every ounce of courage I could muster, I dropped the envelope into the darkness and closed the metal door with a quiet but echoing bang that skipped down the empty streets.

Turning east to head home, I noticed the chilly hint of fall was disappearing from the air. Nevertheless, I inhaled deeply the last hint of it; change was on its way.

CHAPTER ONE

The morning sun was muted, hidden by a thin layer of fog as a repetitive pounding woke me from a well-deserved sleep. During the past six weeks, I had been holding a full-time, seasonal position at the hospital. My job was to plan, coordinate, hire, and be the overall point-person for Alton Oaks' annual Spooktacular Spook Show put on by the children's wing at St. Collette's Hospital on the west side of town. Sadie had bugged me about helping since July, and I finally gave in after I helped complete the Dee Dempsey Greenhouse and Outdoor Play Area for the Alton Oaks' school district. It was the birth of River Oaks Elementary's outdoor education program; the dream of a beloved teacher who died tragically at the end of the school year.

After working fourteen hour days and being endlessly tangled—literally—in the fake spider webbing for six weeks, the haunted house, character parade, and Boo Ball fundraiser went off without too many hiccups. Ever since the hospital was built—a little over ten years ago—these events kicked off a month long bill of fall activities in our town that always drew in Canaries—tourists not from Alton Oaks—who came to visit our renowned Whett River Canal Trail & Bike Path and spiked our local economy.

It started with the hospital's Spooktacular Spook Show and ended mid-November with the Miller's Farm Thanksgiving Table. Their old storage barn would be cleared of tools and machinery and set up for a beautiful potluck and dance—a tradition held since the 1940's when the Miller family first moved to Alton Oaks.

I had definitely earned a full night's sleep after running on coffee and blind hope for nearly two months. As I pulled the quilt from my tired eyes and groaned at the sun, I cursed whoever was making that racket.

The brisk air sent a chill down my back as it crawled up my bare arms and into the ratted holes of my Prey for Chance tour t-shirt that I coveted in junior high. I threw on a pair of warm red socks and the warm, plush hand-me-down robe from my sister, Bailey, in order to investigate and chastise.

The pounding persisted until the noise of wood creaking and snapping sharply interjected. As I climbed down the staircase, I noticed that the plastic canvas that hung at the entrance of the living room was draped aside. The Alton House was so old that parts of it were literally falling apart. The plastic canvas hung at the entrance of the living room for as long as I could remember to keep us out of its cold drafts, leaky holes, and hazardous dilapidation.

Rip Oakley—Alton Oaks' newest resident—was bent over the rotted wood of the window seat with a sledge hammer in his hands. His dark hair was normally gelled back, but was coming loose due to the weight of swinging around the sledgehammer. "What in the heck are you doing?" I asked, noticing the mound of damaged wood piling up in the corner.

Putting the sledgehammer down, and with a grin playing on the corner of his lips, he only reached for the tape measure in his tool belt.

I jumped off the last few stairs, the banister creaking loudly with my imbalance. "Rip!" I exclaimed and dashed towards him with a look that demanded an answer. He was literally tearing apart my house!

"Charlotte May I!" I heard my father's nickname for me and I slowly turned in my stocking feet. The weatherized plastic that hung in the windows swelled and sucked from an outside breeze. "You better put some shoes on," my dad instructed as he rounded the corner in his work clothes, holding a cup of coffee. The necktie he wore was covered in orange pumpkins and curly green vines; I recognized it from my childhood.

"Dad," I started, confused and a bit agitated from the lack of sleep. "What," I said dramatically, "the hell?"

"Rip's starting work today," he explained and then took a long sip from his World's Best Dad mug. He leaned on the cracked archway with a glimmer of happiness that comes from the first sip of morning coffee.

Confusion soaked my expression.

"The renovation..." my dad trailed off, hoping it sparked my memory. I only lifted an eyebrow.

Rip dropped another piece of rotting wood onto the blue tarp a few feet from where we were standing. His eyes caught mine for a moment and amusement at my temperament twinkled in his eyes. I'm sure my disposition, on top of my exhausted expression and frazzled bedhead hair, was amusing to anyone not as irritated as I was.

"Didn't your mother tell you?" my father asked as he backed out of the foyer to be out of Rip's way.

My eyes searched the cracked ceiling for a forgotten conversation with my mother as I followed my father into the dining room. My mother was the Queen of Gossip in our small town and was always talking about something to someone. She could normally be found on the front porch gabbing away with her regular circle of hens.

Slowly, I shook my head in response.

"About a month ago your mom and Mrs. Lupizo— she's the head of the historical society now—found out they were approved for a grant that they applied for in order to fix up the house after it became an Illinois Historical Landmark last winter... or was it the winter before?" My dad scratched the back of his neck in thought. "Either way," he continued, "your uncle suggested we try and keep the work local to support small town businesses. And Rip just happened to start his own handyman business. It was perfect timing."

The little noises Rip made with his tools seemed to prick irritatingly at my aggravation. I wiped my overgrown bangs from my forehead and sighed with impatience. "Doesn't one need licenses and permits to do work like this?" I asked, realizing I was going to lose a lot of mornings sleeping past eight o'clock.

"Got 'em all, Charlotte May," Rip said, dropping more debris onto the tarp on the edge of the foyer with a wink. He was getting a kick out this and knew using my full name would hit a nerve.

I turned back to my father who glanced at his wristwatch. "Sorry, Charli," he said and placed his mug on the scratched dining room table that my grandfather had built my grandmother for their twenty-fifth wedding anniversary. "I have to get going. Ask your mom about it. I'm sure she could use your help down at the library anyway."

Backing up, I stood below the staircase and watched my dad leave the house with a bicycle helmet under his arm. Rip began pounding again, out of my line of sight, and a chill traveled up my legs, settling into my shoulders. I looked up at the stained glass window above the door and groaned.

After a hot shower, and layered in warm clothes, my disposition changed. Sure, it was still noisy and I was still sleep-deprived, but at least this winter wouldn't be as drafty with the updates. The thought of the cold winter air made my shoulders wiggle with a chill. After three years of living in Albuquerque and two years in the subtropical weather of Costa Rica, I wasn't sure if my body was ready for a Midwest winter, despite having spent my childhood in it, undeterred.

"Hey, Charli?" Rip's voice wandered through the first floor until it found me pouring a cup of coffee in the kitchen. The leaves outside the kitchen window were orange and brown in the silhouetted morning light and it made me smile.

"Yeah?" I answered loudly, hoping he could hear me from the living room. I added a splash of milk to the mug, determined not to start my day until I had devoured one heaping serving of caffeine.

"When did you say this house was built?" A loud pound accompanied his answer followed by wood creaking.

"Um," I said in thought and then took several long gulps from my Fozzie Bear mug. My brother, sister and I continued to keep our Muppets mugs in our parent's cupboard despite moving out. Mom said it was to remind us that we always have a place to come home to. I smiled at Alex's worn Gonzo mug sitting next to Bailey's Miss Piggy mug as I closed the cupboard door with a squeaky thud.

Rip's question echoed in my head as I urged the caffeine to wake up the part of the brain I needed to answer his question. As I made my way to the living room, I thought about the research I did on my ancestors this past spring for the elementary school's Heritage Night. "He built it in 1916," I reported, stopping in the archway that led into the living room. I leaned on the chipped varnish and took another sip of coffee feeling the warm liquid travel down my body.

Rip had already ripped out the decaying wood of the window seat and was inspecting the wiring he had exposed. "What about the wiring?" he asked as he knelt beside the mess he had made. He hadn't realized I had entered the living room and his voice was louder than it should have been.

"Not sure," I responded nonchalantly. His head shot up in my direction as if I had startled him. "So what exactly are you doing to the Alton House with this grant money?" I asked as I closed my eyes and took another sip from the nostalgic mug.

There were 1960-era furniture pieces throughout the living room. Two olive green womb swivel chairs sat near the fireplace, though the vinyl was cracked and covered in a thick layer of dust. A white sheet covered the orange tufted sectional. That couch always looked uncomfortable with its low back and painfully flat cushions and low, equally miserable arm rests. A wooden coffee table with a round face and faux-golden bulbous legs stood shakily in front of the couch. The chipped varnish and paint made the table look like a war-torn victim. The multi-level end tables on either side of the couch held lamps with ancient light bulbs that were so old, they were reliable and had yet to burn out. When it would rain, we'd turn on the lamps and lay out buckets for the leaks using the light that escaped from behind the tweed lampshades.

Besides keeping up with rain damage, this room was never used; the furniture smelled musty and old. I did, however, see old pictures from when my mom was a kid and not one thing had changed about the living room besides the amount of dust and darkness. Currently, there was canvas covering much of the ancient furniture and the heavy, dust-coated drapes had been taken down from their perches, letting an over abundance of sunshine permeate the corners that were stained in decades of shadows.

Growing up, our family never spent much time on this side of the house because of the state it was in. It was old. Even Alex had to be careful trekking across the loft above the north wing to get to his bedroom; there was a hole in the floorboards that Uncle Randy and Dad never quite fixed permanently. Until Alex left for college, he carefully crossed the sheet of plywood each sleepy-eyed morning and exhausted night.

The kitchen of the Alton House was slightly newer and my family was either on the front porch or, in the weatherized back porch in the winter. There was an old TV that gave off heat and a potbelly stove to keep us warm, though it was a serious fire hazard.

Rip snuck a glance at me while he fiddled with the exposed wall. "You honestly don't know what I'm doing here?" he asked with a hint of amusement in his voice. "Your mother has talked of not much else for weeks."

I had been so busy with the Spook Show and didn't care much to gossip with my mother and the other women who congregated on our porch. I shrugged at his comment and took a long gulp from the mug; my coffee cooling faster in the chill than I had hoped.

Rocking back on the balls of his feet, Rip looked up at me and said, "I'm fixing up the living room here, the library, and the study." He threw a thumb behind him, at the room in the back of the house that was lined in dusty, dark bookshelves. I feared that any of the ancient books back there would disintegrate with the slightest touch. "It looks like we'll have to put in new insulation in the exterior walls, weatherize the windows, and get an electrician out here to update the wiring—you're practically living in a tinder box," he added. I supposed the two-prong outlets were a bit dated and dangerous when often a spark accompanied plugging in an appliance.

My eyes traveled out the window above Rip, where I could just make out my sister's house. The white farmhouse stood quaint and charming in the distance with its red trim and colorful autumn decor; an image almost as perfect as my little sister seemed to be. I sighed.

"This is the original part of the house, right? Built by Andrew Alton?" Rip asked, getting to his feet. The red and black flannel shirt he wore was unbuttoned and danced around the white t-shirt beneath.

I was surprised at how much he remembered from my presentation four months ago. "Yeah," I answered. "These three rooms, the library, most of the dining room and the front porch. There used to be a bedroom next to the kitchen, but it burned in the fire. When they repaired the space after the fire, they just turned that room into more cupboard and counter space for the kitchen."

Rip's eyes moved around the room as he took off his leather work gloves. "I'm going to have to hire extra help," he commented.

"Is your first real job as Alton Oaks' 'handyman extraordinaire' too daunting?" I asked, half-joking and half-hoping I struck a nerve to get even with him for mocking me with my full name earlier.

Taking a small notebook and golf pencil from the back pocket of his faded blue jeans, he rolled his eyes. "Nothing can be as difficult as fixing Mrs. Fitzgerald's sink," he said, jotting down a few notes.

Mrs. Fitzgerald was widowed back when I was in junior high. As kids we knew to steer clear of her house even if she had free cookies beside her folding lawn chair or when she was handing out king-size candy bars on Halloween. One hello led to three hours of a one-sided conversation monopolized by Mrs. Fitzgerald and her longing memories of "the good ole days." If ever a child was late for dinner, the first place a parent would check was Mrs. Fitzgerald's front yard when we'd welcome and even thank our chastising mothers for salvaging what was left of our afternoon.

"How long did she keep you?" I asked with a smirk.

Lining up the measuring tape to the height of the window, Rip replied exaggeratedly, "Seven *hours*."

A chuckle tripped over my lips and I covered it with another swig of coffee.

"The sink led to fixing the water heater to replacing the filter, to unclogging the bathroom drain. She insisted on giving me a coffee break with freshly baked coffee cake. I fell for it, hook, line, and sinker." Rip gracefully moved the tape measure from one angle to the other and recorded numbers as he explained, "I finally got out of there when I told her I needed to pick up a chilled horizon pin from the hardware store to fix the temperature in the fridge."

"A chilled horizon pin?" I asked, shifting my weight from my perch against the archway. "What's that?" I asked. The first apartment Jackson and I had together was a renovated attic on the outskirts of Albuquerque. Within the first month the refrigerator died. Both Jackson and I tried to fix it until we ended up living out of a cooler for awhile. Perhaps this chilled horizon pin was the piece we could have used.

Rip let the tape measure slap back into its metal container and gave me a guilty look. "No idea. I made it up. I've been telling her it's on back order."

I couldn't help but laugh. "You have to eventually go back, you know," I said and emptied the mug in my hands in one swift gulp. "If you get on Mrs. Fitzgerald's bad side, you won't find much more work here. She's the head of the Women's Guild at the church, and her opinion holds a lot of weight. You tick her off, your business is as good as gone," I surmised.

"I know," he admitted, writing more measurements in his notebook. "But I'm hoping I can hire an intern or two through the high school and just send them."

"That's horrible," I commented.

For a few moments I stared at the faded face of Fozzie Bear and mourned my empty mug as Rip carefully and meticulously took and recorded measurements throughout the living room. He was going to be busy for awhile. He knew what he was going to do each day; each hour filled with purpose. Now that the Spook Show was over, my days were suddenly bleak. Bleak and starkly empty.

"You know," I started, looking down at my comfy brown moccasins. I took a tentative step into the living room. "If you need some help with this project, I could assist you."

Rip cast a doubtful eye to me over his shoulder, resting the tape measure on the mantel of the fireplace. "You?" he asked, almost as if I had told a joke.

Offensively, I remarked, "Yeah. I volunteered at Habitat for Humanity every spring in college. I can install bookshelves, put up drywall, patch up plaster, re-cement bricks in the fireplace." I took a breath and stood a little straighter, looking directly at Rip's doubtful profile. "I can do anything just as good as you can here."

I was pleased when he lifted an eyebrow in surprise. "Like install a chilled horizon pin in Mrs. Fitzgerald's refrigerator?" he asked.

With exaggeration, I rolled my eyes. A strong breeze rustled the plastic on the windows, cutting into the weight of the silence in the room. Rip leaned his head to the side in thought before giving in. "I guess every master needs an apprentice."

Suppressing yet another eye roll, I relaxed the

tension in my shoulders and declared, "I am not going to call you 'master,'"

Rip's eyebrows rose in surprise so that they touched the gelled hair that fell out of place. "Can I at least throw in some 'You're fired!' puns?" he asked in jest, referring to the television show *The Apprentice*.

It was almost scary at how good his Donald Trump impression was. With a smile, I crossed my arms over my chest and shook my head. "Absolutely not."

CHAPTER TWO

After spending six weeks living and breathing Spook Show, and catching sleep and eating when I found available pockets of time, the sudden void in my day was difficult. It reminded me of the culture shock I got when I first moved to Costa Rica: The disorientation of seeing everything in another language; having to work around the weather: the full-on downpours every afternoon that prevented any kind of travel; the extremely strong sun that burned any part of my Norwegian exposed skin; the dirtiness, the busy streets, the currency, the dialect—how to communicate basic needs using my American school-taught Spanish. Everything I once knew was gone and I had to adjust to a different world in order to survive.

The word *vacuous* echoed in my head, which probably was what led me to vacuum my room. It was a task that I'm not sure had been done since I was a senior in high school—nine years ago! Dragging the large behemoth (that had to be at least ten years my senior) across the no-longer black and white checkerboard-printed rug in my room, led to vacuuming the hallway. And then the museum of dust in Alex's and Bailey's old rooms. And the spare room beside mine that I'm sure had at least one rodent resident amongst the boxes and plastic bags of storage. I was about to tackle the cob webs in the worn down loft above the library and study when the beast moaned and screamed to have its bag changed.

The Alton House was drafty, especially during

breezy days like this one, but I was working up a sweat. I wiped away the beads of hard work on my forehead with the crook of my elbow as I came down the stairs, holding the full, dust-covered vacuum bag at arm's length. As I reached the bottom stair, I suddenly wondered if we even had a replacement bag, or if they even made replacement bags for that heirloom anymore.

When I emerged from the kitchen, shaking the dirt and dust off my hands, Rip was squatting by the front door, closing his metal toolbox with a clank. "Done for the day already?" I tisked.

Rip glanced at his stainless steel wristwatch whose deep blue face looked too big on his wrist. "It's two o'clock," he reported. "I'm taking a lunch. Hungry?"

I raised my eyebrows at his offer, surprised. My stomach quaked in response and I realized all I had consumed that day were two cups of coffee and the last chocolate chip cookie in Dad's Star Wars-themed cookie jar. "Yes," I said and grabbed my fleece sweater from the front hall closet. "Oakie's?" I asked.

"My treat," Rip said with uncharacteristic kindness and followed me out the door.

The air was warmer outside despite the breeze and complimented the perfect autumn blue sky against the changing colors of the few maple trees on Oak Street.

"I didn't know you were home," I remarked, surprised to see my mother perched on the porch between our neighbor Mrs. Kratsky, my sister Bailey, and Mrs. Sullivan—the co-owner of The Buzz Coffeeshop downtown. It was unusual to see her on this side of town, but I figured she made a special delivery of muffins and coffee to the town's Gossip Queen since scandalous news was at an all-time low. "Oh, hi, Mrs. Sullivan," I greeted and nodded to the regular crew on the front porch.

"You were busy upstairs," Mom shared. Her eyes followed Rip as he neglected to acknowledge them and made a beeline towards his motorcycle. It was parked in the gravel driveway beside Mrs. Kratsky's golf cart, which was decked out in metallic pumpkin garland that fluttered in the breeze. That city boy still had a lot to learn about manners in a small town. "I didn't want to bother you," my mother added, her eyes returning to me.

I wasn't yet sure if she didn't like, or just didn't trust Rip. Or possibly both. She, much like many other residents of our small-minded town, didn't like outsiders. They were always quick to point the finger of any wrong-doing to the stranger from the city. To her credit though, my mother chose what was best for the town over what was best for her and hired a local for the house. I'm sure the prodding elbow of her older brother, who happened to be the town mayor, and the gossip that would ensue to her mutiny had affected her decision too.

Rip kick-started the motorcycle and it roared to life as if to tell me to hurry up. I waved to my mother to cut short our conversation. "I'll be back," I informed. "Food," was the only detail I shared as I ran from the porch, leaving my mother's reply to be eaten by the sound of the roaring engine.

"You know I hate this thing," I said when I caught up to Rip. He was sitting comfortably on the bike and extended his helmet to me before I even asked for it.

It wasn't my first time on his motorcycle. This past summer Rip gave me a ride home which ended in a jaunt in a police vehicle. "Can't we walk there?" I asked. Taking the helmet from him, I looked longingly down the road, my stomach rumbling.

"I'm not sure I trust your mother," Rip said, stealing a glance behind me, "not to put saw dust in the gas tank or 'accidentally' hit my bike with a pipe."

I lifted my eyebrows in surprise by his bluntness; I didn't doubt there was truth on both parts. "Fine," I said, giving in.

Oakie's Bar & Grill was Alton Oaks' only restaurant. My dad had been working there since he was in high school, when he commuted from Sheridan in his sky-blue 1962 hand-me-down Ford pick-up truck. It's where he met my mother—despite attending the same high school—as she desperately spent a roll of dimes trying to get a small, plush Star Wars Ewok from the claw machine near the entrance door.

Oakie's was where we grew up, having dinner with Dad after he was promoted from Kitchen Supervisor to Assistant Manager and eventually to Head Manager. It was where every Alton Oaks high schooler went with their date before homecoming, which was this past weekend. The outdoor patio was still decorated in the extra lights and outdoor heaters with decals of the school's mascot stuck to every window. Oakie's was such a huge part of being an Alton Oak citizen that heaving open the heavy interior doors was like coming home. I smiled when the scent of Oscar's bacon-wrapped appetizers greeted me as if they were a warm smile welcoming me back.

"Charlotte May I!" my father's chipper voice called to me from behind the counter of display pies. His pumpkin-themed necktie swayed as he turned round to the front, simply glowing. This was my father's happy place, there was no doubt about that. He emerged from behind the counter with a rib-cracking hug. I don't think he had quite grown accustomed to me being back in town and popping in to see him now and again.

"Rip Oakley," my dad greeted and extended his hand in greeting. "Nice to see you again. How's the first day at the house coming along? Are you taking a break to finish your tasting of the World Tour of Beers?"

Rip gave my dad a firm handshake. "You know I'm partial to the German darks, but I think I'll leave the Swedish Pale Ales for another, more daring day. Besides," he added in good humor, "I don't drink in the middle of a job; very unprofessional."

"Smart man," my dad said approvingly. The skin beside his eyes creased with his smile. "Are you two sharing a table?" he asked without waiting for a response. He grabbed two menus from behind the host's podium and said, "Follow me. I'll get you set up right away."

We followed my father's frame through the dimly lit entrance and into the restaurant where only a few of the red and cream vinyl booths were occupied by late lunchers like ourselves.

Fluttering a hand, he showed us to a table beside the fireplace. It wasn't a real fireplace, but an LCD screen inside the hearth showed the image of a crackling fire on chilly days. Currently, an arrangement of pumpkins and other colorful gourds sat around a cauldron where a vibrantly colored frog sat beside an owl. They both looked as if they belonged amongst a young girl's stuffed animal collection. I suddenly wondered what happened to Bailey's and my old stuffed animals.

"Here you go," Dad said as he handed us the menus. "I'll have Sandy come by to take your drinks." He disappeared into the kitchen without another word, leaving Rip and me to an uncomfortable silence.

I opened the leather bound menu, already knowing what I wanted, but scanning for new dishes amongst the pages never hurt anyone.

A loud thump suddenly turned everyone's heads to the nearest window. Outside, a truck was unloading an acorn the size of a fire hydrant onto the sidewalk outside Oakie's. It was an Alton Oaks tradition that the local businesses loved. The night after the acorns were placed, employees of local business would creep out in the middle of the night and claim an acorn by painting it with a clever or colorful advertisement. It was always exciting to see the town installing the acorns because everyone knew that night would contain thrill and excitement. Many people discreetly rushed to the hardware store and nonchalantly bought a few spray cans of paint like it was an every day purchase. I'm not sure how the tradition of sneakily doing it at night happened, but it made co-workers feel a sense of camaraderie. Even now, at Oakie's, I could see the servers exchange clandestine smiles.

"This town goes all out, doesn't it?" Rip asked and then returned his gaze to his menu. "Can't wait to see what you all do for Christmas," he muttered with a hint of sarcasm.

His comment rubbed me the wrong way. "Just because you wouldn't know fun if it bit you in the butt doesn't mean—" I stopped myself before I had any regrets. Sure, Alton Oaks wasn't the perfect town, but it was home. It was a place that still cherished tradition.

I straightened my silverware on the cloth napkin and counted to ten before I added, "You should at least try to be part of the town spirit if you want this to be your home—especially if you want more clients. The Fall Festival starts tomorrow. You should probably check it out before you criticize it." I mean even Jackson read the *Twilight* series before he very publicly criticized it... to anyone who would listen. *Any. One.*

Rip's eyebrows arched. It was like he could see a storm behind my eyes and was waiting for it to die down, dumbfounded by its presence. "A Fall Festival?" he asked, critically. "How utterly and alliteratively creative."

Trying a new tactic, I sat up straighter and adapted a persuasive, excited tone. "It's a lot of fun. The Miller's Farm creates a corn maze—and the first person to find the scarecrow gets to present the Parade of Scarecrows along the Canal next week. There's hayrides, pig races, taffy apples, pumpkin carving, live music, bon fires..." I trailed off, getting lost in the happy thoughts of my past.

"Sounds cliché," Rip pointed out frankly.

He had a point. But this is Illinois—the heartland: Farmland of the great U.S. of A. This was tradition. "What, are you afraid you'll have fun and tarnish your image?" I asked, dripping with attitude. My tone completely shifted and I even surprised myself with the amount of gusto in my words.

I could see in his eyes that I hit a nerve. A spark flew into his hard, amber eyes "I'm regretting bringing you to lunch," he admitted. His lips quivered with the words he was holding back.

Smugly, I folded my hands and innocently responded, "Oh?"

Rip moved slowly, building anxiety as to what he'd do next. Closing his menu and placing it on the table, he picked up his fist that was tanned by working outdoors all summer. He measured barely a centimeter between his thumb and forefinger as he said in a gravelly voice, "I am this close to ordering a four-course meal, including a steak, eating it through a charming but unbelievably fake smile that ignores every word out of your mouth. Then foot you with the bill as I walk out of the front door without looking back."

He didn't scare me, but I didn't dare roll my eyes at him either. I knew that most of the time he was all bark and no bite. "Aren't you country girls supposed to be charming anyway? Seen, not heard?" he asked in a lighter tone. He found what he was looking for in my eyes and justly picked up the menu, returning his gaze to the page of red meat.

Without a thought, I slapped his menu onto the table. The metal corners thunked onto the surface, turning the heads of the elderly couple close by. "I," I started, piercing Rip's eyes with the fury of a woman, "am not that kinda country."

He didn't look away and I refused to back down. After what seemed like an hour, I pulled my hand from the plastic pages of the menu and in a lighter, silvery voice added, "And that comment was very condescending to all women."

Rip let out a small breath of impatience. He picked up his menu and continued his browsing without a word. I watched his eyes move back and forth across the options from behind my own menu and wondered if he had the nerve to dine and dash, leaving me with the bill. I knew he was all talk. I had met so many boys like him in college who spoke so many words, but offered very little action. Getting on each others' nerves was becoming a regular occurrence between us. I sighed. Things had to change.

"Come to Fall Fest with me tomorrow. You'll see," I offered.

Clearly irked by my uncensored female tongue, he replied coldly, "And why should I do that?"

Swallowing the wrong reply, I offered, "If you go through the corn maze and are the first one to find the scarecrow, I will work as free labor for your company until Christmas." I neglected to remind him that he'd have to present the Parade of Scarecrows, but at least this way it was a win-win for me.

His eyes lit up with intrigue. Finally he extended a hand and, with a smile, replied, "You've got a deal."

Until Sandy—a gray-haired woman with the spunk

of a twenty-year old—arrived to take our orders, smacking her gum, our chatting was non-existent after that. While we waited for our food, I played with my silverware, went through two glasses of coke, and people-watched. It had gotten to the point where I almost forgot Rip was there, as he stoically, and with very few movements, scrolled through the screen on his phone. It wasn't an uncomfortable silence, but after spending so much time around my gossiping mother and Sadie, who was always brimming over with questions, it was a subdued—almost surreal—company to be in.

Just after Sandy dropped our hot plates onto the table, I saw Sadie and Alex round the corner, looking for a place to sit. "Sadie!" I beckoned her over with a smile. "Alex!" I exclaimed even more excited to see my older brother than my best friend. Sadie and Alex had been dating for not quite a year and a half now, despite not telling me for the first ten months. I didn't blame them though, I had been busy in Albuquerque and didn't come back to Alton Oaks very often. They were my two favorite people in town, so the news only made me ecstatic.

I popped out of my seat for a hug while Rip looked up briefly from cutting his steak. "What are you guys up to?" I asked, leaning against the booth, not yet ready to rejoin Rip's company.

"It's one of those weird, scarce days where we both are off work," Sadie responded, sticking a hand into the pocket of her skinny jeans. Her eyes traveled down to Rip and back to me. I knew I would get pummeled later by her inquisitive text messages.

"Technically, I'm on-call," Alex shared and ran a hand over the pager clipped to his belt. My brother was a doctor at the hospital while Sadie worked as a nurse in the children's wing. They also lived a few houses from each other in downtown Alton Oaks.

Alex wore a thick, tan coat that didn't make him look so lanky. "What are you guys up to?" he asked, pushing his wire-framed glasses up his nose.

"We were just talking about Fall Fest tomorrow," I shared and glanced down at Rip who filled his mouth with a forkful of steak and potatoes. "I talked Rip into finding the scarecrow."

Both Sadie and Alex's eyes widened in surprise as they swept their gaze past me, to Rip. He was still chewing and failed to comment.

"Are you guys going?" I asked, hopeful.

Sadie regretfully shook her head.

"Sorry, Charli May," Alex said. "Work."

Sadie looked crestfallen. "I have practice in the morning," she shared. I had all but forgot that she was the new head volleyball coach at the high school. She ripped up the court back in the day, despite her size; she even got a partial scholarship to Loyola University. "Then I have to run to Springfield and drop off one of my mom's tables," she added. Before Sadie's dad retired from his law firm and her parents moved to Florida, her mom was a skilled woodworker. Sadie still had her mom's tools and many of her pieces in a storage shed.

I guess I shouldn't have been too upset that I wouldn't see her. After all, I was with her for nearly six weeks, running the Spook Show. We were always seeing each other in the halls of the children's wing and leaving each other cups of coffee and amusing, hand-drawn, post-it note cartoons. "Oh well," I remarked.

I guessed Sadie felt the same as she also sighed. "Oh!" she exclaimed, suddenly perking up. "We have a home game tonight. You should come! When was the last time you saw the high school? Graduation, right? You should come too!" Sadie said, extending the invitation to Rip.

I found it comical that he had just shoveled another forkful into his mouth and couldn't verbally decline the invitation. Jumping on the chance to make Rip uncomfortable, I replied, "Yes! Definitely! We'll be there!" And though Rip gave me a look that could curdle milk as he chewed, I thought that maybe it would be the dose of small-town he needed to change his pessimistic city-boy mind.

"What if I had plans?" Rip asked as we walked into the late afternoon air outside of Oakie's. He was *still* complaining about having to go.

"Do you?" I asked, raising an eyebrow as we walked to where his motorcycle was parked.

He ignored the question and grumbled, "I didn't even like going to my own high school."

"That's 'cause you've never been to a high school out here in the sticks with us country folk," I mocked, putting on the helmet and mounting the bike.

More to himself than to me, he remarked, "Please don't let it be in a little, red, one-roomed schoolhouse." The bike then roared to life, cutting off my chance at a comeback.

The ride up Oak Street didn't take more than ten minutes with his ignorance regarding the speed limits and no passing zones. It was almost four o'clock when Rip parked the motorcycle in his driveway. The clouds in the east, just behind the Alton House, were already blotting out light with the promise of an early evening. I was surprised to see a vehicle parked in the Alton driveway and wondered if Mrs. Sullivan ever left or if a new, nosy resident had stopped by for gossip.

I didn't complain to Rip about how I'd have to walk the thousand or so feet to the Alton House from his front yard—he had zero charm—I just sighed as I handed him the helmet. At this point, I was just happy he didn't ditch me at Oakie's with the bill.

With no sarcastic remark leaving my lips, I began trudging up the road, knowing full well he wouldn't be around when it was time to go to the volleyball game. A few yards later, he caught up to me and kept pace. "Are you suddenly being a gentleman?" I asked, shocked that he was walking me home.

Without an eye roll, sigh of agitation, or any hint of emotion, he replied, "Don't flatter yourself. I still have some work to do and I'd rather not leave my bike near your mother." He nodded towards the Alton House where I could make out shapes of people on the porch in the distance. "Besides," he added with a hint of amusement, "if I can make your life a little harder, why not?"

His tone was in jest and it was clear that our friendship would be the kind that kept poking fun at each other, when we weren't grating on each other's nerves. Giving in, I replied, "Charming as ever, city boy."

As we approached the gravel driveway of the Alton House, I noticed that the vehicle was not Mrs. Sullivan's white van with The Buzz Coffeeshop's logo emblazoned on the side. This was a plain white van. With a patch of rust near the rear bumper in the shape of the letter T. One with New Mexico license plates.

"Oh no." I panicked and froze. My feet were heavy, suddenly rooted to the spot as I knew exactly who that van belonged to.

Rip stopped a few feet ahead, suddenly aware that I wasn't walking beside him. "What?" he asked as if I was about to comment on how annoying he was walking, or breathing, or being. His demeanor changed as soon as he turned back and saw my face.

"Charlotte!" Jackson called from his perch inside the

sliding side door.

"Who's that?" Rip asked, looking from the man in ripped jeans and a paint-splattered t-shirt to me.

"Jackson," I said. The word was unpleasantly sticky in my mouth. "My husband."

CHAPTER THREE

I wanted to cry. Then I wanted to scream. I wanted to explode... just *not* in Alton Oaks, *not* in front of my mother and her gossip club who were looking on with obvious interest from the front porch. Their mugs of coffee and tea were frozen at their lips as if I couldn't see them hiding behind them with wide eyes.

Instead of fighting, I took flight. I did not want to tarnish Alton Oaks—my safe haven of a hometown—with the splatter of my failed marriage. Turning on the spot, I kicked up dust in the driveway as my face grew warm and I gritted my teeth. A torrential downpour of swear words were muttered under my breath as I took off down Oak Street. I was careful not to run because it seemed childish. For some reason running meant crying and I was done wasting my tears.

"Charlotte! Wait!" Jackson called after me. My chest burned with fury and I unzipped the fleece sweater as my feet carried me across my escape route.

"Wait," Rip said, jogging to catch me. "Is that—?"

"Yes," I said through clenched teeth, staring straight ahead. My eyes did not leave the path in which I was following. My fists were balled at my side. I could feel my fingernails piercing the flesh of my palms and I concentrated on the pain. I really wanted to hit something and I didn't mind it being Rip.

"But didn't he—?" Rip continued, jogging once more to keep up with me.

"Yes," I replied once again in a tone that would turn Medusa to stone.

The sound of a vehicle approaching from behind made me pick up my pace. "Charlotte!" Jackson called from the driver's seat of his van. "Just stop for a minute."

"I owe you nothing," I spat without hesitation, seeing Rip's motorcycle getting closer with each step.

"Charlotte, come on," Jackson said as if I was being childish.

It never crossed my mind that he might be here to patch things up. In my head it was already over; he was here to make me feel worse for leaving him. But isn't that what he always did? When I would talk to him about his staying out all night, "working in his studio," or after an "all-night gallery opening," he would make me feel like I was not supportive. "You don't believe in me or my work, do you?" he'd ask, feigning a face that cracked with hurt feelings. "I'll just give up my dreams and get a desk job for you, I guess," he'd add with a measured amount of guilt. Eventually, I'd give in and encourage him to spend as much time in his studio as he wanted. I wouldn't be lonely. I would be okay; I was just being childish.

"I told you I would contact you when I was ready!" I said too loudly and lowered my voice. "You don't get to decide when that is!"

I swept up Rip's driveway as Jackson once again pleaded for my attention. "Charlotte—"

"—Look," Rip said, cutting him off and coming between the van and me as it began to pull into his driveway. "Man, you should—"

I was thankful for how intimidating Rip was at that moment with his bad boy swagger and dark threatening gaze. The poor guy had nothing on me though, and I cut him off. "—Let's go!" I demanded, saddling up on the motorcycle.

Rip ran up beside me as Jackson pulled the van

along the road. I knew Rip really wanted to go off on me for touching his bike—for so fiercely getting on and probably nicking it. "I don't think—" he started with an I-know-better-than-you gaze.

With a look that could wilt flowers, I demanded in two clear, distinct, devil-evoked words, "Get on."

Surprised and grateful that he complied, I silently urged him to speed faster as we merged onto US-16 and left Jackson's headlights somewhere near Blackhill Avenue.

My nails dug into Rip's leather jacket. The wind ferociously tossed my hair and ripped at my face. When I realized that I'd neglected to put on the helmet, I didn't care. I was throwing caution into the wind. No amount of physical pain would hurt as much as what Jackson had put me though... was putting me through.

After we passed into Sheridan, Rip pulled into the visitor's center parking lot. The sun was low in the sky, but it was still bright. It filtered between the maple leaves almost making them seem as if they were on fire. Fallen foliage littered the ground and covered the picnic tables like a tablecloth.

Rip cut the engine and jumped off the bike. "Get off," he said flatly. Now that Jackson was gone, I didn't doubt that Rip was going to, well, rip into me for using him and his bike the way I did. If he wanted to argue, I would be more than happy to oblige.

I slipped off the leather seat and popped up alongside him, ready to yell and scream if he was to provoke. My adrenaline was still pumping and I wanted to holler and stomp away the pain that transformed into anger when I saw Jackson's face.

Puffed up with angry energy, I jabbed Rip in the back with my finger. "If you think—"

Rip turned, put up his palms, and cut me off. "Punch me," he demanded.

"What?" I said, taken aback. If he was taking this matter lightly, it would only add fuel to my fire. I was tired of men not taking me seriously. Did he really want me to hurt him? He was actually inviting me to cause physical harm? He was going to be sorry.

"Seriously," he said with his palms still up. He looked directly into my eyes, completely serious. "Punch my hands," he said again. "As hard as you can."

He planted his feet and bent his knees to field any blow. Without hesitating, I punched as hard as I could with my right hand. It felt good. Again I punched and Rip didn't wince or flinch. He stood calmly and watched my fists.

The punches came one after the other. Even when what felt like empty tears fell, I punched at my blurry targets. One, two, three, four. I threw punch after punch until my knuckles were raw, the collar of my shirt was damp, and I started to feel the cold breeze instead of the warm blood coursing ferociously through my body.

Finally, my hands fell to my sides and I took a deep breath of the dusk, laced with the scent of burning wood.

"Better?" Rip asked. His palms were red, but he didn't portray a hint of pain.

I nodded. The wave of anger subsided.

"Home?" Rip asked, putting his hands down.

The world seemed clearer now, like someone had removed the aged newspaper from a boarded up window. I shook my head in response. Home was not where I wanted to go. Home was full of questions and gossip... and Jackson. No, I needed a distraction. "Volleyball game," I said and reached for the helmet tucked in the compartment in the back end of the motorcycle.

"Oh good," Rip said sarcastically as he threw a leg over his bike. "You didn't forget."

As we approached Riley C. Shepard High School—
my alma mater—we could see that the parking lot was
packed. The game must have already started. A group
of teenagers were sitting on the football bleachers
across from the parking lot and they looked up when
Rip pulled his motorcycle to a stop just below them. I
wasn't about to argue with him about the legality of the
spot he chose and just handed him the helmet.

Lights from the high gymnasium windows were lit
up, illuminating the red brick building and shedding
light on the banner advertising the dates of the school's
fall play. We were obviously late, which made me book
it across the parking lot.

Pulling open the heavy door that I walked out of
every day as a teenager to catch the bus to Alton Oaks, I
was greeted by the smell every high school carries:
hormones, perspiration, and stale learning. Muted
sounds of gym shoes squeaking on wooden floors,
cheering families, and the whistles of referees came
from the two doors on the right side of the hallway as
we rushed towards them. The sounds had instantly
taken me back in time to when Sadie and I played for
the school's volleyball team more than ten years ago.

The bright lights and amplified sounds of the gym
pounced on us as we walked past the green doors and
into the gym. I stopped and scanned the room, finding
Sadie standing on the sidelines by her players on the
bench. She was in her purple and orange Riley C.
Shepard Coach windbreaker with a whistle around her
neck and a clipboard in her hands. Her focus was on her
team and her eyes bounced with the ball. As the right
side hitter spiked the ball over the net, scoring for the
home team, she cheered. Sadie's eyes swept past me in
celebration and she smiled brighter. She threw a thumb
over her shoulder before shouting affirmations at her

team. Behind her, I spotted Alex in the wooden bleachers. His tall frame barely fit on the wooden benches and his knees almost seemed to comically reach his chin. He hunched over, his arms resting on his knees as he watched Sadie. Those two seemed perfect for each other—how did I not see it sooner? How did it take them this long to find each other?

Alex waved us over and Rip followed me as we walked around the opposing team and stuck to the sidelines. Rip seemed horribly out of place. He was a sore thumb; a shifty-eyed city boy who probably never attended any school functions. Many eyes turned our way—*the new guy—what's his name?—he was at the high school volleyball game!*—they would whisper to each other around town in the morning. I was hoping it would help him be welcomed by the town instead of shunned.

"Hey guys," Alex said, scooting over. I sat down beside him, relieved to be back in a normal setting; in my normal, Jackson-free, Alton Oak life. "What happened, Charli May?" Alex said, suddenly looking like an over-protective brother. His eyes darted to Rip. It reminded me of a time in third grade—and Alex was in seventh—when Matt Finley was picking on me outside of school and Alex ended up interfering as I tried to walk home one day. Alex never laid a finger on Matt, but that was the last time Matt ever picked on me. If only it could be that simple with Jackson.

Rip's hands went up in defense. "It's nothing," I said, putting my hands between them.

"Jackson—" Rip started.

I shot Rip a look that demanded he not say another word. "It's nothing," I repeated thickly. This was my own battle; my own demons.

"Then you might want to do something about your hair and face," Rip muttered insensitively. Riding across the highway without a helmet and shedding tears probably did take a toll on my appearance.

Alex's eyes widened. He never liked my husband. We didn't talk for a long time because Jackson and I eloped in Vegas. However, this past spring Alex and I reconciled and he promised he wouldn't get in the middle of my choice in men anymore, unless I asked him too. It's probably what stopped the words that quivered on his lips, begging to be said.

Cutting the tension, as I avoided eye contact with him, his beeper sprang to life. "Darn," he said as he pulled the clip from his belt. "I have to go," he shared, reading the screen. Turning to me, he asked, "Will you let Sadie know I was called in?"

I nodded as I watched him unfold his legs from the bleachers. "We drove separately in case this happened," Alex added, clipping the beeper back to his belt. "Sadie has to leave for Springfield right after the game anyway." He looked at me as he pulled out his cell phone and added with an eye roll, "Those Canaries couldn't wait twelve extra hours for that table."

Alex's finger hovered over the screen of his cell phone, but he hesitated to stand. "You know my house is open to you, right? If you need anything?" he asked, trying to say more than his words did.

I nodded again and tried to give him an encouraging smile. As always, he saw through it and gave me a half-hearted noogie as he scooted past us. "Be good, Charli May," he said with a big-brother smile.

In a nail-biting conclusion, the home team won by an embarrassing error by Beecher High School's server. Cheers erupted from the bleachers, making Rip jump. He spent most of the time on his phone, and I thought for sure when he stepped out for a few moments that he wouldn't return. Now, with the excitement billowing from the crowd around him, he looked like an animal that heard a menacing noise in the forest and was on full-alert. Rip was so painfully out of his element that it was almost amusing.

As the flushed-faced teams marched across the gym exchanging high fives, I stood and stretched my legs with a smile. It was silly to feel as happy as I did in my old high school—considering I spent most of it as an awkward shadow beside Sadie—especially when compared to Bailey or Alex—but it was such a wonderfully normal setting, full of pep and spirit and camaraderie, that I couldn't help myself.

"Great job, Sadie," I congratulated as she gathered her things from beside the team bench.

Her auburn hair was pulled back into a ponytail that bounced with her proud movements. Her blue eyes were wide and bright, matching her smile. "Thanks, Charli." She paused as Rip slowly caught up to us, his eyes on the screen of his phone. "You actually got him to come?" Sadie muttered, shocked. I only shrugged in response.

Sadie pulled the strap of her duffle bag onto her shoulder and gathered a water bottle and a few stray towels from the bench as a parent cut-in, yelling a compliment to the coach from across the court. Smiling and grateful, Sadie put up a finger to signal she would be right over. "Don't leave yet," she turned to me and said before I could comment on Rip's presence or mention my run-in with Jackson. "Gotta do some coach stuff. I'll meet you outside in a few, okay?"

As a former player, I knew Sadie had to talk with the team, make sure the towels were collected, do some paperwork, and lock the locker rooms after making sure they were clean. If Rip wasn't with me, I'd offer to help, but I didn't quite trust Rip not to take off and leave me stranded. I nodded in response and watched her bounce off to high-five one of her players.

"Time to go," Rip said more as a statement rather than a question.

"Would you chill?" I didn't mean to sound impatient, but based on Rip's eye roll, I'm sure he took it that way.

The gym emptied quickly. There was only a small group of adults talking at the bottom of the bleachers when Rip and I headed towards the exit. Two small children chased each other across the court, running into the legs of the adults. They'd laugh, bury their faces in their parent's pants, and take off running again.

That's when I saw him.

CHAPTER FOUR

The familiar face lumbered across the court, dismantling the volleyball nets. His wispy red hair was the same as it was in high school, though his forehead seemed bigger. His cheeks were permanently flushed against his fair complexion, and he seemed to double in size. He reminded me of a large dog that wasn't quite aware of how big he was, and still tried to crawl onto their owner's lap.

My mind searched for his name as memories of seeing him in the cafeteria—where he always walked around eating a heaping plate of tater tots drenched in ketchup and mayonnaise—came flooding back to me. "Hi, Sean!" I waved as we passed him on the court.

His eyes lit up and he immediately recognized me. "Hi, Chaw-lee," he said with an exaggerated wave. He still couldn't pronounce his *R*s without them sounding like *W*s. I tried teaching him how to once, when we were paired up for the school's Turkey Trot, but failed. He scooped me up in a hug that squeezed the breath from my lungs.

"Aw you Chaw-lee's boy-fwend?" Sean asked Rip after he released me from his grip. He had no sense of discretion.

"No, no," I responded too quickly with my hands up. "This is my friend, Rip," I introduced.

"Hi, Wip!" Sean said with a smile and pulled him in for a hug.

Sean was much larger than Rip. I watched in good humor as his eyes widened, suddenly constricted in this stranger's arms. If it had been anyone else who'd pulled Rip into a hug, I'm sure he would have pulled away and hit them. But Rip, much like everyone else, never knew how to interact with Sean's autism and developmental delays. "Okay, Sean," I said. "That's enough."

Immediately Sean dropped Rip and turned to me. Behind Sean's large frame I could see Rip was shaken. He ran a hand through his hair and shook his arms to bring life back into his leather jacket.

"Chaw-lee," Sean said, grabbing my hand and pulling me towards the exit. "Come see the muw-all. We painted it fo' the jew-ball-lee."

Without much of a choice, I let Sean pull me into the biting air of night. The sun was absent and the only light was from the bulbs that sang like cicadas outside the school building; they lined the parking lot and some were perched above the doors.

Just around the corner of the building, Sean stopped. He stood on one of the cement slabs in the parking space nearby and raised his hand to show off the mural. It took up the entire brick wall of the gymnasium. In large letters it read: "Riley C. Shepard High School, Home of the Bobcats." It portrayed the school mascot, woodworking classes, the 4-H program, and other highlights of the school including some teachers and students—even the one famous alumni we had: Darlene Magda, a student who'd made it as one of the last ten finalists on *American Idol*.

"Look, ovaw in the caw-naw," Sean pointed. Rip caught up to us, but stuck to the shadows. I think he was hoping to become invisible to Sean in order to avoid the same reaction when we did leave.

Sean was busy balancing on the cement slab as if he was a tight-rope walker. I followed Sean's finger to the bottom right-hand corner, not far from where we were standing. "I painted that pawt," he said proudly. "They let me because I wok in the gym evwee day. They put me in chawge of the supply clowset, they let me push the button fow the basketball nets and pull out the bleachews, and clean the flo' with the big loud polishaw. I live so close, but I get to dwive a golf cawt. My mom lets me dwive ouw Jeep sometimes, too," he added with pride. "But shh, don't tell," he added.

Sean had pointed to a very rudimentary painting of a girl with long brown hair dissecting a pile of white daisies. "It's you!" Sean said with a smile. "Wememba' when we wuh pawtners in science class?"

It was a sweet gesture from him. I volunteered to be his partner during my junior year for a botany project. He was nearly in tears when he saw the other students slicing open their flowers with scalpels. He had a tick where he would sing, "You, you, you, you, you, you, you," like a singer warming up their voice to the scales. "Just pretend you're a doctor," I told him, cutting off his little ditty. "And the plant needs your help."

"Like Operation?" he asked, looking up, glassy eyed.

"Yes! Just like Operation," I urged, thinking back to the coolest board game we had as children.

I was in charge of the scalpel, but Sean was handling the tweezers. As he picked at parts of the flower, I would periodically make a loud buzzing sound—like the game board did—that set Sean off in a fit of giggles. I couldn't believe he remembered that day from so long ago.

"Sean and Charli, sittin' in a tree," Rip taunted from behind me. I ignored it, just as I did from my classmates in high school.

"That's sweet, Sean. You did a great job!" I complimented.

"It's you!" he said again. He was so excited that he jumped off the curb as if he was a gymnast, nailing a landing. Headlights from the other side of the parking lot swept over the mural like spotlights. "You, you, you, you, you, you, you," I heard Sean singing in a whisper. The sound momentarily transported me back to our high school years. He never did grow out of that.

"I know it's me," I replied with a smile. "It looks just like me! You did a fantastic job, Sean," I added, touching the smooth paint on the cold brick wall.

Sean's face turned red with the compliment. He covered his face, not from embarrassment but from the car whose bright headlights were pulling up alongside of us. It irritated me that they had their bright lights on. I muttered an insult under my breath.

Wait, no. That was not a car. No. Dammit, no! It was a van.

"Charlotte," Jackson said out of breath, as if he had run to Sheridan from Alton Oaks rather than driven. His window was rolled down and his dirty blonde hair had grown so that it got caught in the strawberry-blonde beard that sprouted on his cheeks.

"Jackson!" I yelled. I usually tried to keep my voice measured around Sean, but this was a tone I had trouble controlling. "What in the—? How did you—? Why?!" I stumbled over my words and stepped vehemently towards the van.

As I got closer, I saw movement in the passenger seat. Long blonde hair fluttered in the nipping breeze from the open window. She leaned back to try and stay hidden behind Jackson's frame. I leaned over and confirmed that it was Jessica: the other woman. "And you brought *her?*" I accused, raising my hand and pointing past him.

"Dude, Charlotte, just chill, alright?" Jackson said as he shifted the van into park. He stepped out of the vehicle in his same unkempt clothes, only now I could see how wrinkled they were. "There's no need to go postal," he said condescendingly as he closed the door behind him.

He looked so small at that moment. Maybe it was because I was standing beside Sean who towered over everything.

"You shouldn't talk to Chaw-lee like that," Sean said in a tight voice. "I don't like it. It makes me angwy. You should be fwendly!"

Jackson, very dramatically, rolled his eyes at the comment, as if everything Sean said was below him; it added kindle to my fire. "Look," he said with an attitude. "I just need to talk to you for a few minutes," he explained as if I was a child. "Is that okay with Gilbert Grape and the Fonz over there?" he asked throwing a thumb towards Rip.

"You son of a—" Rip exclaimed and dashed towards Jackson. I managed to squeeze my way between the two of them, after Rip threw the first punch. My hair got caught in someone's grip and I cried out in pain and frustration.

Sean came to the rescue and pulled Rip off Jackson, holding him back effortlessly as Rip struggled to break free.

"ENOUGH!" I yelled, putting my hands up between the two boys. I was frustrated and aggravated at the amount of testosterone coursing through the night air. I was supposed to be the angry one, flying her fists, not them.

Jackson's lip was bleeding and he tried to puff out his chest in an effort to not seem as pathetic. "I want a divorce," Jackson blurted out. The two seconds of silence seemed to last forever. My whole world shook as if Atlas held it with Jell-O jiggly legs. In those two seconds I heard the words I didn't want to face but needed to hear. One hundred and twenty seconds made my world tremble in a juxtaposition of soul-crushing news that freed me from my bonds.

As if on cue, Jessica's slim arm emerged from the window. Her dainty long fingers glistened like diamonds in the moonlight against the red file folder. He grabbed it and waved it towards me like a weapon. "Just sign the effing papers and I'm gone. We can be rid of each other forever!" he exclaimed.

Silence filled the parking lot, leaving a dense fog of tension in the air as all eyes were on me. Before I could respond or react in any way, the metal door of the gymnasium opened and Sadie slipped out. Under the security light, she stopped and took in the scene: Jessica leaning out the window of the van, Jackson with a swollen, bloody lip wielding a red folder whose red divorce papers started to peek out from within, and Sean holding Rip back by his leather jacket behind me.

Without an explanation, Sadie dropped the gym bag with a thud on the asphalt and pushed up the sleeves of her windbreaker, making a beeline for Jackson with a look of fury filling her eyes. She might have been small, but she was fierce. Jackson knew that and backed up against the van as she approached. Standing in front of him, she glowered and said, "I told you a long time ago that if you break her heart, I will break your neck." She paused to crack her knuckles. "And nothing would make me happier right now than making that happen."

I hadn't seen this side of Sadie since we played volleyball. I didn't stop her because, well, I was caught up in the drama and wanted to see what was going to happen next. Seeing Jackson cower in front of little Sadie was amusing and filled me with pride. Coming home to Alton Oaks was good for my soul; there were people here who would always be on Team Charli.

The tension and anticipation were so thick that we barely noticed the Sheridan police cruiser rounding the corner of the building. His bright spotlight swept over the scene before his corn land-drawl did. "Games over, folks," he said. "Time to go home."

The spot light by his rearview mirror swept over the scene and, noticing the tension between Sadie and Jackson, the officer paused. His mustache twitched and he asked, "Is there a problem here?"

"This," Sadie said, stabbing Jackson in the shoulder with her finger, "is the root of every problem."

Jackson immediately rubbed the spot that I had no doubt was already bruised. The officer seemed to debate if this situation called for him getting out of the car. I noticed his gaze swept past the out-of-state license plate. "Sir, you need to go home," the officer said to Jackson from his car window. "Go ahead," he urged. "I'll follow you out."

"Fine," Jackson said through his clenched jaw. He turned to me after he climbed into the van, "But you will sign these papers, Charlotte," he said as if it were a threat.

"Gladly!" I shot back as Jackson stepped on the gas. His muffler jiggled, almost falling off, as he sped over the speed bump twenty yards away. The police car followed him slowly, almost indifferently.

"What the hell?" Rip exclaimed, finally breaking free from Sean's grip.

"Chaw-lee okay? That is not a nice man," Sean asked as he put a beefy warm hand on my shoulder. A chill shook me head to toe with the gesture.

Sadie paced back and forth in a sea of exhaust fumes muttering her G-rated profanities. "That asinine fart-knocker," she muttered, "can kiss my grits..." She turned in her pacing and continued her string of insults.

I watched Jackson drive away until the tail lights disappeared, turning down the nearest block. I stood alone, among my friends. Guilt and genuine curiosity made me wonder why I didn't leave Jackson earlier.

Memories, both good and bad, of my life with Jackson flew around me like mosquitos, playing to the hushed soundtrack of Sadie's profanities and Sean's out-of-tune "You, you, you, you, you, you," ditty.

CHAPTER FIVE

The annoying sound of Rip's motorcycle scratched my eyes open in the morning. I didn't want to leave the warm cocoon of my blankets despite the weak morning sun that lit up the yellow leaves of the young maple tree outside my bedroom window.

Vrrrroom, vrrrrroom. He revved the motorcycle again. Pulling the blankets with me, I dragged my feet over the cold, worn floorboards to the window. Rip was revving the engine and looking up at the windows of the Alton House. He cut the engine, letting the serene silence of morning settle back into the world when he saw me.

I sighed in resignation. He was not going to win over the people of Alton Oaks with that kind of wake up call.

Gathering up the blankets like they were skirts, I descended the stairs and hoped I didn't run into my mother. She would undoubtedly corner me with tight lips, a disapproving look, and a swell of questions about Rip's too-early presence. I'd managed to avoid her last night as I snuck through the back door after returning from Sheridan. I'm sure the Queen of Gossip was being pummeled by questions she couldn't answer about her daughter's estranged husband appearing in town. I took a deep breath to clear my thoughts and tame the anxiety that crept up as I lumbered down the last few stairs.

"What?!" I asked haughtily as I threw open the screen door. I pulled the blankets tighter around me as the lingering night air clawed through the breeze.

Rip leaned on his bike and crossed his arms. "Let's

go," he said. "I have a scarecrow to find and free labor to earn."

I groaned. I must not have been in my right mind to propose that agreement. "You honestly want to go to Fall Fest?" I asked.

"No," he said bluntly, shaking his head. "But I could use the free help on the Alton House." He smiled impishly and added, "And if it makes your life harder, well, how could I pass that up?"

I grumbled dramatically because I wasn't awake enough for a clever comeback. Turning, I disappeared inside with a promise to grudgingly keep. The thought of him presenting the Parade of Scarecrows on the canal, from the back of the Miller's hay bales, piled in the back of their pick-up truck, sent a wicked smile across my lips. "Oh did I not mention this perk?" I would ask innocently when he found out it was the prize for finding the scarecrow.

I was getting used to riding on the motorcycle. The bending curves and wild wind ripping through my jacket wasn't nearly as intimidating as it used to be. My eyelids grew heavy out of boredom rather than squeezed shut in terror. I barely held onto Rip as he cut our way down Oak Street to the other side of town. We passed by residents on their Saturday morning commutes to The Buzz or to Prescott's Grocers. Each one turned their head at the loud contraption roaring through their sleepy town.

Yes, I'm sure they began to notice how often I was on the back end of that new guy's motorcycle. I didn't care. Ever since I was considered a murder suspect this past summer, it seemed like whenever I was around, people were extra observant; like I was a magnet for gossip. I didn't mean to be, but sometimes living in a small town means you're around small-minded people.

Rip parked the motorcycle along with other vehicles outside the Miller's barn. The sun was warming the air and wispy clouds of fog were evaporating over the pond behind the faded and peeling red barn. The warm rays felt good on my back and I closed my eyes to soak it in.

"Here," Rip said and shoved a black charcoal thermos in my direction.

"What?" I asked and took it from his cold hands. "What is it?"

"With everything going on, I thought you could use it," he said nonchalantly.

I lifted my eyebrow skeptically at him as I unscrewed the lid. Warm tendrils crawled into the air with the scent of apple cider. "What's the catch?" I asked. Why was Rip being so uncharacteristically nice to me? My guard was up.

Rip only exhaled with an amused grunt, then turned to tuck the helmet away.

Tentatively, I took a sip and welcomed the warmth it sent billowing through my body. My tongue tripped over the liquid as a rough taste seeped onto my palette and I coughed. A family walking by with two young children in a plastic, red wagon turned to look as they headed towards the Fall Fest entrance. "Did you poison it?" I asked, half-joking, and wiped my mouth.

"Just with apple pie moonshine," Rip shared with a smirk on the corner of his lips.

I shoved the thermos back at him, hoping the action left a bruise. "Are you in the habit of spiking women's drinks?" I asked, horrified by his male-centric ego.

"What?" he said with the slightest chuckle and took the thermos.

As Rip threw the thermos in with the helmet, I took off along the gravel, grumbling about the choices I'd made in my life.

The Millers set up hay bales and a display of pumpkins and corn stalks at the end of the makeshift parking lot. The same orange and black sign they used each year—touched up with fresh paint—hung above it. In boxy letters, it read: Miller's Fall Festival. My heart immediately shed its shell of grumpiness at the sight. How long had it been since I last came here? Ten years ago, maybe. Did I even attend during my senior year of high school?

It was still early and yet to be crowded. Within the hour it would be packed. The odds of finding the scarecrow were in our favor. There was one year, however, when it wasn't found for twelve hours and everyone thought it was rigged. Normally, it's found within the first hour or two of opening day. The ambitious seekers were always first at the gate.

Wooden stands were set up selling Aunt Muriel's Sugar Shop's pies, The Buzz's hot beverages, Aunt Mary's jam, and Girl Scout cookies from the local troop. The sight of the patch covered, green sash the girls wore started endless renditions of camp songs in my head.

The church spun cotton candy and the elementary school sold taffy apples and other foods on a stick as a fundraiser. The Millers had the biggest stand which was full of farm-fresh produce and were selling roasted pumpkin seeds, corn-on-the-cob, and bottles of locally-harvested honey to raise money for next year's festival.

The morning breeze began to chase away the chill of lingering night air. Adults toting strollers and children strapped to their backs eagerly shoveled out cash for a to-go cup of java, while children hovered like bees by Oakie Doughkie's bakery table. The white tent that sheltered the U-shaped folding tables were covered in gingerbread cookies dressed as scarecrows, pumpkin-decorated cake pops, chocolate-covered pretzels made to look like stalks of corn, and wafer cauldrons, brimming with green and orange iced cupcakes. My stomach rumbled as we passed.

The roofed cork board had schedules and sign-up sheets, blowing against the thumbtacks for the day's contests: pie eating, apple bobbing, chili cook off, and pumpkin carving.

"Looks like no one's found the scarecrow yet," Rip said, tapping on the paper that had an empty space next to "Scarecrow Found By:" which looked to be written on a typewriter.

"Get ready to be very busy the next two months. Prepare for splinters, asbestos, and back-breaking labor," Rip taunted. Pretending not to hear him, I took off again; I hated how he always underestimated me.

Pumpkins carved by the folks at Spook Fest were donated and lined the path—I couldn't wait to see them glow at night with candlelight! A group of middle school kids shot by us, their footing slipping slightly on the morning dew. "I'm so goin' to find it this year!" one kid yelled.

"No way, Nick!" another called in response. "I am!"

"They're dreaming," Rip remarked as we followed their trail to the corn maze.

I tried to hide my smile because even though Rip was trying to give me a hard time, he was getting into the spirit of Fall Fest.

The corn grew tall this year, even Rip couldn't see over the top. It waved in the breeze that was laced with the smell of coffee and warm, spun cotton candy. There was a scarecrow at the entrance holding a sign that would soon hold the name of the person who found it. Currently, though, it read *Not Yet Found*. Rip eyed it hungrily.

Pulling something out of his pocket, Rip said, "Let's get this over with." He walked in, making sure no one else was following us.

"What is that?" I asked as I picked up my pace to keep up with him, trying to look over his shoulder in the limited space of the corn maze. After we made a few turns, I pulled on Rip's jacket, demanding an answer.

Sighing, he stopped and turned to face me. Now I could clearly see a compass in his hand. "Are you cheating?" I asked aghast.

Rip checked over our shoulders to see if the coast was clear. "The rules clearly state: no strollers, no unsupervised children under the age of ten, and no alcohol. Nothing about a compass... or guns," he stated and began his decent again.

"You have a gun?" I asked, aghast, catching up to him.

He let out a satisfied laugh and shook his head. "You simple-minded country folk," he commented and kept on walking.

Relieved that he wasn't carrying a concealed weapon, irritation at his comment crept into the forefront. After turning another corner, I gripped his jacket and didn't let go until he turned and faced me with an exaggerated sigh. "What?" he asked impatiently.

"Seriously," I said, surprised that my breathing was slightly labored. "What's the compass for?"

Rip rolled his eyes, ignoring the question and took off again. I grabbed the tail end of his jacket and held on like it was reigns. "Tell me or get used to the extra weight," I taunted, letting him propel me forward. After making three tight turns, he finally stopped and turned to me in frustration.

"Fine," he conceded. "I did some research," he said quietly. "The first corn maze, in 1952, was set up by Fred Miller. His hobby was cryptography and he used patterns in farming his crops, which is why this land stayed fertile all these years. I looked up several of the past year's 'keys' for the maze and found the pattern," he reported and turned to continue his quest.

I wasn't going to let him get away without a few questions and pulled on his jacket again. "When did you have time to do that? What's the pattern? Why hasn't anyone else figured this out?"

Rip turned slowly, he was dramatic in the way he showed his impatience: shifting the weight to his right foot and cocking his hips with the toss of his head; a sigh rushed out that dripped in repugnance. "Charlotte May," he started, knowing full-well that using my full name would hit a nerve. "Not everyone is as smart as I am."

I matched his dramatic and impatient tone, but amplified my body language. "Oh, *please,*" I said trying to make my whole body do an incredulous eye roll.

Rip took a step closer to me and spoke low and fast. It amused me that he was starting to get upset that I was keeping him from finding the scarecrow. "Fine," he spat and pointed to the compass and offered more information. "We started with turning due south, then east—but that was a dead end, so we really had to go northeast, then we went south again, and now we're going west southwest. Since it's 2016 we have to either find the square root of 16 or subtract the two numbers. Since four is the square of sixteen that means every fourth cardinal direction—"

"Never mind," I cut him off, raising a hand. It was too early for this amount of thinking. Plus, it was like Rip was removing the veil of whimsy on a childhood memory. Realizing that there were cold, calculated numbers fueling this pastime made me think of when I found out my mom was the tooth fairy. "Just go do whatever it is you're doing." I said. I highly doubted whatever method he was using would work. But leave it up to Rip to take the fun out of Fall Fest.

I followed the back of his jacket through the maze. Once in a while we'd come across the group of boys who so desperately wanted to find the scarecrow as they ran determinedly down the aisles of corn stalks. We ran into a few scarecrow seekers, but as we got deeper into the maze, we hardly ran into anyone.

Rip wrote down directions on a small sheet of paper as we walked and muttered to himself. Sometimes I'd jump in surprise when a crow fluttered from a nearby perch and shot suddenly into the sky. Or when a squirrel, busy nibbling on a fallen cob, would dash suddenly deeper into the field, sending the corn stalks fluttering angrily in their path, I'd gasp and clutch my chest, startled.

The sun grew brighter and I thought about shedding a layer of clothing; I was starting to work up a sweat. Out of boredom, I pulled out my phone to call Sadie and see how her trip to Springfield went, but remembered that she was at volleyball practice. The poor girl must have had a sleepless night and I made a mental note to stop at The Buzz and deliver some caffeine to her after we left Fall Fest.

As I was thinking about my own lack of caffeine that morning, Rip turned the corner and the aisle tripled in size, revealing the scarecrow ahead, where (ironically) several crows were perched. A triumphant smile flashed across Rip's face before he realized he wasn't supposed to find this task fun. "Looks like someone will be helping me put in new installation tomorrow morning," he said smugly.

"How in the heck did you do that?" I asked, dumbfounded. I guess we didn't get lost after the first few wrong turns at the beginning of the maze.

"I'm good at solving puzzles," Rip simply said as he

pocketed the compass.

Normally the scarecrow was dressed in a bright flannel shirt under a pair of overalls, but that was at least a decade back; things must have changed. Now it was dressed in a purple and orange Shepard High School jersey and a straw hat dipped over its face—instead of that creepy barley bag that gave Bailey nightmares as a child.

"Now what?" Rip asked with his hands on his hips. His black leather belt peeked out from beneath his jacket with the movement.

"You grab the scarf from around its neck or from its pocket or somewhere—it'll have the year on it—then you find your way out, and take it up to the Miller's farm stand," I instructed, shielding my eyes from the sun with my hand. "Unless someone's already taken the scarf," I added.

Rip's hands dropped from his hips with the set of instructions. Two months of working for his company will be worth it just to see him march to the canal, leading the festive town folk to present the Parade of Scarecrows. I planned on bringing my camera.

Rip muttered to himself as he took the first step to declaring his discovery to Alton Oaks. An amused smirk crept across my lips until something colorful caught my eyes from behind the corn stalks. Bending down and squeezing between the leaves that tickled my ears, I investigated. The brightly clothed scarecrow of my childhood was lying on the ground. The nightmarish barley bag had faded painted eyes that stared up at me, pathetically. They seemed to ask, "What did I do wrong?" from the muddy ground of the corn field.

At first I thought it was knocked over by the wind, then I wondered why there would have been two scarecrows... especially since this one had a red scarf tied around its neck bearing the year 2016.

"Uh, Charli?" Rip's voice slowly crawled across the distance between us. Close by I heard those determined boys running through the maze.

"What?" I asked sharply, pulling my head out of the corn stalks and turning from my squatted position to face him.

"I need you to stop those boys from coming in," he said in a measured tone.

"Why?" I asked and stood with an amused smile. I noticed that Rip didn't hold the victory scarf in his hand. "Afraid of losing?"

"Charli," Rip said, standing between me and the scarecrow. He threw a thumb over his shoulder and said, "That's not a scarecrow—"

I cut him off and moved to close the distance between us. "—Geez, he might not be a well-dressed scarecrow or even scare away the crows, but give him *some* credit—"

"Charli," Rip said sharply. His hand stopped me by grabbing my shoulder and preventing me from getting any closer to the scarecrow. "It's a body."

CHAPTER SIX

My eyes flitted from Rip's steadfast gaze to the not-a-scarecrow. Now that the world moved a bit slower, my still skeptical gaze took in the details. It didn't quite have the uneven stuffing of an honest-to-goodness, Midwestern scarecrow. Black crows rested possessively on its arms. And—Oh!—those *were* hands poking out of the jersey. Oh my god! Were those crows picking at its face?

The excited chatter of the boys grew closer and it snapped me out of my horrific shock. Rip pointed to the entrance we came through minutes earlier. "Please, Charli," he urged with sternness and pointed to the entrance.

Not having the energy or a reason to argue, I obeyed. I dragged my sluggish feet to the four-foot wide opening in the corn field. Shock froze my thoughts and, at the same time, made them run a mile a minute.

"And Charli?" he called, snapping me out of a trance. He stood below the deceased as if he was its bodyguard. "Call Deputy Do-Right."

Those ambitious boys intent on finding the scarecrow never did stumble upon it. We heard them come so close that I held my breath, bracing myself to hold them back, but they must have made a wrong turn somewhere. As their chatter got farther away, I exhaled heavily in relief.

My hands were shaking with the realization that I was standing fifteen feet from a dead body instead of a slightly nightmarish, yet wholesome and enjoyable hometown scarecrow. I immediately dialed Jake's cell phone—how often have I called it for situations like this since moving back to Alton Oaks? Far too often.

Three rings. Six Rings. Voicemail. He didn't answer. That had not happened before. I bit my bottom lip, perplexed, and scrolled through my contacts until I found the Alton Oaks Police Station.

"Alton Oaks Police Department. Is this an emergency?" I automatically recognized Seth's voice; he was an old classmate and one of Sadie's adolescent ex-boyfriends. A breeze swept the hair from my face and I refused to turn around and face that surreal scene once more. Would this be considered an emergency?

"Seth, it's Charli Parker," I said, knowing I couldn't put-off reporting this news, but I wished I could in order to avoid the drama that would follow.

"Hey, Charli," he greeted. All formality left his tone. "What's going on?"

"Um," I let the word leave a trail of hesitation as it exited my mouth. Another hometown murder! I was not ready for this. Why was I always caught up in these things? "Well," I began, knowing I had to just spit it out. "You know the Miller's Corn Maze?"

"Did you find the scarecrow?" Seth asked, his voice suddenly very intent and interested. I imagined him suddenly sitting up in the maroon and black swivel chair at the front desk as if this was a life-or-death emergency.

"Um," I said again, letting the syllable drag. "Kinda," I admitted. *Geez, Charli, just spit it out!* "You need to send the chief right away." I winced with the next sentence. "The scarecrow isn't a scarecrow. It's a dead body."

After pocketing my cell phone, I stood nervously

among the waving corn stalks with a dead body not too far away. In the distance, citizens were enjoying the first pig race of the day, or picking the perfect pumpkin to carve, or eating their fill of roasted corn. Knowing half the town was at the festival by now made the minutes go by in slow motion; anyone could come barreling around that corner at any moment! And even though Rip gave directions through the maze, the police plowed a direct path through from the back. As they got closer, we heard them redirecting the ambitious maze-goers to their sudden exit. There was no doubt in my mind that the abrupt police presence sent atomic-force ripples through the town.

Alton Oaks' finest entered from my left and I watched them tackle the corn to the ground. Two disheveled officers entered first and brushed off the farm dust and vegetation from their uniforms as they surveyed the scene.

Then Jake stumbled in, though I barely recognized him. An uneven beard had sprouted on his face and the hair beneath his wide-brimmed deputy hat desperately needed a cut. His eyes went up to the dead body, then took in the attitude Rip was emanating, until they finally landed on me.

Guessing that my guard duty was over, I made a beeline for answers. Sometimes I just couldn't control the Alton nosiness that runs through my blood.

Jake's whole body language seemed to sigh in reluctance when he saw me coming. "Why," he started without an ounce of compassion, "do these things always involve you?"

"Look," Rip cut in, defensively.

"No." Jake's word stabbed us both. He was clearly not in the mood to deal with Rip and his impudence. "Let me tell you how this is going to work." Jake took off his aviators and measured himself up to Rip. He pointed to his right, his unwavering gaze not leaving Rip's face. His voice was hard, like a brick wall stopping us from moving forward, and said, "*You* are going to give your statement to Chief Gomes. *I* will get a statement from Charli, and then *you two* can get out of my crime scene."

I heard Rip's knuckles crack as he balled his fists, staring at Jake in fury and clenching his jaw. I thought, for sure, I'd see Rip tackle him; that I'd witness another altercation with him in less than twenty-four hours. I held my breath waiting for someone to throw the first punch.

"Sir," an officer said, approaching Rip. He put a hand on Rip's shoulder to pry his attention from Jake. Immediately, and with great force, Rip shook off the officer's hand, mumbling about his rights. "Follow me, sir," the officer said, now aware of Rip's hostility and ready to use force if needed.

Rip ran a hand through his hair and tugged on his leather coat as if to reinstate his macho. I watched him walk away and sighed, shaking my head. *This will be a fun ride home,* I told myself sarcastically.

"Charli," Jake started impatiently as he grabbed his Steno pad from the inside of his jacket. "What in the— what happened?" he asked as if he really didn't want to be doing his job right now.

I squinted at the sun behind him. "We went through the maze, found the scarecrow, only Rip said it was a body, so I called you."

"'Rip said?' What does that mean?" Jake asked perturbed at the mention of Rip's name.

His attitude was eating away at my patience. "It means," I said with insolence, "exactly what it means. Rip saw the scarecrow first—he wanted to find it so I let him—only he said it was a body and wouldn't let me get near it. He told me to call you, but *you*," I poked him in the jacket and immediately regretted it when his eyes filled with fire, "didn't answer."

Jake rubbed at the beard around his lips, as if the gesture was wiping away the words he struggled not to say. "Did you come across anyone else in the maze? Anyone suspicious?" His words had a ring of forced pleasantness on them.

Shifting my weight from one leg to the other, I thought about the incredibly boring route we'd taken through the maze. "At first, yeah—I mean no one suspicious, but there was a group of middle school boys we ran into a few times. A few young families: The Dillards and Luke and Eva Swanson. There was no hooded figure lurking through the shadows of the corn field if that's what you mean." I might have been hanging out with Rip too long when I realized how sarcastic that statement was; Jake wasn't the sarcastic type.

Jake clenched his jaw as he wrote the names in his Steno pad. "What time did you arrive? How long were you in the maze?"

Adjusting my tone from a sarcastic/defensive-Rip-setting, to a childhood friend/encouraging tone, I replied, "We got here around nine o'clock. There were a few families here. We came straight to the maze."

Sliding up the sleeve of his jacket, Jake glanced at his simple, brown leather banded wristwatch. "You called the station at 10:00?" he asked, his tone adjusting with mine.

I bit my lip and then answered, "Yeah, I think so."

"It only took you an hour to find the scarecrow?" he asked, finally looking into my eyes.

I shrugged. "I guess so." That's definitely what it looked like.

"Stick around," Jake said when he finally looked away from me. His gaze felt like the light in old police movies that they shined onto the face of the people they questioned. "We might have more questions," he added and motioned for an officer behind me. "Take her to a paramedic," he said, "to check for shock."

The officer was someone I didn't recognize from my past, though I saw him a few times when I visited Jake at the police station. The brass plate on his jacket read: D. Kapersky. He didn't speak much, but his small frame carefully led me through the path the police plowed through at the back end of the cornfield.

An ambulance and two Sheridan police vehicles were parked near the old station wagon that represented the Alton Oaks station. A cruiser from Terryville pulled up while we were exiting, and the two officers who spilled out of the car automatically began setting a wider perimeter that kept the nosy residents of Alton Oaks from creeping closer to the crime scene.

After a nameless paramedic checked my vitals, I leaned against the hood of one of the cars. Deep in thought about what the morning had brought, Rip stumbled out of the corn field with two officers escorting him. He argued about not needing to see a paramedic and the officers on either side of him were clearly over having to deal with the man's attitude.

"This town!" Rip declared as he jumped onto the hood of the police cruiser beside me, the metal moaning with his weight. He said each word as if he had spit them. He had run out of patience; he never had much of it when it came to police officers anyway, especially Jake.

"Then why do you stay?" I asked without feeling. The weight of the world began to grow heavy on my shoulders. With Jackson returning to town, the idea of divorce, seeing Jessica, having to deal with my feelings, coming face-to-face with unanswered questions, the uncertainty of my future, and now another murder made me want to slip away from the world; run away and not come back.

"I have my reasons," he barked.

His tone didn't affect me. I was numb to his jabbing remarks and tiresome attitude. I just wanted to go home.

The sun warmed the day and I wasn't so cold sitting and waiting anymore. Rip and I sat silently beside each other. At one point, Rip lit a cigarette and I didn't have the energy to move out of the path of smoke, or the gumption to call him out on his rudeness.

Jake and Chief Gomes exited the corn field with the stretcher not far behind them. Both men made a direct path towards us. Rip sighed dramatically as he put out the cigarette. I wasn't ready to brace myself for his hardened retorts or for the thick barrier of tension between him and the police. I was done caring for the day.

Chief Gomes stopped to brief the two officers from Terryville who were on crowd control while Jake stopped two feet in front of me with a sigh. "I know," I said, resigned. "Why does it always involve me? I don't know," I said, not caring. I was exhausted at wondering why.

Jake's tough exterior broke. He was no longer a brick wall and it kindled a warmth in me. "No, Charli," he began hesitant. "It's worse than you think." For the briefest moment, his gaze swept past Rip then returned to me. "I need you to come with me."

Panic began to bubble up inside me. My stomach dropped as it did whenever I rode a rollercoaster. This past spring I was under suspicion for a murder at the elementary school and I feared I would find myself in those same shoes again. I began thinking about who I argued with, who disliked me, and what could possibly put me under suspicion for another murder as I followed Jake towards the ambulance.

The stretcher with the body bag sat just outside the open doors of the ambulance. The gentle hum of machines filled the air and the gravel beneath the paramedic's feet crunched as they gave us some space. Jake stopped on the other side of the stretcher and looked at me hesitantly as Rip stepped up beside me. "I need you to identify the body," Jake said as he pulled the zipper on the black bag.

Before I could ask what he meant, he pulled apart the black exterior. Without a whim of caution, I looked down and there he was; his crow-eaten face staring up at me pitifully. His left eyeball was a void, pecked out by the birds, and his skin—where there wasn't dried up bits of blood—was a ghastly, paper-thin white. Gasping, I covered my mouth at a scene too horrifying for nightmares.

"Jackson," I said in disbelief and threw my hands up to cover my face. Squeezing my eyes tight, I hoped to stub out that image, but it burned onto the back of my eyelids.

"Jackson," I said again in a cracked whisper as I felt the salty warmth pierce my eyes and pour down my face. "Jackson," I repeated.

CHAPTER SEVEN

"What the hell is your problem?" Rip asked, offended. His hand reached out and punched Jake in the shoulder from beside me. He moved to scare Jake on the other side of the stretcher when one of the Terryville police men came between them. "Don't they teach you pigs sensitivity training?" Rip called out as the police officer used his forearm against Rip's chest to push him away from the stretcher. "What the hell was that?" Rip called, disgusted.

"Sir, we're just doing our job," the police officer said, pushing Rip further away until Rip didn't need a physical barrier anymore and paced, constantly running a hand over his hair. His eyes traveled to Jake and me every time he turned in his perturbed tramping.

A vein popped out on Jake's neck from beneath his scraggly beard as he clenched his jaw. He relaxed—if ever so slightly—when his gaze left Rip and returned to me. His lips twitched to say something, but he only pierced them shut. I looked back down at the black bag that contained my husband. Was this a joke? Was that someone who just looked like Jackson? Were the cosmic forces that made him appear in Alton Oaks—a place he never wanted to visit with me anyway—now placing him in a body bag? No. That couldn't have been Jackson.

But that face beneath the vinyl material burning into my mind. It had the same strawberry blonde facial hair, the same crooked eyebrows, the same three birthmarks by its right ear that reminded me of something I'd see in the night sky. It really was Jackson, wasn't it?

The crunching of gravel under Jake's boots caught my attention and I looked up at the hard exterior of my childhood friend. For a moment, his warm hand touched the small of my back, directing me away from the stretcher. "I need you to come to the station," he said, almost regretfully, leading me to the ancient station wagon.

"I'll take her," Rip declared, cutting in and putting his hand on my arm.

Jake's face hardened as he put his hand on my shoulder. Through clenched teeth and with a fiery look, he retorted, "Let me do my job, or I will have you detained for obstructing justice."

Jake opened the back door of the station wagon and tucked me inside. "I'll meet you there," Rip said, offering a look of determination. His face turned to stone when Jake slammed the door as if to end his sentence.

I studied the back of Chief Gomes' white hair and the bushy outgrown dirty blonde hair of Jake's head as we rode down Oak Street with only intermittent chatter on the police radio to fill the space. Shocked silence was my riding partner as curious people on Oak Street strained to see who was in the backseat. I slouched, letting my hair fall into my face, and avoided eye contact. Not too long after we approached Main Street I heard the roar of Rip's motorcycle catch up to us. I caught myself wishing I had held onto that spiked apple cider to calm my thoughts and ease my nerves.

Many people were milling about downtown on this sunny Saturday, despite the opening day of Fall Fest. Naturally, when the police car pulled up in front of the station, nearly every head turned to catch wind of potential gossip. I could almost hear the enthusiastic whispers race down the street like a strong breeze when

Chief Gomes opened the door and I stepped out. Rip's motorcycle turned into the parking lot across the street, and my eyes quickly returned to my feet.

Without words, Jake led me to the interrogation room. I sighed when I walked inside; this room was becoming way too familiar to me. I was frequenting it so often the past six months that I even noticed an extra chair in the room and that layer of dust on the filing cabinet was disturbed as if someone's elbow had scraped across it, or a heavy file folder had been dragged from it. Jake and Chief Gomes had me wait so long that I even noticed an old white board peeking out from behind the filing cabinet. I counted the number of pens in the cup on the table, the number of sections in the drop-down ceiling, and the collective number of legs on the furniture in the room. I was desperately trying to keep myself distracted from thinking about Jackson's demise.

Right in the middle of counting the number of right angles in the room, Jake walked in and I was relieved to see him. Closing the door behind him, he took his time sitting down. He placed a file folder and his Steno pad on the table before looking up at me.

"Charli," Jake said exasperated. For that one word, his face broke from the always-serious, work-face mask he wore with his uniform and let his soft, friend-face break through. I missed that face.

"Why—" Jake started but stopped himself. He seemed to collect his thoughts and with those thoughts came the brick wall that didn't let emotion or friendship cross the line of work-Jake.

"In his statement," Jake began, consulting the file folder, "Mr. Oakley identified the victim as Jackson, your husband. When identifying the body, can you agree to his testimony?"

I heard the ticking of my wristwatch as his words

took root. "Rip said what?" I asked, thinking back to the moment when Rip refused to let me get closer to the scarecrow. *He knew?* My eyes prickled with emotion. I bit my bottom lip and looked up at the ceiling where one of the six bulbs, scattered in the small space was burnt out.

Inhaling slowly, I tried to push away the tears, but a few escaped and trickled down my cheek. "Jake," I pleaded. "I can't—" a crack in my throat made my voice trip over a few more tears.

"Charli—Ms. Parker," Jake said, catching himself. His eyes swept across the camera in the corner of the room. "Can you please, for the record, identify the body found in the corn field?" his tone was impatient rather than consoling.

Tugging on the sleeves of my sweater, I pulled them over my fists and used them to wipe away the tears. "It was Jackson," I said and sniffed. "Jackson Neilson. My husband." I took another deep breath and urged myself to pull it together; to not let my emotions run away. I could let it all out once I stepped out of the police station. But right now I needed to keep it together, answer the questions, and then I could process everything else once I crossed the threshold of the Alton House.

"Did you know that Mr. Neilson was in town?" he asked, his eyebrows slightly jumping.

I nodded. "Yeah. He came by the Alton House yesterday and then showed up at the high school last night after the volleyball game."

Without looking up from his Steno pad, Jake asked, "Can you please explain why he was in town?"

I stomped down the emotions that desperately wanted to explode when I thought of Jessica's slender hand giving Jackson the folder from inside the van... and the angry words from Jackson's mouth... and the sledgehammer of divorce that shook my reality. "He wanted to talk; he wanted a divorce," I admitted and stared at the empty tab at the top of the file folder in front of Jake.

"Were you upset?" he asked without an ounce of concern in his voice.

Again, I nodded and began to bite my thumb nail.

Briefly looking up from his notes, Jake asked, "Did anyone witness this exchange?"

My eyes felt tight and scratchy but I didn't dare rub them or squeeze them shut to soothe them. I didn't quite trust that the tears wouldn't break through. "When he came to the Alton House, my mother, Bailey, Mrs. Kratsky and, I think, Jenna were on the porch. I was walking up the street with Rip when I noticed Jackson's van. I didn't want to talk to Jackson, though." My eyes once again traveled to the burned out light bulb so that the tears wouldn't fall. "Rip gave me a ride to the high school and we watched the volleyball game. After the game, Rip and I were outside the school waiting for Sadie when Jackson pulled up." I stopped myself for a moment; that was the last moment I shared with Jackson before his death. The upsweep of emotions was almost overwhelming. Taking a deep breath, I tried to neatly fold it all into a drawer, deep in my mind, so that it wasn't so overbearing.

Jake was jotting down information in his Steno pad. "And then what happened?" he inquired.

"Jackson was upset because I was upset because Jessica was there and—"

"Who is Jessica?" Jake asked, carelessly throwing the name into the conversation when it should have been said in vile disgust.

I bit down on my bottom lip until I tasted blood. When I felt like I could talk without grinding my teeth, I replied, "The other woman." I rolled my eyes and snorted at the thought. "Our old neighbor. The woman who has been sleeping with my husband for lord-knows-how-long."

Jake's blank face studied mine for an uncomfortably long time. Creases formed beside his eyes as he thought. Finally, he tilted his head and returned his attention to his notes. "Please continue," he instructed with a curt nod.

"Jackson made some stupid comments about Rip and Sean—"

"Sean?" Jake asked with an arched eyebrow.

"Sean Walters. He was there too. We went to high school with him. Big, tall, red hair. He was showing us the mural on the side of the building after the game when Jackson showed up." Jake didn't nod in realization, but continued to write in his Steno pad. "Rip punched Jackson, I tried to stop it but just ended up in the middle of it until Sean pulled them apart. Then Sadie came out and—" I stopped myself and wished I had left Sadie out of the conversation.

"And?" Jake asked. He acted as if he knew I was avoiding something.

"Well," I started, knowing it was too late to keep Sadie's name out of this mess. "She wasn't happy to see Jackson either."

"So everyone who came in contact with Jackson had a reason to be upset with him?" Jake asked.

"Well, yeah," I admitted unwillingly. "He was being a jerk to everyone."

Jake leaned back in his chair and tapped the eraser of the pencil on his pad of paper in thought. "How long has Jackson been in town?" he finally asked.

"I'm not sure. He came by the Alton House yesterday around four o'clock, I think. It might have been earlier, but that's when I got home from lunch."

Jake looked down at his notes. "And this woman,

Jessica, where is she?"

I choked down the response I really wanted to give him and instead reported, "I don't know and I don't care."

Jake licked his lips. The pause seemed to let my words echo around us and I felt guilty for saying them. "And when was the last time you saw Jackson?" Jake finally asked.

"After the volleyball game last night. A Sheridan police officer drove through the parking lot and told us to stop loitering. He followed Jackson's van out of the parking lot."

Glancing at Jake's paper, I could see him write a note to check this fact with the Sheridan police department. "In which direction did Jackson leave the parking lot?"

I studied the old picture of the police station that hung on the opposite wall and I thought about it. "He made a right out of the parking lot, I think." I bit my lip and tried to picture in which direction his tail lights disappeared that night.

Jake turned the page of his Steno pad with a sigh. With the pencil hovering over the clean page, he asked, "Can you please describe the vehicle Jackson was driving?"

That van. The one we nicknamed Tito the Traveling Van. The same van he bought in Costa Rica three years ago in order to stay with me until my Peace Corps term was over. The same van we traveled through Latin America in, and crossed the border in, and arrived in Albuquerque in. The van that never seemed to need new parts or break down despite how old and horrible it looked. It was the well-behaved child in our relationship. I described the make and the model and the T-shaped rust stain in the back and the license plate number and the bumper stickers we added as we traveled... back when we were happy and young and naïve.

When I rattled off my last sentence I felt like I was going to explode with tearful emotion. I feared that my next breath would break the dam I'd constructed and I did not want to break down in front of Jake. I did once, over the summer, and he proved to be a great friend through it, but now he was acting different. I feared that if I broke down in front of him, and he did not give me a consoling hand or a single encouraging word, I would be hurt by another man and I just wasn't ready to gamble on that.

"Thanks for coming in, Char—Ms. Parker," Jake said, catching himself again. "We'll be in touch if there's anything further," he said standing up and pushing in his chair. He paused at the door a moment and said in a softer tone, "Feel free to leave when you're ready."

Still holding in the break down that desperately wanted to burst through, I squeaked out a small noise of understanding and nodded.

Jake opened the door, letting in the sounds of the busy station rush in momentarily. As the door closed with a metallic click behind him, I let my face fall into my hands and let myself go, stuffing the sleeve of my sweater into my mouth to muffle the wails.

CHAPTER EIGHT

It was only three o'clock—just mid-afternoon—when I got back to the Alton House. Rip offered to give me a ride on his motorcycle, but I declined. "Do you really think you should be alone?" Rip asked as he followed me down Main Street. Curious residents watched me from the corner of their eyes as they went about their Saturday afternoon business.

My face was stained in bitter salty tears and was red with fury, sadness, and shock. I broke down hard in the police station where no one would bother me or watch me with worry. "Do you *really* want to be around me right now?" I snapped back, each word a bullet of torment.

We were in front of the firehouse, just past the Westbrook Attorney offices, and Oreo, the resident firehouse Dalmatian, was watching us from his spot beside the fire engine. The garage doors were open and two firemen were cleaning the engine with rags in their hands. They turned their attention to us with concern.

"Look," I said in a quieter tone that still brimmed with moxie, "I know you're trying to be nice, which is a rare character trait for you, but I can't be nice right now. I want to tell you how stupid your hair is, and how stupid this town can be, and I don't mean any of it. I'm just upset and I need to burn it off." I turned and paused before storming away. "*Alone*," I added and took off down the street. I was going to regret being so cheeky later, but I didn't have room in my emotions to care right then.

Luckily no one was home when I stomped up the steps of the Alton House. It was odd that the Gossip Club wasn't congregating on the front porch despite this morning's events, but it was Saturday; they were probably all in town, doing their homework by gathering even more gossip to share after dinner.

I didn't know where to go once I stepped over the threshold. Sweat had gathered beneath the layers I put on this morning. My hair was a knotted mess and my face could use a wipe down. At least I was home, that was what mattered, but my feet were glued to the floor and my back leaned against the heavy oak door. Do I go to the kitchen and think about eating while that grotesque image of Jackson's crow-eaten face hid behind my eyelids? Do I go up to my room and think about how that was my only bedroom now? That the one I'd had in Albuquerque belonged to a different me... when Jackson was alive and I was blind to the fact that he used that bed to cheat on me? Or do I go into the living room that was broken and lost to the past?

Drafts of cold air blew the plastic canvas and moaned throughout the house while the birds chirped in the trees outside. Before I had to make the choice of what to do next, Rip's motorcycle roared up the driveway. I was grateful for it, but I would never tell him that.

I walked into the living room as if I had planned on that all along. I heard Rip's heavy-soled boots climb up the stairs and guilt started poking holes at my gut when I realized I would have to apologize for my behavior. *Eventually*, I convinced myself. *Not today*. I walked towards the built-in bookshelves and inspected their sturdiness as Rip walked in the front door.

He threw his leather jacket onto the drop cloth that covered the couch before he saw me on the far side of the room. "What?" he asked. He looked as if he was unsure if he should be mean to me or concerned, or attack me with our back-and-forth mock insults.

"'What?' What?" I asked, turning my head from the bookshelf.

Rip only lifted an eyebrow as he picked up his tool belt and secured it around his waist.

"A deal's a deal," I said and leaned on the wall paper that was cracking with age. "You get me as free labor until Christmas."

Any gentleman would have denied this and let me out with the loophole that he didn't technically find the scarecrow... but Rip wasn't a gentleman. And, honestly, I needed the distraction. I needed to put my energy into something productive to keep my mind on other matters.

"Great," Rip said as he bent over his toolbox. "Grab a bucket and start scraping off that wallpaper."

I was going to argue that I could do more than that—that these shelves needed new joints—but I let it go. There was enough squabbling going on inside my head that I didn't need to contribute to more of it on the outside. Obediently, I walked into the kitchen where I grabbed a rag and filled a bucket with warm water and a hefty dose of fabric softener.

We worked in silence for a while. The sound of scraping was the background beat as Rip began pulling out the warped wooden shelves from either side of the fireplace. "What happened today?" Rip's voice broke through the monotony suddenly. "At the police station," he clarified.

I shook my head without looking up from the faded wallpaper. "No," I said. "Ask me another question. Something else. Entirely."

The scraper was covered in bits of wallpaper and I put it down on the drop cloth as silence passed between us. As I picked up the rag and began washing another section of the wall, I could hear him throwing another piece of wood into the pile behind him. Warm water ran down my arm and it tickled. For a split second I let myself smile and found joy in that moment. It ran away when Rip said, "Then tell me a story."

"About what?" I asked. I was never good at telling stories. Even when I had my classroom in Albuquerque and I encouraged the students to make up stories with the English words they were learning, mine were never imaginative. "The fish swam quickly," I would share while my students told tales of their fish swimming behind a devil rock or getting lost in the ocean or meeting a shark. I wasn't good at making up exciting stories.

"Andrew Alton," Rip said as if he didn't have to think about a topic.

My great-great grandfather was an enigma to me. The more time I spent in Alton Oaks, the more interested I became in learning about him. However, resources were limited here. I had done research all spring on him and scoured every resource I could find at the library in order to present a history lesson on Heritage Night at the local elementary school. Andrew Alton died on the steps of Town Hall in 1920 and no one knows why or who did it. That mystery was like an itch I kept scratching, but couldn't get any relief.

No story I could tell would give him justice for the things he did for our country and our town, but I was going to try. "Well, Andrew Alton was a successful U.S. Marshall. It was clear that he loved his job. He caught his first fugitive—Mad John Brown—when he was only twenty years old."

The rag plopped back into the bucket of water, and I picked up the scraper. My mind traveled back to sitting in the basement of the library last spring and the hours I spent sifting through old periodicals on the microfilm archives. "There was one fugitive he could never quite catch. One reporter at the *Oak Leaf Press* said it was a cat-and-mouse game between Andrew Alton and D. B. Williams."

I pulled a large scrap of wet wallpaper from the wall and let it plop into the pile on the drop cloth. "D. B. Williams was a bank robber and murderer. He was the only fugitive Andrew Alton couldn't catch."

"D. B. Williams was never caught?" Rip asked, in between pounding his hammer into the wood.

I picked up the bucket and moved it five feet to the left, just beside the archway entrance of the front hall. A draft from the foyer made me shiver as I held the wet rag. "Well, technically, no," I admitted and ran the rag on the wall over my head. I had missed at least two feet of wallpaper below the high ceiling, but I'd worry about it later, when I could find a step ladder or drag in a kitchen chair.

"Technically Andrew Alton caught him, but D. B. escaped and wasn't caught again," I admitted. The research I had done vaguely mentioned this downfall in Andrew's relatively successful career.

"Was never caught again period, or never caught again by Andrew Alton?" Rip asked. It sounded as if he was holding his breath and I snuck a peek behind me to see him trying to pry a piece of wood from the stud with the back of his hammer.

"Never caught," I clarified and began scrapping off the wallpaper again. "It was like he ceased to exist after that." I grew frustrated when I couldn't find any more research on D. B., it was like he vanished into thin air.

Rip grunted as the wood finally gave way and it moaned as the nails scraped their way out of the studs. "I have a theory," I said, getting lost in how gratifying it was when the wallpaper came off in long strips instead of having to scrap away at the patches that got stuck.

"Oh?" Rip asked noncommittally. He pounded the nails out of the wood without asking a follow up question.

"My theory is that D. B. Williams had an accomplice." It was the first time I told anyone that and I wasn't sure if it was worth sharing. Andrew Alton's murder would probably never get solved, but it was an interesting case, especially since he was my ancestor.

Rip was quiet and I wasn't sure if he was processing my theory or if he didn't care. "So no one's really lived on this side of the house?" he suddenly asked as he threw the piece of wood into the growing pile. I guess my theory didn't have the wow-factor I secretly hoped it had.

"No. Not really. Not since the late fifties. I mean there's pictures from Christmas in this room when my mom was little, but it smells funny, it's too cold in the winter, the fireplace might be a fire hazard, and it leaks," I shared.

"It's kind of like living in a museum, isn't it?" he asked.

Without answering his question or even giving it much thought, I turned and asked, "Are you hungry? I'm starving. Want a sandwich?" I was suddenly famished and put down the scraper. I had bits of wallpaper all over my arms and sweater. I probably should have changed clothes before starting this project, but I didn't care; this was a good distraction.

"And coffee!" Rip called after me as I left the living room.

It was getting darker noticeably earlier these days. The sun was still out and it was still considered daytime, but the light was moving west fast. I could tell because the kitchen was much darker than usual, despite its lone window facing south. I pulled the cord on the florescent lamp that hung above the sink and counter space, and its subtle but annoying hum filled the air.

Moving from the cabinets, to the breadbox, to the fridge, I went about making ham sandwiches—carefully avoiding my mother's faux vegan lunchmeat which I didn't understand the point of. As I plopped a puddle of mayonnaise on the bread, a commotion started on the front porch. After wiping my hands on the hen-and-rooster themed dish towel that hung from the stove, I curiously made my way to the front hall where Rip was standing. He had his hands on his hips, just above the tool belt, and he peered out the small narrow window beside the front door.

"Who is that?" he asked.

Beside him, I watched as a blue Prius peeled out of the driveway—probably an Uber driver from another town—leaving a severely intoxicated woman yelling and tripping over her own two feet. "That," I said, my anger anew, "is Jessica."

Rip turned to me with an eyebrow raised. He clearly did not get a good view of her from the passenger side of Jackson's van last night. "The other woman," I clarified.

CHAPTER NINE

We watched as Jessica fell onto the gravel several times. Each time she pulled herself up, and she'd swing her small purse over her shoulder. The strap was long and it would wrap around her at least once before smacking her in the back. Her long blonde hair was ratted, as if she had run her hands through it several times and grabbed it in frustration. "*Chew!*" she yelled, slurring her words as she grabbed onto the banister at the bottom of the porch stairs.

I pulled open the door and stepped onto the creaking floorboards of the front porch. The screen door didn't slam shut behind me; I pretended it wasn't upsetting that Rip stood behind me like a bodyguard or a nosy neighbor.

"*Chew!*" she exclaimed again, pointing to one of the many me's I was sure she was seeing while squinting her eyes. Her whole body swayed and she held on tighter to the banister. I doubted that she would even make it up the stairs in her severely inebriated state. "Chew killed 'im, didn't chew?" she slurred. Pain dramatically deepened her features and, for a short moment, I felt empathetic. She really did love my husband. The feeling passed when I realized I was more angry, than emotionally upset, at Jackson's demise.

"Jessica," I started, suddenly thankful we lived so far from town. If this spectacle had happened on Main Street, half the town would be gathered around by now. "Do you need a ride back to your hotel?" I asked wanting to be rid of her.

"Chew-ar-ah murderer!" she yelled and pulled herself up to lean over the banister.

I held in the words I so badly wanted to yell at her. I held my flailing fists to my side and choked back the screams I wanted to unleash. "Let's call you a cab," Rip suggested as he descended the stairs. He softly but suggestively grabbed her arm to lead her away from the house.

Jessica pulled herself from Rip's grasp and fell onto the grass. It was like watching a toddler have an over-dramatic fit at a toy store. Rip only turned and watched her crawl several feet away. He looked at me with confusion as Jessica tried twice to stand up before she found her balance. Grass stains appeared on her gray jeans that hugged her toned legs.

"Chew two!" she wailed, pointing her finger in the air like a sword. "Chew two did-didn't chew?" she cried. "I loved him!" she yelled so loud that I'm sure the people on Main Street could hear her. "An chew killed 'im!" she fell over again but didn't try to get back up. She rubbed the dirt, grass, and gravel from her palms onto her off-white crew neck sweater that was stretched out and rumpled. The term "rock bottom" came to mind.

"He didn't wanchew!" she screamed with tears. "If you couldn't haffim, no one could, sat right?" Her accusations added gasoline to my fire, but I contained the explosion.

I looked down Oak Street and noticed my mother barreling towards the house with her shopping cart kicking up a trail of dust behind her. She was on her way home from her Saturday morning grocery run that usually ended up taking all day with her usual gossip stops at The Buzz and the after church group.

"Look, Jessica," I said as I walked down the stairs. "I didn't kill him—*we* didn't kill him," I declared and walked towards her. "He was my husband," I said and squatted down to her level. "Now let me—"

Before I could finish my sentence, Jessica reached out and grabbed my hair. She pulled me down to the ground and let loose a torrent of drunken anger and irrational decisions. When Rip pulled her off me, blood trickled down my nose and Jessica was holding a clump of my hair in her fist. Before I could release a string of curse words directed at Jessica, my mother rushed up beside us just as the ancient Alton Oaks police station wagon entered our driveway. Even Bailey had rushed out of her house and sprinted across the lawn—though I wasn't sure if it was to make sure I was all right or to get a firsthand account of the newest town gossip.

I cried out in pain and frustration. "What is wrong with you?!" I yelled, grabbing the throbbing spot on my scalp. "Are you so moronic you'd actually—?" I was cut off by Jake and another police officer walking up to the scene.

"What seems to be the trouble here?" Jake asked as they surveyed the situation.

Rip had let go of Jessica and she fell to the ground, sobbing. I felt the blood trip over my lips and I wiped it away with the sleeve of my sweater—little bits of wallpaper that stuck to my sweater scraped my face with the movement. A strong October breeze and the rustling of dried leaves covered the sound of Jessica's sobbing and my heavy, angry breathing.

"She showed up drunk as a—" Rip began, but Jake cut him off.

"Charli, what is going on?" Jake asked perturbed. He acted as if this childish behavior was below me; that I knew better; that I was wasting his time.

Rip didn't protest with my mother standing beside him. He pursed his lips together and balled his hands into fists instead, shifting his body weight from one leg to the other.

"This *idiot*," I said the word dramatically and pointed to Jessica because my scalp *really* hurt. "Showed up drunk and accused me of murdering Jackson."

With being called an idiot, Jessica tried to stand up once more, but failed. She drunkenly tried to crawl my way like an inebriated exorcist until the thin, dark-haired officer beside Jake stepped between us. He looked down at Jessica and raised his palm towards her. "Ma'am," he started, "you need to calm down or I will have to restrain you."

"Ma'am," Jake started, turning his attention to the woman we were all standing over, "what is your name?"

"Jessica," she said, looking up at us. "Jessica Neilson," she stated, clear as day. Mom gasped and my jaw dropped. "Well, it woulda been if *she* woulda signed the divorce papers!" Jessica pointed to me accusingly. She carefully tried to enunciate her words. "Bu' she hadda go an' kill 'im instead."

Jake looked from Jessica to me with confusion. "Ma'am," he started again. "What's your name?"

"Jessica Quincy," she stated sadly.

Then, without a trigger or cause, Jessica popped up and pounced on me, sending me backwards onto the gravel driveway. The skinny police officer managed to pull Jessica back while Jake explained, "Ma'am, you are clearly disturbing the peace and are severely inebriated. You're going to have to come with us."

Jessica muttered a string of slurred swear words as she half-heartedly fought against the officer.

"I have to hand it to you, sis," Bailey said amused as we watched them deposit Jessica into the station wagon and drive away. "Alton Oaks hasn't been this eventful until you moved back."

At that moment, I did not want to hear that. I did not want to acknowledge that all the drama in Alton Oaks was because of me. I did not want to point fingers. I wanted someone to ask if I was okay, or tell me how crazy Jessica was. With my head throbbing, I wiped away another trail of blood with my sleeve and marched inside the house.

I wanted to beat a punching bag and run until my legs turned to Jell-O. I wanted to yell until I had no voice left... but not with my mom, sister, and Rip so close by. Walking into the living room, I saw the sledgehammer that Rip had used to tear apart the window seat yesterday morning.

It was heavy when I picked it up; I had to use both hands to carry it to the wall that separated the study from the living room. With the anger I spent all day stuffing deeper inside me, I picked up the hammer and slammed it into the wall. It hit with a satisfying thwack, breaking through the drywall and revealing the studs.

"What are you doing?!" Rip asked, running into the room and taking the sledge hammer from my grasp. He held it effortlessly, like it didn't weigh as much as it did. Mom and Bailey followed, but hesitated entering the living room. They stood under the archway and waited, like players on the sidelines of the field.

"Work," I said matter-of-factly. "Aren't we putting a new wall here?"

Rip glanced at the north wall that separated the living room from the library, and that's when I realized I was tearing down the wrong wall. Instead of correcting me, Rip handed the sledgehammer back to me and said, "Yeah. We're tearing down all the walls."

CHAPTER TEN

Mom and Bailey congregated on the porch for a few minutes, but when Mrs. Kratsky and Jenna didn't show up, they decided to hop in Bailey's car and make a stop at The Buzz.

It turns out that I didn't have enough anger to demolish the entire wall. I abandoned the sledgehammer when blisters began to form, my shoulder cried out in pain, and my stomach clawed with hunger.

The house grew darker with the setting sun. Rip turned on the clamp lights that let more light into the living room than the past fifty years combined. Walking into the living room was like walking onto a stage. I sighed as I looked at the entire wall I'd nearly de-wallpapered today and then to the wall I'd barely demolished. Rip had picked up the sledgehammer and inspected the damage I had done as I continued to scrape away at the wallpaper.

"Hey," Rip said several minutes later. I was just getting into a rhythm of scraping and was thrown off by his voice. "Come here," he instructed.

Rip was peeling back some of the dry wall from the hole I had made in the wall. I braced myself for a comment about how weak I was or the work he was about to make me do. "What is that?" he asked, pointing at something inside the wall.

Getting closer, I saw that his hand was running over the interior wood. Rip repositioned the clamp light nearby so that it shone into the wall. On the stud there was a crest with a knight and archer burned into the wood. "Do you know what it is?" Rip asked sounding excited.

"That's the Alton family crest," I said, running my finger over it. It was tradition in the Alton family to get the crest on one's eighteenth birthday. There was a long line of only male heirs until my mother was born. Nevertheless, I got a necklace with that same crest when I turned eighteen, Alex got a ring, and Bailey was given a charm bracelet.

"What's it doing on an interior stud?" Rip asked confused. I could see a million questions racing through his head when I looked into his eyes.

I shrugged. "Maybe it's something builders did back then? Andrew Alton did design and oversee the building of this house."

"Charli!" I heard my mom's voice outside. Her quick footsteps were full of purpose as she climbed the porch stairs. She sounded breathless and I feared something was wrong.

I jumped up and turned towards the front hall. "Mom?"

The front door flew open and the springs screeched in protest. "Charli!" my mother exclaimed as she appeared under all the spotlights in the living room. Her face was flushed and her short blonde hair was windswept. "Quick," she breathed and motioned for me to follow her. Her eyes were heavy with regret and desperation. "It's Sadie."

CHAPTER ELEVEN

When I flew out the front door, Bailey was sitting in the circle driveway, the car idling. "Hurry," she said and threw open the passenger door. "I'll give you a ride."

"What happened?" I asked, breathless, reaching for the seatbelt. "Is Sadie okay?"

Mom had jumped into the back seat and Bailey sped down Oak Street. "We were at The Buzz," Mom said, trying to catch her breath. "We had no idea."

"What happened?" I said more forcibly. I'd had a rough day and did not want to end it with my best friend's death.

"Alex called Mom," Bailey shared as we pulled onto the paved part of Oak Street.

Mom nodded. She turned in her seat to face me as best as she could. "Sadie was at home. Alex got called into the hospital," Mom shared. "The police showed up and asked Sadie questions about last night, with Jackson. One thing led to another and, well," Mom avoided my gaze. "Sadie's been arrested for Jackson's murder."

Her words echoed in my head before I could comprehend their meaning. "What?!" I finally spat out. I ran last night's events over in my head several times; what gave her the means, motive, and opportunity more than Rip—who punched Jackson—or me, who is (or was?) extremely upset with him.

"I don't get it either, Charli," Mom shared and shook her head. "But you should be there, we all should be."

Moment's later, Bailey turned left on Main Street

and found a parking spot behind the art gallery across the street from the police station. I had run out of the house without a jacket on. My sweater was covered in bits of wallpaper and stained in my blood from Jessica's earlier outburst. None of that mattered to me as I high-tailed it across the street with Bailey and Mom trying to keep up with my determined pace.

As I opened the heavy door to the police station, I was ready to cause a scene in order to get Sadie free. Arresting her for Jackson's murder was the most ridiculous thing I had ever heard of and someone was going to get an ear-full, and I did not mind that person being Jake right now. But the first person I came face-to-face with was Alex and his long face and sulking eyebrows; it immediately washed away my anger.

He was sitting on the long, hard wooden bench to the left of the front desk. His eyes were focused on the Styrofoam coffee cup in his hands. The cold gust of wind that walked in with me caused him to lift his gaze. Automatically, I pulled him into a hug because it sure did look like he needed one.

"You heard?" he asked as we parted. Mom and Bailey walked in then and Alex nodded, understanding.

"How?" I asked.

"Did you call Jillian?" Mom asked, pulling Alex into a hug.

"Yeah," he said and nodded. "Mr. Westbrook should be here shortly."

The four of us squeezed together on the wooden bench as the police station continued its bustle without our presence making a difference. "But how?" I asked again, still confused as to how Sadie could be booked for murder.

Alex shook his head, not quite comprehending it either. "She threatened him in the past and last night," he shared.

"Yeah, but it was just a threat—an empty threat at that," I said. I was positive—one-hundred percent sure––it was an empty threat. I did not believe Sadie could be capable of murder.

Alex nodded and stirred his coffee. "Remember that table she was dropping off in Springfield for her mother?" Alex asked.

I nodded. "Yeah," I responded. "That was the reason why she couldn't go to the Fall Fest with us, well that and the volleyball practice this morning."

"She has no alibi," Alex shared almost defeated. "She didn't buy gas or stop at a store. She didn't even meet the people who bought the table. They instructed her to leave it on the back patio. There's nothing to prove she wasn't with Jackson last night."

"But that's just suspicion of murder," I said. I was under suspicion of murdering the elementary school's principal in June and I was never arrested, how in the world was this different?

Alex took a deep breath. "Charli," Alex said painfully. "Jackson was found wearing Sadie's high school volleyball jersey."

CHAPTER TWELVE

"This is ridiculous," I kept repeating. Long after Mom and Bailey left, long after the clock struck midnight, long after Alex's fourth cup of coffee, I muttered, "This is ridiculous."

Those are the three words I wanted to tell Jake when I saw him come towards the front desk two hours after I arrived. When he saw me, though, he made a U-turn and avoided the front of the station.

They were the words I couldn't stop muttering as I paced the four-foot by eight-foot space as Alex's head jerked when he nodded off to sleep. And, finally, when the skinny cop who took Jessica away earlier in the day (or was that yesterday already?) came to the front desk and escorted Alex and me to the interrogation room to see Sadie, those three words were replaced with, "Are you okay?"

Sadie sat at the table in her sunflower-printed fleece pajama pants and her eyes were swollen with shock. Alex scooped her up into a hug before I had the chance. Her pale hand cupped the wispy locks on the back of Alex's head and she nodded to something Alex whispered into her ear, letting a small tear escape.

"My dad is taking the next flight out of Miami," she said when Alex let her go. His arm lingered on her shoulder even after I squeezed some life back into Sadie. "He thinks this whole thing is a misunderstanding—completely ridiculous," she shared as she sat back down and we followed suit. She tugged on the sleeves of her white thermal shirt, her eyebrows furrowed in worry.

Sadie's father used to own a successful law firm in downtown Alton Oaks before he retired. He represented anyone in town who needed him, but he also had clients from all over the state, ranging from Bloomington to Carbondale to Gurnee. "It *is* ridiculous," I said from my seat at the head of the table. "We know you didn't do it, Sadie."

Hesitation soaked Sadie's expression. "What is it?" Alex asked, rubbing her shoulder. "It's worse," she admitted. She bit her lip, looking from me to Alex. "I only just heard," she explained, wringing her hands. "Based on the wound on the back of Jackson's head, they have a pretty good idea the weapon was unique—a U-shape."

My lips were dry as I hung on her every word. "They found my mom's old hand saw in the back of my pick-up; the curved wooden handle is missing. It's apparently a good fit for the murder weapon." Sadie's expression teetered between an incredulous eye roll and fearsome disbelief. "It was in the toolbox in the back of my truck; I'd been meaning to stop at the hardware store to get it fixed," she admitted.

Silence covered the room for a moment, hovering like cigarette smoke, as this news seeped into a stone-cold fact. "That's ridiculous!" I finally declared, breaking the tentative atmosphere. "Why use the handle of the saw? You'd think the sharp end would be easier!" I passively dismissed the bluntness of my words.

"Charli," my brother's soft but firm voice cut me off. The last thing Sadie needed was my outburst. Alex's eyes gave me a warning, but turned tender when I had realized what I was doing. "Charli," my brother started again, rubbing Sadie's shoulders, "they found a bit of blood on the saw."

The sentence was hard to swallow. How could this

have happened? "I told them it was probably from my mom; she had to have nicked herself," Sadie explained at a loss. I thought back to our childhood. Her mother was a craftsman; a skilled woodworker, but she often had bandages around her fingers. Sadie's theory made sense.

Nevertheless, I rubbed my face in my hands, frustrated at the situation. "I'm sorry, Sadie," I offered, remorseful, feeling how warm my face had gotten.

She offered a sympathetic smile and Alex grabbed her hand for support. The look they exchanged made it clear that they loved each other and it filled my heart with warmth, despite the circumstances. "Are you okay, Charli?" she asked, a spark rekindled in her eyes. "I only just heard before..." she trailed off, but I knew she meant she found out about Jackson's demise when the police showed up at her door. Sadie was usually Miss Questions McInquiry—a nickname I never called her to her face. She was always eavesdropping on gossip, but after spending most of the night driving and then coaching the volleyball practice, I didn't blame her one bit for falling behind on her bad habits.

"I'm fine," I lied. Sadie needed help first. Besides, the pain and anger I felt wasn't going to go away over night. I needed to make sure Jackson didn't take Sadie down with him. I needed to help prove her innocence. Her father could take on the legal part, but I was determined to tackle Jackson's angle. "You're innocent, Sadie, and I am going to prove it. I will find out who murdered Jackson and it most definitely wasn't you."

Sadie was the Watson to my Sherlock when I was determined to clear my name in June. She was by my side through it all and I wasn't going to just let the police handle this.

Filled with fervor, I left Alex and Sadie behind and marched into the chilly air that stagnates in the middle of the night, just before dawn. I hated the drama that Jackson brought into my life, even after his death. I would clean up this mess like I cleaned up all of his other messes, but this time it wasn't for the sake of our marriage. It was to save my best friend.

I groaned when I realized what I had to do: I had to track down Jessica.

CHAPTER THIRTEEN

I sat on the bench outside the Alton Oaks' Bank & Loan on the corner of Oak & Main, and pulled out my cell phone. After I called several motels and inns around Sheridan and asked for guests under the names Quincy or Neilson, I didn't have any luck.

Alton Oaks residents were beginning their Sunday morning commute to The Buzz or the sunrise church service as I began to feel defeated. What if Jessica had left town already? Was she allowed to? The Alton Oaks police had taken her away from the Alton House yesterday afternoon completely inebriated; she couldn't have gotten far.

The sun grew stronger from behind me and I welcomed the little warmth it offered. Alex let me borrow his jacket when I left the police station, but it was so big—despite my brother's tall, lanky frame— that it attracted pockets of cold air. I decided to warm up inside, but my only options were The Buzz and the church... and the inn. The only place for Canaries to stay in town since The Daisy Mountain Bed and Breakfast closed sometime after I left for college. I thought I'd try my luck there.

The air was warm and smelled like a buffet breakfast filled with maple syrup, sausage, and scrambled eggs. Hunger clawed at my stomach as I walked past the festive display of pumpkins near the crackling fireplace when I walked to the front desk.

"Hi," I greeted the middle age woman with gray roots and a lipstick-covered smile. Her short, curly hair bounced across her face as she looked up from the computer screen. The game of solitaire that she was engrossed in reflected in her brass name plate bearing the name Patti.

"Welcome to the Alton Oaks Inn, do you have a reservation?" she asked, minimizing her solitaire window.

"Actually," I said, feigning exhaustion. "I have a friend from out of town and I think she's staying here. We went out yesterday for a birthday celebration brunch. One thing led to another and, you know," I said and made a motion with my hand that implied drinking. "Anyway, we were so out of it, I don't know how I got home. I just wanted to make sure she made it back."

Patti's eyebrows raised with realization. "Yes, I remember her." Her fingers danced across the keyboard. "Sounds like you guys had quite the time. The police brought her in."

"Oh!" I exclaimed, sounding shocked with a hand to my mouth. "Is she all right?"

Patti looked at the numbered keys hanging behind her. "Room 12, go ahead and check on her yourself. She might need some help this morning."

"Oh my goodness, thank you," I said and turned towards the green and tan oak-leaf printed carpet that led down the hallway.

Scanning the brass numbers on each door, I didn't find room twelve until I turned the corner. It was the last door on the main floor. A baby was crying somewhere down a long hallway, but silence came from behind room twelve. Though I knocked firmly on the door, it didn't sound very loud. After several moments I knocked again, bruising my knuckles by trying to be louder.

I heard stumbling, followed by a loud bang and swearing. Opening the door slowly, Jessica leaned onto it for support. Dark circles swelled beneath her mascara-smeared eyes. Her blonde hair was a forest of tangled knots, and she reeked of vodka.

"Not you," she replied, as if the words caused physical pain. Her voice was scratchy and I'm sure she was dehydrated. She moved to close the door, but every one of her movements was slow and weak, so I slipped my foot over the threshold to stop it.

"Look," I said, gazing down the hallway and then back to her. "You want justice for Jackson. I want to clear my best friend's name. Just give me ten minutes."

Looking down at her, I felt like a puppet master. In her state, I could probably make her do anything I wanted... maybe that's why Jackson ran after her. I shuddered thinking about it and removed my foot to give her a chance to say no.

Jessica's smeared makeup outlined her dry, red eyes as she looked up at me. "Five," she hoarsely stated and stumbled her way to the bed where she collapsed.

I found an empty plastic pitcher next to the sink and filled it with water. "What happened that night?" I asked, letting my voice and the sound of running water echo in the small space.

Jessica didn't answer so I shut the water off and filled a disposable cup. She was lying on her stomach, eyes closed, and a tear was caught on her eyelashes. "Here," I said, handing her the cup of water and putting the pitcher on the nightstand. "Drink," I said.

She sat up slowly, grabbed it and asked, "What? Did you poison it?" Instead of waiting for an answer, she gulped it down quickly. I watched as a trail of water leaked from the corner of her lips and dribbled down her chin. This was the same person who would knock on our apartment door, dressed in a sports bra and running shorts, or a tight sundress and ask if we needed anything from the store or farmer's market. For the longest time I thought of her as an endearing (if not sometimes intrusive) neighbor. But all of it was a facade; ulterior motives to initiate secret rendezvous with my husband.

Pushing the anger aside for Sadie's sake, I sat on the opposite bed and asked again, "What happened the other night with Jackson?"

Jessica had wiped the water off her chin with the sleeve of her shirt... Jackson's shirt. I only then noticed that she was wearing one of his paint splattered Santa Fe shirts and I tried not to let it bother me, despite suddenly grinding my teeth. Jessica only looked at me as if answering my questions was below her.

I sighed and let my eyes sweep across the room. The room was delightfully decorated in shades of red and gold. The heavy curtains did not let in the light of the rising sun and the deep red bedspread against Jessica's pale legs made me think of Snow White. The only things that looked out of place in the room were Jessica's pants, crumpled at the floor of the bed, and her purse and keys on the bedside table. "Why did you guys come to Alton Oaks?" I asked, noticing the paintbrush keychain I put in Jackson's Christmas stocking our first year in Albuquerque.

Jessica poured herself another glass of water and downed it in one gulp. "He got your letter. He didn't want to play your games anymore and wanted a divorce so we could get married," she stated, matter-of-factly. "Jesse needed a ride to Boston so we made a trip out of it," she added with a shrug.

"Jesse?" I asked. "Jesse Randall?" He was Jackson's roommate in college and his best friend. Jesse was the witness at our wedding in Vegas. Jesse, who was always coming over on my payday when I'd gone grocery shopping and ate our food. Jesse, who one week wanted to be a hip-hop street dancer and the next train dolphins.

"Yeah," Jessica replied as if it was a stupid question. "He met a girl rock climbing in Colorado and they're planning to get married. We were all going to have a double wedding after you signed the divorce papers." Jessica's anger suddenly turned to sadness and she let a flood of tears pause the conversation. "He was going to be my husband," she said in between gasping for air. I fought the urge to argue with her, that he was still technically, *my* husband.

"Is Jesse still in town?" I asked without sympathy towards her emotional outburst.

"Your guess is as good as mine," she said, curling up in the fetal position on the bed, hugging a red and gold striped pillow. "Last I saw him," she said through a whimpered yawn, "was Saturday night."

Jessica slipped her bare feet beneath the comforter and added, "We went out to a bar after we left you at the high school." After taking a deep breath, she instructed beneath her closed eyes, "Now go away."

Without arguing, I slipped out of the room. The brass knocker on the wooden door jingled slightly as I shut the door behind me. *This trip wasn't a total waste of time,* I thought to myself as I walked back to the lobby. Jesse was with Jackson the night he died. And after knowing Jesse for several years, I could honestly say he was born to be a murder suspect.

CHAPTER FOURTEEN

As I walked out of the maple-bacon smoked scent of the inn, I realized my next step would be to track down the sketchiest nomad I'd ever met.

I had known Jesse almost as long as I knew Jackson. He would either be at the closest bar or outdoor adventure. Since Oakie's Bar & Grill was closed, I decided to check out the bike shop before I asked Rip for a ride to the closest bar that was open on a Sunday morning.

Bike Lite was a popular shop among the Canaries who were into cycling. It wasn't too far from the Whett River Canal Trail and all the Canaries stopped there before hitting the bike path. I had never been inside because I never had a reason. Mr. K. was our local bicycle repairman at a far less cost. When he fixed up my road bike this summer, his payment was a jar of my mother's dill pickles and a loaf of banana bread—my grandmother's recipe. He refused the money I tried handing to him; I don't know what the locals would do without him.

When I stepped into Bike Lite, I felt like I had left Alton Oaks behind me. Besides the wooden floorboards, everything was bright, new, and shiny. Bicycles hung from the walls and displays of safety gear, accessories, and protein gel packs were strategically placed on the sales floor. Near the registers in the back of the store, there were racks of clothing: padded bicycle shorts, nylon pants, and thermal tops that reduced wind resistance.

"Hiya!" A tall man with a long brown beard greeted me from behind the register. He was putting out packages of hand warmers next to the display of headlamps. The man couldn't have been much older than I was, but years of being out in the elements made tanned wrinkles prominent around his eyes.

"Hi," I greeted. Something about the commercialism of the store unnerved me. I had been surrounded by the small-towniness of Alton Oaks for so long, being in Bike Lites was almost surreal.

The man quickly looked me up and down and said, "You're a local, aren't you?"

"How can you tell?" I asked, letting my shoulders relax a little.

He laughed. "Locals are direct. They go straight to what they want. Canaries amble. They stop and go," he paused and studied me again. "You seem to be on some kind of mission."

I nodded. "I'm looking for someone," I said.

"Drake doesn't work on the weekends," he said with an eye roll, like he got that question all the time and moved to finish stocking his display.

"No," I said. "I'm looking for someone who might have come in here, probably to rent a bike."

"We get a lot of bike rentals on Sunday." He moved to the computer at the register and after a few clicks said, "All but two of our bikes have been rented or reserved." Turning from the screen and giving me a smile, he reported, "Lucky for you, we've only been open for an hour. We rented bikes to a family of four and a young man."

I bit my lip in hopeful thought. "About this tall?" I asked, putting my hand a few inches above my forehead, "With rusty-brown hair?"

The bearded man nodded. "He walked out seconds before you walked in. You might be able to catch him.

He rented the bike for the day. Otherwise he should return it around five."

I sprinted out the door as he finished his sentence. "Thank you!" I waved and was slapped by the still chilly morning air. Bike Lite had been well-heated, and now I had pulled my brother's very large coat tight around my waist as I scanned for a bicycle. I cut through Town Circle and was met by the bracingly cold air coming off the river. The sun was incredibly beautiful, rising over the river and through the autumn-colored leaves, but, *dang*, it was cold.

To the right of the western gardens surrounding Town Circle I saw him. He was unmistakable. The bike leaned against a bench as he bent over to tie his shoes. He didn't look like a seasoned bicycler with a skin-tight outfit. Instead, he wore a black fleece sweater over a forest-green thermal, and a pair of jeans that were frayed at the bottom. I shivered thinking about how cold his ankles were about to get. "Jesse!" I yelled and picked up my pace to catch him. Even across the distance between us, I could see his exaggerated eye roll.

"Charlotte," he said, faking pleasantries. "What are you doing here?"

He didn't just ask that, did he? I thought. "I live here," I stated matter-of-factly. "What are *you* doing here?"

His whole body was jittery and couldn't be still, as if he had just downed an entire pot of coffee. He shifted his weight from leg to leg, moved his hands from his pockets, to his belt loop, to behind his back, and his eyes didn't quite stay on me for too long. "Just passing through. You know, old school road trip with Jackson."

I lifted my eyebrows at how evasive he was acting; how carelessly, without emotion, he threw out Jackson's name. "The last time I saw you, you and

Jackson had a fistfight. You showed up at his family reunion in Santa Fe and I found you guys trying to rip each other's heads off. You swore off his friendship and left."

Jesse shrugged. "I was an idiot," he simply stated. The look on my face must have portrayed something other than naïve belief in his story because, with more agitation, he then added, "Jackson told me about this girl he was secretly seeing and I liked her better than you, so I hung around." Jesse paused for a moment, looking up and down the bike path, and then added bluntly, "And now he's dead."

If I hadn't been so tired, Jesse's provoking probably would have triggered anger, but instead I suppressed a sigh and ran a hand over my face. Jesse grabbed the bike and began walking east. My time to get answers from him was limited. "You don't seem very upset," I pointed out.

"Neither do you!" he shot back. I fully expected him to climb onto the bike and pedal away, but instead he stopped and said, "Look, we all grieve in different ways. Since I'm in the middle of the flattest damn part of the country, there's no rocks to climb. So let me take this bike and burn off my sadness with a twenty mile bike ride, okay?"

"Just tell me what happened that night. That's all I want," I pleaded.

Jesse flew his leg over the bike and put the bicycle helmet on his head. As he fastened the straps, he explained, "Charlotte, we had a few drinks at the bar a few miles out of this god-forsaken town. Jackson was clearly upset about what had happened between you and your *bodyguards*." I moved to argue this point, but decided not to; I needed what information I could get from him while he was willing. "We made it back to the inn and parked the van. He said he needed to take a walk. Jessica and I went inside for a nightcap and that was the last time I saw him alive."

"Didn't you think to—" I started, but Jesse had already sped away.

I watched him ride into the rising sun, wishing he'd answer the questions still swimming around in my head. Turning towards Town Circle to put a barrier between the cold river breeze and me, something about the conversation I'd had with Jesse didn't sit right. If Jesse's only alibi was Jessica—who was too drunk to know up from down—the police should know. Though I had left the police station not quite two hours ago, I decided to go back and talk to Jake. He was always there to listen during Sara Zimmer's murder in the spring and I expected him to act the same now. It was only half a block away and the desire to be out of the chill quickened my pace.

When I walked into the station, I immediately went through the partition that separated the inner workings of the station from visitors. I didn't have time to explain—shouldn't they know me here by now?

"Jake!" I called as I saw him exit the chief's office and circle around to his desk. He looked forlorn and lost... the uneven beard didn't help his image either.

When Jake saw me, I swear I saw him roll his eyes and it made me falter. "Charli," he scolded, dropping a heavy pile of papers and file folders onto his desk, "you can't just come back here whenever you feel like it."

Ignoring him, I said, "I need you to check out—"

"—No," Jake stated, turning to face me. His piercing eyes were only a foot from mine and I froze. "You cannot tell *me* what to do. This case is personal for you. You cannot get involved."

Jake looked away and busied himself with organizing the papers on his desk. We were all tired, physically and mentally. "With or without your help,

I'm going to prove Sadie's innocence," I said, though it sounded more like a warning.

A heavy, frustrated sigh exited Jake's lips before he turned his swivel chair to face me. "Please, Charli," he said, holding his head in his hands. "Leave this to the professionals."

Perhaps it was exhaustion that caused my outburst, or maybe it was all the churning, unorganized emotions from Jackson coming to town with Jessica, a divorce, a murder, and my best friend arrested for his murder whirling around in my head. Whatever the explanation, I swiveled his chair so fast that his head spun to face me. I leaned my hands on the arms of his chair and, full of conviction, said, "Lotta fat good you professionals did on the last two murders. Correct me if I'm wrong, but Sadie was the one who figured out who killed Ms. Dempsey *and* Ms. Newton last June. Sadie deserves a lot more attention than what you're giving her."

"We're doing all we can," Jake said through clenched teeth, clearly upset.

Straightening out the oversized coat that hung off my frame, I stood up and replied, "Then you tell me: Have you questioned Rip like you questioned me? Because he threatened Jackson too that night. Do you even know who Jesse Randall is? Because the last time I saw him before this morning, he was trying to rip Jackson's face off in a fist fight. And he's here in Alton Oaks."

Before Jake could even muster a reply, I turned on my heel and left in a huff. Sadie would not spend another night in this police station; I was determined to prevent that.

CHAPTER FIFTEEN

"Are you *just now* getting in?" Rip asked, shocked. He'd had the luxury of a hot shower, and probably a breakfast while he was making that thermos full of coffee he was currently pouring. I could tell he had cleaned up the remnants of my temper tantrum last night because there were no hazardous splinters or broken wood ready to impale a clumsy employee (*cough*, me).

"Why are you working on a Sunday morning?" I asked, sticking out my hand and bottom lip, hoping he'd give me his cup of coffee.

"I'm heading out to Bloomington to pick up some lumber and supplies. I needed to take a few more measurements before I left," Rip explained and handed me the plastic mug. As I greedily gulped down the hot liquid, I silently hoped he hadn't spiked it like he had the last beverage he'd offered me.

Rip's lips twitched as if he debated whether or not to tell me something. Finally, he asked, "Do you want to see what I found last night?"

I shrugged and took another gulp that seemed to open my eyes a bit wider. Rip moved to the study on the other side of the wall I had bulldozed and returned with an aged envelope. "I was inspecting the built-in shelves on the other side of this wall last night, to see if I needed to replace or reinforce anything, or if we really had to get rid of the whole wall. I found this on the top shelf, wedged behind a loose panel."

He gingerly handed me the contents of the envelope

one-by-one: World War II bonds, U.S. Marshall
vouchers, payment vouchers and receipts from Andrew
Alton's work as a U.S. Marshall. I looked at each
yellow, aged paper in amazement. "And the *pièce de
résistance*," he said triumphantly and handed me a
brittle sheet of paper that was worn where it had been
folded: an arrest warrant for D. B. Williams, dated
1908. On the bottom, in long pen strokes of faded black
ink, were three words: *He is mine.*

The full weight of history held my silent
astonishment. These were certainly my great-great-
grandfather's—some of these documents were not only
a testament to our family—to the Alton House, but to
our town's history. "This is amazing," I stated, looking
at the papers in front of me. "You need to give them to
Mrs. Lupizo down at the library; she's the head of the
historical society," I said, still marveling at the papers
in my hands.

Rip nodded noncommittally and very carefully
began to collect the papers. "How's Sadie doin'? She all
right?" he asked, changing the subject.

The plastic mug was nearly emptied when I removed
it from my lips to reply. "No," I said, shaking my head.
"Well, yes," I stumbled. "Physically she's fine, but
she's pretty shook up. I can't stay and talk," I said
suddenly and downed the last bit of coffee. "I just came
home to change clothes, grab my coat, and some food,"
I reported, handing the mug back to him and then
dashed up the stairs without another word. I was
grateful he didn't ask follow up questions as I took
every other stair with determination.

The mirror on the inside of my closet door caught
my gaze as I reached for the first available shirt and
pair of clean jeans. I was a fright; I still had blood
crusted on the side of my nose from the altercation with

Jessica yesterday—why hadn't anyone pointed that out?

I probably should have taken the time to shower, but if Sadie didn't have that luxury, then neither did I. Everyone I encountered would have to deal with the greasy roots of my hair, the bags under my eyes, and the split lip from Jessica's earlier lashing that I tried to ignore.

The banister along the stairs was loose and I tried not to touch it for fear that I'd fall to my death. Not that I needed it—I flew down the stairs with a plan. Running smack dab into Rip was not part of that plan. "Oh, sorry!" I said, putting my hands up.

Apparently the force of my body weight flinging into Rip didn't phase him. He still had his hand on the knob of the storm door and looked at me questioningly. "Sometimes I think you're a hazard to humankind," he remarked.

"Ha, ha," I said sarcastically as I grabbed my coat off the hook on the hall door and followed him outside.

Rip had a black pick-up truck parked on the side of the house and before we parted ways, I grabbed the sleeve of his leather coat momentarily. "Hey, can I ask you something?"

With a raised eyebrow of impatience, he jutted his head in response. "What?"

I looked from the dead leaves beneath my feet to the old tire swing on the oak tree in the front yard and then to Rip. "You didn't kill Jackson, did you?"

"No," he said immediately in a dark tone. "Why would you ask that?" The cracking of Rip's knuckles made me want to find a way out of this conversation, but I didn't.

"I'm just trying to clear Sadie's name and I've reached a dead end." Frustration tainted my features. I felt like there was a clue right under my nose, but I just couldn't see it. "I can't find anything," I admitted.

Honestly, I lacked the courage to do this alone. I always had Sadie beside me, or Alex, or my dad... or Jackson.

Rip began walking backwards to the truck with an air of indifference. "When I can't find something, I retrace my steps," he said simply and turned to open the door. "But I still haven't found my shackle bolts," he mumbled.

Feeling helpless with his advice, I gave a half-hearted wave anyway. "Drive safe," I said and bit my lip.

I did miss Illinois in the fall, especially Alton Oaks. I forgot how festive and colorful the town became. I used to love walking into town and hear the crunching leaves under my feet, seeing the flocks of birds flying south overhead, or cutting through the forest of oak trees, hearing acorns dropping all around me as I went to Sadie's house. I had the sudden urge to call Sadie and see if she wanted to play in the leaves or carve pumpkins. But she wouldn't answer and I frowned with the realization. I decided to stick with my original plan and stop at Froz T's and bring Sadie our traditional treat of ice cream tacos. It might be cold out, but it might make her feel a tad bit better.

As I walked down Main Street with an ice cream taco in a Froz T's take-out bag, I didn't expect it to be a problem. However, as I walked past the partition at the front desk and made a beeline to the interrogation room, Jake cut me off. "And what do you think you're doing?" he asked, looking down at me with a hand on his hip. The bags under his eyes were just as bad as mine; he probably hadn't gotten any sleep either.

"Visiting Sadie," I stated as if it didn't need to be said.

"You can't bring that inside," he said, pointing to the brown bag blazing the name Froz T's in purple ink.

Taking the transparent plastic container out of the bag, one could clearly see it was only an ice cream taco, with the vanilla ice cream already beginning to ooze out of the waffle cone shell and leaving a trail of green-tinted coconut shavings. "Seriously, Jake?" I asked, cocking a hip with attitude. "Do you really think I stuck a file in the ice cream? Geez, you know me. You know Sadie. Please, just let me do this."

Jake narrowed his eyes at me and I expected to either be escorted out of the station, or to get a tongue lashing. "Fine," he spat. "Do what you want, like always."

His last sentence didn't register until he stomped away. "What is that supposed to mean?" I asked, taken aback, but he didn't hear me. I watched him plop down at his desk, throw a file folder onto its corner, and rub his face with his hands. *What was his problem lately?* I wondered.

I pushed aside the urge to talk to Jake and instead opened the door to the interrogation room. Mr. Wilder was there in one of his old, expensive suits. When he retired to Florida, he seemed to live in cargo shorts and flower-print or Gator-themed tops, which was hard to swallow when my entire life he was Sadie's dad: the intimidating lawyer who wore dark suits, power ties, and never smiled. Seeing him back in his old garb gave a small sense of normalcy to my world again.

Beside him, and among a sea of papers, notebooks, and file folders, was Mr. Westbrook, the lawyer who took over Mr. Wilder's firm and who once worked for Sadie's dad. Looking small and meek on the other side of the table, was Sadie. She carried the same pained look she had when she was grounded for bad grades or when her parents forced her to take honor's algebra.

All faces flew in my direction as I entered the room. "Sorry," I said as I closed the door behind me.

"Charli," Mr. Wilder greeted with a nod.

"Daddy," Sadie said softly, "Can we have a minute?" Her eyes glistened and I wasn't sure if it was real emotion or a tactic she'd learned when dealing with her father.

Mr. Wilder glanced down at his notes. "Mr. Westbrook and I need to go over a few things," he said as he placed his briefcase on the table. "I'll bring you a proper meal from Oakie's," he said, eying my ice cream with distaste. "Then we'll rehash some of this," he shared, but it sounded more like a warning than it did a comfort. Mr. Wilder was always that way.

"Thanks, Daddy," Sadie said, giving him a hug. She looked so tiny in her baggy pajamas and even more pale with her lack of sleep.

As the two men exited the door, Sadie enveloped me in a hug. "You have perfect timing," she said, nearly in tears. "Now I remember why I didn't follow my parents down to Florida."

I handed her the ice cream taco and asked, "That bad?"

Sadie immediately opened the plastic container and dove in, ravenous. "It was the first time Alex and my dad met in like twenty years. It wasn't a fun experience," she said with her mouth full. "The tension was insane, like they were competing over who could make me feel better the most." She took another bite of the taco, half of it already demolished. "I finally told Alex to go home and get some sleep in case the hospital called." After swallowing the last bite, she licked her fingers and said, "Honestly, Charli, besides getting a free ice cream taco, this is a nightmare."

Sitting down in the closest chair, I said, "I know, Sadie. We'll figure this out."

Instead of returning to her seat, the ice cream seemed to give her some energy and she began pacing in the tiny space. "Do you remember Jackson's friend Jesse?" I asked. The last time Sadie came to visit me in Albuquerque, Jesse was crashing on our couch and kept hitting on Sadie. It was what had probably prompted Sadie's sudden urge for a road trip to Flagstaff during the remainder of her visit.

Sadie put her hands on her hips and rolled her eyes at me as she paced. "Don't remind me," she said and continued her gaze to the floor.

"He came in with Jackson and Jessica," I shared.

Sadie grabbed the back of the closest chair and leaned towards me with interest. "What?" she asked, intrigued. Ice cream tacos and gossip: two things that could make Sadie feel better, however briefly.

"Apparently," I said with disdain, "the three of them were on their way to Boston to meet Jesse's fiancé and have a double wedding."

Sadie's jaw dropped in shock. "Are you kidding?" she finally spat out.

I shook my head. "Nope. Their idiotic plan was to get the divorce papers signed one day and married the next."

Sadie's jaw seemed to drop further and she ran a hand through her straight yet frazzled hair. "But I thought he and Jackson—"

"Me too," I agreed, remembering the black eye on Jackson and the blood pouring from Jesse's nose the last time I'd seen them together.

"Then why—?"

I cut Sadie off, slightly irritated by the information. "Jesse told me that he liked Jessica better than me so he came back around."

Shaking her head, Sadie said, "But that doesn't make any sense!"

"I know!" I said, throwing my hands in the air. "But when did Jackson and Jesse ever make any sense?

Every time they get together they make bad choices." My mind flitted across the memories of their failed business plan to develop Beer World, or how I stopped them from planning to bungee jump off the Hoover Dam.

Sadie sank into the black, faux leather chair and slumped her shoulders. "I'm sorry I can't be there for you through all this," she admitted.

Dumbfounded at her priorities, I responded, "Me? Sadie, you're the one under arrest. For murder! Don't worry about me." I leaned over the table towards her. "My breakdown will undoubtedly come later. For now, we worry about getting you out of here." Sadie offered me a sympathetic smile. "Do you remember anything about that night, before you left the school?" I asked as Sadie tugged on the sleeves of her shirt.

Sadie shook her head defeatedly. "The police asked me, Alex asked me, my dad and Mr. Westbrook asked me. I've been replaying that night in my head non-stop. There's nothing out of the ordinary or useful." She shook her head and picked at the bottom of the table. "After Jackson drove away, you walked to Rip's bike, I walked to my car. I followed you guys out of the parking lot before Rip hit the gas like a bat out of hell— why are you hanging out with him?" she asked, momentarily making eye contact with me.

I shrugged. The answer was probably convenience, but I didn't dare interrupt Sadie's train of thought.

"I got on US-16 and took 67 down. I didn't take the toll road because I forgot the I-Pass on the kitchen table and they have that stupid rule now where you pay more if you don't have the I-Pass with you. Having that would have been useful," she added as an afterthought. "I listened to my iPod—some Prey for Chance and Maroon 5 to keep me awake and then some podcasts on the way home. I dropped the table off at the address my mom gave me. I saw no one." Sadie sat up and admitted, "I know it all seems shady, but I can't figure out a way out of this."

"You delivered the table, there's proof right there!" I said.

"But no one *saw me*," she said, frustrated. "I could just as easily hired someone to deliver it for me, as Jake pointed out," she explained with a hint of irritation.

"What about gas mileage?" I asked.

Sadie shook her head. "There's no proof of what my mileage was. Besides, those things are easy to stage." She sighed. "If only I'd stopped at a gas station for a coffee, or gotten an oil change the previous day. There are so many should-ofs going through my head right now that I can't focus on the right-nows."

"What about your jersey, Sadie? How did it get on Jackson?" I asked.

Sadie shrugged. "I had it with me," Sadie admitted. "I wanted to show the girls—my team—to hype them up. I didn't know it was gone until the police asked how it got to Jackson." Looking up at me, she added, "And I don't know how it got on Jackson. I honestly don't."

Seeing Sadie so deflated hurt. She was always the strong, feisty one. Perhaps I depended on her too much. Either way, my fervor to prove her innocence was anew. "I won't give up, Sadie," I said. "There's always something."

"But *what?*" she asked, her blue eyes glistened as she looked up at me.

No matter how hard I tried to form words, to give her an answer, nothing manifested. I had to find something.

CHAPTER SIXTEEN

As soon as Mr. Wilder and Mr. Westbrook returned with Oakie's aluminum carry-out trays of Oscar's breakfast scramble and three extra large to-go cups from The Buzz, I left. I took the hint and excused myself, promising Sadie I would return with good news. That was my goal, anyway.

Outside the police station, once again I saw the rest of the world going on with their lives. How could their lives be so normal and mine be so upside down? How did tomorrow come for them when I was still stuck in yesterday?

Across the street, the church bells tolled, and the last morning congregation left the church. Where was I supposed to go from here? It felt like Sadie's life was in my hands, despite her father and Mr. Westbrook working hard on her case.

A bitingly brisk breeze shook the long skirts of the women leaving the church and made my shoulders wiggle. I let my feet carry me towards Oak Street, trying desperately to come up with a plan: How was I going to prove Sadie innocent of Jackson's murder? Thoughts of unvisited gas stations and non-existent receipts filled my head. Maybe the people who received the table saw her from the window, or maybe a neighbor caught a glimpse. Or maybe the house had a security camera that captured Sadie's image with a timestamp! But I was sure that the police would follow-up on that angle.

Oh! Maybe her footprint was in the dirt of their

backyard, or if they had a dog, maybe some of its, *ahem*, D.N.A. was on her shoes! I began to bite my thumbnail in discouragement as each theory and idea I came up with was even more ridiculous and far-fetched than the last.

"This is getting me nowhere!" I muttered to myself as I passed the Kratsky's house.

"Hey, cupcake!" Mrs. Kratsky called from the top of her stairs.

I turned my head and saw her leaning on the railing. Her old bones carried her surprisingly quick down the stairs. She had on a long camel-fur coat with black earmuffs. "Do you need a ride? I'm headed over," she shared, adjusting her black cotton gloves.

As much as I wanted to be alone, small town obligations made me reply, "Sure, that'd be great."

I mentally tried to prepare myself for questions that I did not want to answer as I climbed into the Halloween-decorated golf cart. Since the weather had turned, Mrs. Kratsky put on the plastic cover that kept most of the eye-watering wind from our faces. A black plastic cauldron was secured to the dash board with Velcro and filled with rock hard Twizzlers. "How's Sadie doin', hun?" she asked, concern coated her words instead of a thirst for gossip.

I nodded, words escaping me in the moment as desperate ideas flung past me on how to save Sadie.

Mrs. Kratsky pulled out of her driveway and onto Oak Street. The hum of the battery accompanied the churning wind. Just as we passed the fork to US-16, the road transitioned from paved asphalt to a gravel road and the hardened licorice jumped in the cauldron along with the solar-powered plastic pumpkin lights that hung from the soft top frame. "If you want my advice," Mrs. Kratsky said as she glanced in my direction, "That guy, Rich, knows something. I can't believe your mother is letting him tear apart your house." She shook her head in disapproval.

Of course, she meant Rip; she still didn't trust the new kid in town. Her advice was just as bad as Rip's: "When I can't find something, I retrace my steps," I rolled my eyes as we passed his house.

As we pulled up the Alton driveway, I saw Mom and Bailey were already perched on the porch swing. Mrs. Kratsky grabbed her red and black thermos and climbed the steps without hesitation or trace of arthritic pain. I followed behind, slowly, dragging my feet. "There was a break-in at the high school this weekend," I heard my mother divulging as Mrs. Kratsky made herself comfortable on the rocking chair.

"Was anything taken?" Bailey asked. Her long blonde hair fell over her shoulder and a manicured hand with dark red nail polish tucked it behind her ear.

"No. The storage shed was missing the lock, but nothing seemed to be missing," my mother finished. "Did you ever find that horseshoe medallion you had hanging from your rearview mirror? I'm thinking maybe it was stolen," my mother added.

Bailey shook her head as I grabbed the rough, splinter-populated railing, and replied, "No. I'm thinking so too. I talked to the police about it, but I don't think it will turn up. I mean, why steal *that*? There's no value in it. The twenty dollar bill I keep in the car wasn't missing, or my iPod. It makes no sense."

My mother shook her head in disbelief. When she noticed me climbing the stairs, she patted the bench beside her. "Oh, Charli, honey, come sit with us," she nearly pleaded. "How are you doing?"

Hugging myself to stay warm, I sat down. "How is Sadie doing?" my mother asked and I was grateful the subject of her questions was not me.

"She's holding up," I said, though my voice sounded

far away. "But it sounds like there's a strong case against her."

"No one believes *Sadie Wilder*," my sister said her name with incredulousness, "is capable of doing, well, you know..." my sister trailed off and glanced at my direction. The image of Jackson's bloodied and torn face came front and center. A violent chill ran down my shoulders and scared away the image.

"No, no," Mrs. Kratsky added, shaking her head, "not Sadie."

"Did Jake say anything? Why has she been arrested?" my mother asked, though I wasn't sure if it was out of concern or gossip.

My heart broke thinking about my best friend sitting in jail, being accused for my husband's brutal murder. Guilt and pain choked me.

"Oh, no, never mind about that," Mrs. Kratsky seemed to almost chastise my mother. She turned in my direction and pointed a gloved hand in my direction, "All you need to know is that we're here for you, no matter what you need. You poor thing; your best friend and your husband. I can't begin to imagine how you're feeling." She leaned forward in her rocking chair and added, "You know what you need? Some of my chicken noodle soup. I will bring some over tonight. You let me know if there's anything you need, you got that, Charli?"

Love for my neighbor—the grandmother image in my life—filled my heart. I nodded, my eyes full of gratitude.

Before my mother could make amends, we turned our heads towards Oak Street as the Alton Oaks station wagon approached. The tires crunching on the gravel of the driveway made me cringe. We watched without a word as Jake exited the car. Anxious anticipation filled the air as he walked up the porch stairs.

"Good morning," Jake said brightly to the women on the porch, tipping his wide-brimmed deputy's hat.

There was a chorus of niceties from the women on the porch. I studied Jake's body language; how fluid his movements were, how confident and sure he was. When his eyes swept across me, he tensed for a moment; his jaw setting and his back straightening. "Sorry to disturb your morning, but I needed a word with Mrs. Sloane," he informed.

Everyone looked at Bailey, surprised. Relief melted away the tension in my shoulders that he wasn't seeking me, but it turned to regret when my sister seemed to lose some color. "Me?" Bailey asked hesitantly.

"Yes ma'am," Jake replied with a hand on his gun belt.

CHAPTER SEVENTEEN

"Whatever it is," Bailey started, "you can say it in front of my family." She gestured to the women on the porch with her palm.

Jake's gaze swept across us as he shifted his weight to one foot, cocking his hip. He pulled a manila envelope from beneath his arm that I hadn't seen was there. "It's regarding the inquiry you filed about a possible theft," he informed, opening the flap on the envelope.

"We found a variety of items recently and were wondering if the item in question is the one you're missing." Jake pulled an 8 x 10 photo from the envelope and handed it to Bailey.

"Yes! That's the horseshoe medallion that's been missing from my rearview mirror!" Bailey exclaimed. She showed the picture to my mother, pointing to the item in question. I couldn't help but lean over and glance at the photo myself.

A variety of items: the horseshoe medallion, a large broken Carabineer, half a set of dentures, the letter from a varsity jacket, a Master lock, and a D-shaped shackle bolt were strewn on the ground. My heart leapt into my throat when I saw the wooden handle of Sadie's handsaw among the items. "What does this mean?" my mother asked, handing the photo to Mrs. Kratsky. Jake had given the old woman two seconds to look at the picture before placing it back in the envelope.

"Mrs. Sloane," Jake said with formality, but was cut off by my sister.

"Jake, you've known me my whole life. You can call me Bailey," my sister said. Her demeanor relaxed when she realized Jake was only there to return her lost good luck charm.

Jake rubbed the uneven beard growing over his chin before replying, without addressing my sister by either title. "I need you to come to the station to answer some questions," Jake instructed.

"For this tiny little trinket?" my mother asked incredulously.

"Ma'am," Jake started, "there was blood found on it, along with the other items, and it's evidence in a current case."

"Was it Jackson's blood? I had nothing to do with it!" Bailey protested. "It was stolen from my car a week ago—before Jackson came to town!" Panic began to rise in her voice.

"I understand that," Jake said. "Which is why we need you to come down to the station and answer some questions. It will help us figure out what happened."

"Yes, of course," my mother said, grabbing my sister's elbow. She turned her attention to Bailey and said, "Let's go to your house and get your purse. I'll drive you downtown." Bailey nodded and both women rose.

"And Ms. Parker." Both my mother and I looked at Jake questioningly. Jake's attention was on me and my shoulders slumped. "If I could have a word?"

My mother and sister exchanged concerned glances with me, but I nodded to let them know I'd be fine. I watched them walk down the stairs and head towards Bailey's house.

Mrs. Kratsky rocked back and forth, her eyes on Jake and me, not getting the hint that Jake wanted a private conversation. His heavy-soled boots walked across the floorboards to the other side of the porch and

I followed. "Charli," Jake began, pulling out his Steno pad from his jacket pocket.

Using my first name was a small reassurance for me. "I need you to give me a description of your friend Jesse," he requested.

"He is not *my* friend," I clarified. "He's Jackson's."

"Regardless," Jake said, starting to grit his teeth, "please provide a description."

I studied his features, wondering why he suddenly needed this information. Was he finally following up on this lead? Did new evidence come to light? Was there an incident with a Canary that the police wonder was connected to Jackson's murder?

"You saw the items in the photograph, correct?" Jake asked with a hint of impatience.

I nodded, putting a hand on my hip.

"The Carabineer had a name written on it in permanent marker and we are investigating." He lowered his voice and inclined his head ever so slightly in my direction. "I'm trying to see if there's a connection."

I bit my thumbnail for a moment, letting this information sink in. "Was the name on the Carabineer Jesse?" I asked, but no hint of recognition crossed Jake's face. "His last name is Randall," I offered and saw a glimmer in Jake's eyes before he turned his attention to the Steno pad.

"Can you please spell it?" he asked. I thought back to the witness name listed on my marriage certificate. "R-A-N-D-A-L-L," I said in between biting my thumbnail. It was just like Jesse to label his rock climbing gear, even the smallest Carabineers: what's his is his, and no one else's. "He's about this tall," I said, my hand hovering an inch or two above my own height. "Dark brown hair, brown eyes. He has a scar on his right forearm."

Jake looked up in question. I wasn't sure if he was questioning how Jesse got the scar or how well I knew him.

"It was from a rock climbing incident. He loves outdoor activities: trail running, rock climbing, skiing, kayaking, et cetera."

"How long have you known him?" Jake asked without looking up.

"Since Jackson and I moved to Albuquerque after the Peace Corps. He stayed with us often. He moves from couch to couch, sometimes town to town."

"What does he do for a living?" Jake asked and shifted his weight to his other foot.

I shrugged. "He's never been able to hold down a job. I think he works long enough to buy what he needs or to go where he wants and then quits."

Jake murmured in thought. "Is he still in town?"

Again, I shrugged. "I don't know. He came to town with Jessica and Jackson, and Jessica is at the inn on Main Street. She would know."

Jake closed his Steno pad and seemed to debate whether or not to share more information. Eventually, his face softened and he took pity on me and my situation. "We know Jessica is at the inn; I've spoken with her," he said and a short sigh escaped his lips. "Because you are the deceased's..." Jake seemed to struggle finding the right noun and settled on, "widow, I can tell you that Jackson's blood alcohol level was 0.12 at the time of his death. Jessica remembers passing out that night, but someone was sober enough to drive the van back to the inn."

"You think it was Jesse?" I asked finding humor in that statement. Jackson and Jesse always seemed to match each other's drinks. There was never a time when one was more drunk than the other. I wouldn't have put it past Jesse or Jackson to drive while intoxicated.

Jake's lips moved to answer my question, but any kind of connection was shut down when Rip came out of the screen door carrying a sheet of plywood. "Yo, Charli!" he said jubilantly.

Tipping his hat in my direction, Jake turned and left the porch. I wanted to keep talking to him, but Jake made up his mind and descended the stairs, stone-faced.

"You are the most unmotivated worker I have," Rip said, taking the plywood to the saw horses on the front lawn.

I shrugged, watching Jake get in the station wagon and slam the door. "You get what you pay for," I said, hugging myself as a breeze rustled the dead leaves on the porch.

"Are you saying because I didn't pay you anything, I'm not getting much from you?" Rip asked. He pulled at the orange extension cord and plugged in the saw.

"Is that your experience with women?" I shot back.

A raucous laughter shook the other side of the porch and Mrs. Kratsky rose from the rocking chair; I had forgotten she was there. It was no wonder she was so good at collecting town gossip. Mrs. Kratsky put a hand on my shoulder and gave it a squeeze as she headed towards her golf cart. "Charli, don't you ever change," she said in good spirits.

A small smile tugged at my lips.

I watched as her golf cart ran into the dust that didn't quite settle after Jake drove down Oak Street. The screech of the table saw filled the air for a minute or two until Rip shut it off, satisfied with the cut. He carried the plywood up the stairs and I turned towards him. "Can I ask you something?"

He put the bottom of the plywood down on the porch but continued to hold the top in his leather gloves. The one lock of hair never seemed to stay gelled back and fell just above his left eye. "Are you sure you didn't kill Jackson?" I asked bluntly.

"What?" he asked, his forehead crinkled with the question.

"The police found some random items with Jackson's blood on them and one just happened to be a shackle bolt," I said. I didn't think Rip killed Jackson, but it was satisfying to see him squirm.

"How do you know it's mine?" Rip asked defensively. His grip seemed to tighten on the plywood.

I shrugged. "It's just weird that you mumble about missing a shackle bolt and all of a sudden one shows up with the potential murder weapon."

Rip grew increasingly irritated. "*Mine* were new— two of them—still in their packaging. I left them with my motorcycle. Bought them Friday morning. I don't think you have much of a case proving that one's mine," he said in a tone that would have frightened me if I hadn't known Rip. He picked up the plywood and went inside in a huff.

"Okay, okay," I said with my hands up, defensively. "Don't get your panties in a twist," I called after him. "Just a weird coincidence!"

Grabbing the railing of the front porch, I looked past the yard, past the distant houses, and down the dusty road that eventually led to Alton Oaks proper. I digested my conversation with Jake, grateful that he'd followed up with Jessica and now Jesse. Why hadn't he asked me about Sean, though? Why hadn't anybody followed up with him?

In the distance, past the falling oak leaves, I could make out my mother and Bailey coming out of my sister's front door and heading to the garage for the car. An idea struck me and I took off from the front porch, flying down the stairs and down the road, hoping I could catch the car before it took off down Oak Street.

My feet carried me steadily on the uneven terrain as I watched the car slowly back down the dirt driveway, lined in blooming mums, in between the tulips that long-since died. I waved my hands and called against the breeze, "Mom! Wait!"

I thought for sure they didn't hear me and would take off as soon as they pulled onto the road. "Wait!" I called again, thankful the rear red brake lights were still glowing.

The car grew closer, but was still a good fifty yards away. Relief slowed my pace when my mother stuck her head out the window and called, "Charli! Is everything all right?"

Catching up to the car, I fought for breath. I'm sure my sister and mother enjoyed the dramatics. "Fine," I said, breathing heavily. "Everything's fine." I took a moment to take a deep breath through my nose. The crisp autumn air filled my lungs. "Bailey, can I borrow your car?" I asked.

The scent of pumpkin spice drifted out from the car from an unseen air freshener. "Charli, you heard Jake: I have to go down to the police station," Bailey said from the passenger seat.

"I'll drop you off. Please?" I asked. "I need to run to Sheridan."

My mother looked at Bailey and my sister sighed. "All right," she relented. "Get in the backseat. You can get behind the wheel when we get to the station."

After my sister and mother got out of the car, I eagerly pulled onto Main Street. It had been a long time since I'd last driven a vehicle. As I made a right turn onto Oak Street, I thought about that memory—Jackson passed out in the passenger seat as we drove back to Albuquerque from Santa Fe just over two years ago. A tear blurred my vision as I pulled onto US-16 and I pushed it away; there would be time to mourn later. I wasn't ready to feel the sharp knife of reality and the churning emotions of death.

Driving the speed limit down US-16 was agonizing. I just wanted to get there and find the clue I hoped would be there. I had to find Sean.

As the yellow and red maple leaves fell over the road, my thoughts collected the bits of information I knew: Jackson came to the high school parking lot with Jessica, afterwards they met Jesse somewhere and went to a bar outside town. If I was right, it would be The Dead End, which straddled the town line between Sheridan and Alton Oaks. That would be my next stop, if I needed more information.

Afterwards, Jesse, Jackson, and Jessica drove to the Alton Oaks Inn where Jessica passed out, Jackson went for a walk, and Jesse—well, what he did from there is unclear. What if Jessica and Jesse were in on it together? No, that was ridiculous. I wouldn't put it past Jesse, but I couldn't see Jessica doing that. If all else fails, I'd have to walk the streets of Alton Oaks and ask questions—maybe Prescott's Grocers caught something on the security camera they installed after Sara Zimmer's death!

"First things first," I said to myself as a soft sixties-era song played on the radio. I had to focus on the first task on my list. Leave no stone unturned!

I pulled up to a small, red-painted, converted barn house that was across the football field from the high school. The paint was peeling and old rakes, snow shovels, and a push broom were weathered and rusty on the small front porch. Everyone knew this was where Sean lived with his mother. I had never visited before, but it was probably the reason Sean had such a deep connection with the high school.

I pulled my sister's car along the curb and got out,

pausing before approaching the house. The window on the far left side of the building was open a few inches and the white curtain played in the breeze. The scent of wood burning danced with the air, sometimes giving way to a horrid stench that reminded me of a dead raccoon I'd found in the shed one summer.

Climbing the steps, I had hoped to see Sean pop around the corner or catch his large figure lumbering across the football field; I didn't want to scare his mother. There was no doorbell on the old building, so I knocked on the door.

There were newer, well-kept houses nearby, though most were cottages with one or two A-line houses nestled deep behind the maple trees that lined the road. Long, vast front yards housed children's toys, roofed glider swings, cars on cinderblocks, and many types of Halloween decorations.

Turning back to the door, I opened the screen door and knocked a little louder on the storm door. The door hadn't closed completely when the last person left and it opened slightly; I heard the television on in the background, the volume high enough that I could hear audience laughter. "Mrs. Walters?" I called out, peeking my head inside.

I choked on the scent of dank uncleaned drains, mixed with something you'd find rotting in the back of the fridge, and urine—but I wasn't sure if it was human or animal. Sean's mother must have been reaching an age where she couldn't keep up with those household chores. I made a note to call Jenna about it when I finished here.

I took a deep breath before tentatively poking my head inside. "Mrs. Walters?" I called again, following the sound of the television. "I'm Sean's friend, Charli," I identified myself hoping I wouldn't scare her with my presence.

The floor plan was pretty open, it once being a barn. I saw the television in the far corner, two empty chairs facing it. "Mrs. Walters?" I called again, trying not to let the smell of the house get to me too much.

A light was pouring in behind the adjacent wall, which I guessed was the kitchen. The shudders above the breakfast nook were closed and covered in dust and grime; they hadn't been opened in a long time.

Rounding the corner, I saw the source of the odor. It wasn't just the flies hovering around the spoiled meatloaf and mashed potatoes that sat with the curdled milk in glasses on the table. It wasn't just the bowl full of peas growing white mold on it. It was Mrs. Walters, hunched over on her plate. Her skin ashen, with maggots crawling from her short gray hair and down her neck.

My gag reflux was in prime shape and I rushed out the door, dry heaving over the ledge. If I had eaten anything, it would have ended up on the overgrown hemlocks below. A middle-aged couple who were walking their Great Dane looked up at me curiously. "Call the police!" I said, leaning over the railing, my gag reflux kicked in again. "Hurry!" I urged.

CHAPTER EIGHTEEN

"Charli—I apologize—tell me one more time why you're here," Chief Gomes said when he arrived on the scene.

I had given my statement to the Sheridan Police Department after they surveyed the scene. A little over an hour later, Chief Gomes appeared in the station wagon without Jake. His adjusted his belt, anchoring it just below his Santa-like abdomen. He let out a heavy sigh with his request.

"Sean's my friend," I explained. "I wanted to check in on him because Jackson had said some pretty mean things to him that night at the high school." I shifted my weight, glad we weren't downwind from the breeze that passed through the house. "Sean's a bit *different*, as you know," I explained. "I just wanted to check-in on him."

Chief Gomes scratched his bushy white beard, surveying me. "And where is he?" he finally asked.

I shrugged, my eyes looking past him at the football field. "I don't know," I admitted. "He wasn't here when I got here."

"Are you sure about that?" Chief Gomes asked without skipping a beat. What? Did he think I was covering for Sean? That Sean was capable of this? I was offended for him.

"Absolutely," I said. "I haven't seen him since the night of the volleyball game."

Neighbors were watching from across the street and two houses down. Many of them stood with their arms crossed, children at their feet, whispering about what they guessed had happened. I turned around when the screen door opened so violently, it slapped against the house. A black body bag was being carried down the stairs on a stretcher.

"Can I go now?" I asked, returning my gaze to him.

Adjusting the back of his belt, he nodded. "Go ahead. I'll call if I have any further questions. But Charli?" he searched for my gaze. "Be careful. *This* is becoming a dangerous hobby," he warned. I knew he was referring to how often dead bodies popped up around me. Deep down I hated feeling guilty about that—it wasn't in my control!

"Yes sir," I said, looking down at the patch of dead crabgrass we stood on.

Without hesitating, I fished the keys out of my pocket and hurried to Bailey's car. I was almost pinned in between the ambulance and a Sheridan police car. Luckily, most of the vehicles dispersed when the ambulance left. Following suit, I pulled onto the road, but my hands were shaking so badly, I had to pull into the high school parking lot to collect myself.

I thought that by running home to Alton Oaks, I would find solace; a place to heal and start over again. It seems like I'd brought a curse with me: our wholesome hometown had had four murders in the past six months! I couldn't help but think that Alton Oaks was changing because of me; something that haunted *me*. Suddenly my world was made out of glass, each step had to be carefully calculated or it would all shatter. Perhaps I was being dramatic, but with everything happening in my life, I think I deserved a small break down in the parking lot of my old high school.

I looked up at the rudimentary image of myself in the mural. Getting out of the car, I leaned against the hood and let the wind erase the beads of sweat that gathered on the back of my neck with my panic attack. The trees bent to the wind and leaves scraped across the parking lot, collecting in corners and against the curbs. There was no football game or volleyball practice, no fundraiser or fair. Without the sound of students filling the air, it seemed eerie, like a scene in a horror movie.

I shook my head to get those ideas out. Walking to the entrance door of the gym, I let the ghosts from that night fill my memory. I stood here, Jackson's van was there, Rip muttered in the corner there. My eyes swept across the leaves swirling in a mini tornado as I tried to tame my hair as the wind picked up again. I walked along the corners and against the parking cement slabs hoping to find a clue.

What happened that night? What did I think I would find at the high school? I should be looking outside the Alton Oaks Inn. I was so distracted with looking in dark corners—both literally and metaphorically, and kicking leaves, and filling my mind with what-ifs, that I never heard him come behind me. And when I realized that I should scream, a large hand covered my mouth from behind me.

"Boo! I scawed you!" Sean said, releasing me, and clapping his hands in a fit of giggles. "Twick-or-Tweat! Happy Halloween!" His face was glowing with glee.

With a hand to my chest, I urged my heart to slow and thanked my genes for blessing me with a strong bladder. "Oh! Sean! You scared me!" I said, trying not to sound too upset.

"Twick-or-Tweat! Happy Halloween!" he said again, clapping as if I had complimented him.

"You shouldn't do that!" I scolded.

"Chawli's not happy?" His finger poked my cheek with the question.

"No," I said. "I was scared."

All glee drained from his face. "I'm sowwy. I only

want you to be happy."

An idea hit me as Sean slumped his shoulders and kicked a pile of leaves between the building and a cement slab. "Maybe you can help me," I suggested.

"Helping people is good," Sean said. "Helping makes people happy."

"Yes it does. Remember the one friend who didn't make me happy? Jackson?" I asked, trying to read Sean's facial expression, but he kept his face down, kicking the leaves.

"He is not a fwend. Fwends don't make you angwy and sad. Only mean people do that," he remarked.

I was getting somewhere with him—I could feel it. He knew something. "Yes they do," I agreed. "Did you see that mean man again? The next day maybe?"

Sean stepped onto the cement slab and jumped into the pile of leaves he kicked together. "Yes. The mean man called me names," he admitted.

A new lead! I could jump for joy! "Sean," I said putting a hand on his arm for a moment. "This is very important: where did you see him? Was he with anyone? What did he say?"

Sean jerked his arm from my reach and his, "You, you, you, you, you, you, you," ditty turned into an agitated moan. He rocked back-and-forth and flapped his hands rapidly.

"Sean, Sean, it's okay," I said, trying to soothe him. I remembered one of my ELL students was autistic and had a passion for anything electronic... and candy. I pulled an orange Starburst from my pocket. "Here, Sean," I said, putting the candy in his eyesight. "Do you want a piece of Halloween candy?"

The sugary treat broke his trance and his face lit up. "Owange is my favowit colow!" he said, greedily unwrapping the candy.

I suppressed a sigh of relief. "I like when leaves are

orange and purple," I offered, testing the waters.

"The colows of ouw school!" he said excitedly, clapping. Munching on the piece of candy, Sean began walking along the parking curb—one foot on the curb and one foot down on the asphalt, in front of the school mural. "I gave the mean fwend ouw colows," Sean admitted, scraping his black and white beat-up gym shoes across the dead leaves.

"You did?" I asked, feigning an impressed tone.

"Yeah," he said, still chewing the Starburst. "I felt bad fow being so mean to him, so I gave him ouw colows and let him play with my fwends to feel bettew." Sean turned and walked towards me, up and down the curb.

A dark cloud momentarily traveled past the sun and darkened the world in the parking lot. "What do you mean?" I asked, my heart skipping a beat as the sun popped back out.

Sean said nothing and turned back around, going up and down the curb again.

I took out my phone and dialed Jake's cell. As it rung, Sean noticed a change in my demeanor. "Did I make a bad mistake?" he asked and then began to rock and moan again, sitting on the curb.

I dug in my pockets for another piece of candy, but didn't find one. Out of candy, and Jake's phone going to voicemail, I hung up and tried a different approach.

Crouching down to Sean's eye level, I said gently, "Sometimes I say mean things when I lose my temper." Sean's face still scrunched up his features and his hands continued to flail. "But then I apologize because I didn't mean it and everyone's happy again."

It took a few moments for the moaning and rocking to die down, but when it did, Sean turned and asked, "If I apologize, will you be happy again?"

Looking down at him, he didn't seem so big and

menacing. I felt bad for him. "Let's see if it works," I said with a shrug.

"Okay," Sean said, giving in. "I will apologize."

Smiling, I reached out my hand. I looked over the football field towards Sean's house; of course the police cars had cleared by now! That was my luck! "Come, then," I said. "Let's go to Alton Oaks and apologize."

Sean followed me to the car, hopping over the cracks in the pavement.

As soon as we got in the car, I very carefully drove back down US-16, wondering what Sean meant when he saw Jackson. Sean's massive frame made me feel like a mouse beside him. Leaning over the console, Sean played with the buttons on the dashboard. I knew Bailey would complain about it, but it didn't matter right now. I would get her car detailed if I had to.

Discreetly, I tried calling Jake's cell phone again, but he never answered. Silently, I cursed him as Sean talked in detail about HAM radios.

After what seemed like an eternity, we pulled onto Main Street in Alton Oaks and I pulled Bailey's car into a spot behind the Oakie Doughkie Bakery. "Okay, we're here," I said, taking off my seat belt. I got out of the car quickly and ran to the passenger side.

In good spirits, Sean emerged from the car and happily bounced alongside me, walking on the balls of his feet as we spilled onto Main Street. "You, you, you, you, you, you, you," he sang. The police station was directly across the street. As I stepped onto the street, Sean froze in his spot, his eyes glued to the police station. "Will I be punished?" he asked, concerned tears beginning to form in his eyes. "I don't like consequences."

Standing between two parked cars and looking up at Sean, I said, "I don't know, Sean, maybe. But that's part of being a grown up."

He hung his head, watching his beat-up mud-encrusted gym shoes back-up onto the curb. Shaking his head, he whispered his ditty nervously.

In an attempt to comfort him, I reached for his hand, but he began flailing his arms and ran down Main Street. Swearing under my breath, I tried to run after him, but he took off like a bullet. Standing at the corner of Oak and Main, I watched him disappear west, leaving me and the Sunday brunch crowd confused.

CHAPTER NINETEEN

With everything going on, I wanted to place the blame for all of these situations on someone else, and I knew just who to take it out on. Fuming, I directed my legs towards the police station with tunnel vision. I let the door fly open with the wind's extra strong hand and ignored the purpose of the partition, walking right past it.

Jake was hunched over his desk. His hair was even more unruly without his wide-brimmed deputy's hat. I wasn't sure if the added chaos was due to the lack of sleep, or if he had just woken up. Approaching his desk in a huff, he turned to face me when I slapped my palm on his desk.

"Look," I started, not caring if I was making a scene. "I don't know what's up your butt lately, but you need to answer your goddamn phone!"

Jake looked up at me unimpressed, undeterred by my lash-out. "Would you like me to detain you for harassing a police officer? Is that the route you're going?" he asked. His tone was encrusted with contempt, that I wouldn't have noticed if we hadn't spent our childhood together.

His unalarmed reaction only made me more irritated. Heat flushed my face as I tried to keep my tone down. "While you're in here, moping around and avoiding my calls, I found a lead."

The optimistic, naïve half of me expected him to jump out of his seat, ready to tackle this new lead. The realistic part of me wasn't surprised when he sighed and turned in his swivel chair to face his computer screen. "Oh yeah?" he asked, uninterested as he clicked an icon on the screen. "What?"

I groaned loudly in frustration at his lack of help.

"Young lady!" Chief Gomes' deep voice was chastising as his large stomach approached Jake's desk before he did. His long white beard made his face seem more flushed than it was. "Follow me a moment," he said, waving his hand towards his office.

It had been over twenty-four hours since I'd last slept and I'm sure it had taken a toll on my judgment, but this was a big deal—a huge break! Why wasn't anybody listening to me?

I sighed away the words I wanted to say and made my way into the chief's office with heavy but determined feet. I had never been inside his office before and it seemed very small; the desk seemed to hold its breath in order to fit inside with the paperwork and filing cabinets. As Chief Gomes squeezed behind his desk, the room felt even smaller.

The chief leaned his hand on his desk but didn't sit down. His blue eyes looked at me from under his bushy white eyebrows with fatigue. It seemed to take several minutes before he spoke instead of several seconds. The blinds on the window beside him showed the busy officers bustling here and there with file folders and memos in their hands. Somewhere beyond the door that the chief kept open was the ringing of telephones and conversations that were not clear enough to understand.

"I remember nearly every child I've spent my career protecting in Alton Oaks and you're not an exception. I've sworn to serve and protect the citizens of this town just like every other officer out there," he said, gesturing to the door behind me with his sausage-like finger.

"Every day we put our lives on the line. I know these

aren't the streets of Chicago or New York City, but these officers miss out on family dinners, witnessing a milestone in their children's lives, or even forgo having a family because of the demands of being a public servant. Then you march in here and tell one of my most over-worked and dedicated heroes that his work isn't good enough? That's where I draw the line." His baby blue eyes were anything but innocent as they bore into me with consequence. Shadows of the horrors he had seen—horrors I didn't even know lay beneath the veiled corners of our town—darkened the crow's feet in the corners of his eyes.

My shoulders slumped with the chastising. I hadn't given Jake any grace, had I? Since I had moved back, he'd given to me unselfishly: friendship, support, protection, advice. I just took and took and took, without offering anything back. No wonder he had been such a pistol lately. I needed to change that.

"Look," Chief Gomes finally said as a heavy breath tripped over his whiskers. "I know you've been of some help to this station in the past—and we are grateful." He leaned against his desk to seem less threatening. "But you need to let us handle it."

Without worrying about decorum or gossip, I said defensively, "Why do you think I'm here? I want to let you handle it! You guys are far more equipped to handle this than me. I am only a concerned citizen here with a tip about my *husband's* murder. A big tip." I flourished my hands for exaggeration. "I need your help and I'm not getting it. Surely you understand why I'm so frustrated!"

I waited for the chief to say something as his mustache twitched. I feared that he was fishing for the noncommittal words that would make me leave the station without a scene. I had a deep respect for the men and women in this building, but it felt like I clutched the puzzle piece everyone was crawling on the floor searching for and no one had heard that I'd found it. With that thought, I raised a finger and caught his gaze. "And if you just pat me on the shoulder with empty promises and show me the door, so help me I will go after this lead myself. And if anything happens to me, that's on you."

Chief Gomes didn't react to my statement, but studied me for several moments while scratching his beard. Finally he sighed and hit the intercom button on his phone. "Vega, get in here," he ordered and then turned to me. "We will take your statement," he said without flexibility in his tone. "We will investigate it, but that's all we can do."

He leaned over his desk, his stomach bulldozed a pile of papers before him. When he held my gaze, he added stonily, "And if I see or hear you harassing any one of my officers again, there will be consequences, Ms. Parker."

Immediately, Jake leaned into the office, holding onto the door frame. "Yes, Chief?" His voice was optimistic until he caught my gaze, then his shoulders dropped.

"Please take this young woman's statement so we can follow up on a possible lead in the Neilson case," Chief Gomes instructed as he pulled out his desk chair and sat down with an audible groan.

"Yes, sir," Jake said then looked at me in defeat. "Follow me," he said and waved me out of the office with his hand.

He escorted me back to his desk and I couldn't help but glance at the door of the interrogation room, only twenty yards away, and frown knowing Sadie was inside and worrying about her future. "So," Jake started, opening his Steno pad, "what is it?"

His hair was in need of a cut, but the length

reminded me of a younger Jake; the one in junior high who looked almost comical in the baggy pants he had begun to wear. The year when he shared fewer and fewer words with Sadie and me on our morning commute to school. I knew then he was retreating from our friendship in the name of puberty and I didn't do anything to stop it. By the time we walked across the stage for our eighth grade diploma, I hadn't spoken to him in months. Had I always been so selfish in our friendship? I had taken—dare I say?—*stolen* so much from us and had only given grief in return. His eyes showed exhaustion and I told myself to start giving. "I think I know who last saw Jackson alive, and it isn't Sadie."

Jake sighed and tapped the eraser of the pencil on his desk. "Of course you don't think it's Sadie," he started, disenchanted. "You have a personal tie to this case. You're gonna let your emotions get in the way of facts."

I bit the side of my tongue in frustration; I needed to handle this exchange matter-of-factly. "I'll admit I'm trying to help Sadie," I shared, "but I am also looking at the facts."

Jake raised his eyebrow as if he was challenging me to prove it.

"I was in the high school parking lot," I said, shifting in my seat. The temperature in the police station was warm, but I was determined not to take off my coat.

"And you found some sort of 'proof,' did you?" Jake guessed, cutting me off. He used air quotes that scratched away at my thin layer of patience.

I licked my lips to stop the words I wanted to say. "No," I said rancorously. "I ran into Sean Walters. He was there that night too."

"Sean Walters?" Jake asked with mild interest, but it seemed more out of curiosity than a possible lead.

"Yeah. I told you about him. We went to high school

together," I explained but recognition did not light up Jake's face. I got more frustrated at this since it showed me that he didn't take my earlier statement seriously and question everyone involved.

"Anyway," I said, pushing those feelings aside, "he told me he saw Jackson afterwards and that Jackson was calling him names—"

"Sean Walters, isn't he the slow red-headed kid from science class?" Jake asked, interrupting me.

I gave a curt nod and continued, "Jackson was being mean and Sean said he didn't like it, but felt bad for what he did. I don't know," I admitted, fingering the metal-plated corner of his desk. "There's something more there, Jake. He knows something, I know he does, but I can't." I sighed, trying to find the right words. Catching Jake's sleep-deprived eyes, I admitted vulnerably, "I can't do it alone. I need your help."

Jake looked at me skeptically, not writing any of this information in his Steno pad. "Charli, you haven't slept in thirty-six hours, do you think that maybe you're imagining these connections?"

A feeling I can only describe as a gut-punch came over me with his words. Shock, surprise, pain, and a lack of breath came and went in a moment. His reaction gave me the most painful and sobering realization of the damage I had done to our friendship in the six short months I had been in Alton Oaks.

I opened my mouth, but words failed me. What had I done? Shakily, I rose out of my seat and only looked down at my feet in disbelief. My brain still couldn't form any words and, dumbfounded, I walked out of the police station. Jake didn't call after me or follow me outside. That realization hurt. How could I save Sadie without Jake? How could a useless, horrible person like me think I could help Sadie without making a bigger mess?

Disbelief turned into self-directed anger as I left the warm station and onto the chilly street outside. Almost immediately I bumped into Alex, who was distracted by his thoughts. He had his hands stuffed deep into the pockets of his coat and his head was bent down to avoid the wafts of biting wind.

"Oh, Charli, I'm sorry," Alex apologized, taking his hands out of his pockets and placing them on my shoulders. "Are you alright?" he asked as his usually messy hair was worsened by the wind.

I shook my head and choked back tears. Desperately, I tried to keep back the river; Alex didn't need to deal with that right now. "No," I said, my voice cracking. "But that's nothing new," I said, climbing over the lump in my throat. "Sadie is who we need to focus on."

Alex's mouth dipped. "Charli," he said with worry. "What's wrong? What happened?"

"Nothing," I said stubbornly. "Just do me a favor?" I asked, ready to give up on the world.

"Anything, Charli May," he said as concern deepened the shadows below his eyes. He guided me closer to the building with a hand on my shoulder as people walked by, giving us long, curious looks. I didn't doubt they were trying to eavesdrop on our conversation as they passed.

A few tears escaped and I erased them with the sleeve of my sweater earnestly. "I need someone to check-in with Sean Walters."

"Sean Walters?" my brother asked, confused.

I nodded and leaned against the cold brick building for support. "He was there that night," I shared as I fought off a wave of exhaustion. "He knows something, but I can't do it; I can't figure it all out. I need help. Someone in there needs to find him," I said, pointing to the door of the police station.

"Listen, Charli," Alex said, pulling me into a hug;

the same hug he gave me when I was ten years old and our dog died, and when I didn't get into Columbia University. It still smelled of Mom's fabric softener and strong, black coffee. "I'll see what I can do. I'll let her lawyers know. You go home and get some sleep. Promise me?" he said, releasing me and catching my gaze.

I nodded. I accepted that Jake was probably right: I needed sleep to think clearly.

"Do you want to take my car?" he asked, fishing for the keys in the pocket of his jeans.

"No," I said, suddenly relieved that I didn't have to walk all the way back to the Alton House. "I have Bailey's car."

Alex's eyebrows arched, but he didn't ask any follow up questions. "Go home," he said reassuringly. "I'll call you right away if anything happens, okay?"

I nodded and embraced Alex in another hug. I was trusting Sadie's fate entirely in the hands of others, for a few hours at least. It was hard to relinquish the responsibility and yet surprisingly easy. I knew I needed sleep in order for the world to make some kind of sense again.

CHAPTER TWENTY

After collapsing in bed as soon as I got home, I slept until two o'clock in the morning. The wind blew through the creaks in the windows. Shadows of bare tree branches frolicked across the room. For several hours I tossed and turned, getting tangled in the bed sheets. Like a record on repeat, I kept playing the events of the past forty-eight hours in my head. I consciously tried not to process my feelings about losing Jackson and tried to be objective, but every time I thought about why Sadie was sleeping on the cot in the lone Alton Oak's jail cell, I would turn over with a groan.

Did they get a hold of Sean last night? Were more unanswered questions being asked? Was Sadie any closer to being free?

The blue light flashed on my cell phone, letting the wicker bedside table illuminate a soft shade of blue. I had become accustomed to this: it was all those text messages and voicemails from Jackson cluttering up my mailbox, my life, my emotions. I didn't want to deal with the few messages he had left since Sadie emptied out my mailbox over the summer. I wasn't ready to hear him say my name, to hear his voice, to relive memories and emotions. I wasn't ready to deal with the finality of our marriage; his life.

For Sadie's sake, I picked up my phone and hoped there was good news waiting from my brother. The missed call that came while I was sleeping was from my cousin Jillian, who worked with Mr. Westbrook.

Maybe she had good news. I accessed my voicemail and scrolled through the unheard messages from Jackson and highlighted Jillian's, putting the phone to my ear.

"Hey, Charli," she began as I propped myself up on my elbows in the glow of the moonlight. "I just wanted to let you know that no news is good news. Mr. Westbrook and Mr. Wilder are following up on your claim regarding Sean Walters. Sadie is still optimistic, but she could use a few minutes with you. She wanted me to pass along a message that the police station opens at nine o'clock. Alright, kiddo, I'll see you soon. Love you."

As I put my phone back down, a pang of guilt stabbed my heart: Sadie was in jail and here I was lounging in bed! After untangling myself from my bed sheets for the fourth time that night, I knew I had to start my day.

The wind howled in the darkness as I carefully avoided the creaking floorboards outside my parent's bedroom and climbed down the stairs. As I reached the bottom, the grandfather clock loudly chimed, signaling it was half-past five. Jumping from the sound, I swore under my breath as the shadows caressed the walls. If I was going to see Sadie today and tackle the town to prove her innocence, I needed sustenance and, more importantly, caffeine.

As the coffeepot started percolating, filling the kitchen with the scent of rich, dark coffee beans, I put two pieces of bread in the toaster and tip-toed to the front door to see if I could grab the morning paper. The sharp teeth of the morning air bit right through my sweatpants as I bent for the most current issue of *The Oak Leaf Press*. Winter was definitely coming early this year.

The scraping of the kitchen chair against the

linoleum seemed too loud against the dark, quiet house. Sitting down with a cup of coffee, I rolled the rubber band off the newspaper and wasn't quite expecting to see pictures of Jackson and Sadie on the front page. Nevertheless, there they were.

The picture of Jackson was one I hadn't seen before and I assumed it had been taken after I left him. Tears started to prickle the corners of my eyes when I realized that I hadn't seen him smile like that in a long time; the smile where I could see both rows of teeth and his eyes crinkled in the corners. I hadn't made him smile like that in years.

And in the corner was a small picture of Sadie, cropped from a group picture at the hospital, I assumed, since she was in her scrubs. HORROR IN THE HARVEST was the headline emblazoned across the front. I bent over the paper, letting my long, tangled hair fall over my shoulders, as I read the article.

> Sadie Wilder, 28, of Alton Oaks was arrested Saturday afternoon for the murder of Jackson Neilson, 29, a tourist from Albuquerque, New Mexico.
>
> The Miller's Farm hosts its annual Fall Festival October twenty-second through the thirty-first. Families of all ages enjoy live entertainment, food vendors, games, and contests. On opening day, the quest for the scarecrow was in full force so that someone could earn the title of Grand Marshall and lead the Parade of Scarecrows along the Whett River Canal Trail. It is reported that Alton Oaks resident Charlotte Parker was the first to discover the scarecrow with fellow citizen, Rip Oakley. Upon further inspection, the

scarecrow had been discarded and replaced with the beaten body of Neilson, who happens to be the estranged husband of Parker.

A pediatric nurse at St. Colette's hospital for four years, and head volleyball coach for the Shepard High School Bobcats, Wilder was arrested for the murder due to the lack of an alibi, threatening Neilson the previous night, and owner of the evidence that the deceased was found wearing: Wilder's high school volleyball jersey. Wilder also happens to be a close friend to Parker. Though a clear player in this situation, Parker's stance is unclear. She has been unavailable for comment.

"We are still looking into the details of the murder and following up on witness statements and tips from concerned citizens," explains Alton Oaks' police chief, Sheriff Gomes. When asked about the growing murder rate in Alton Oaks over the past six months, Gomes ensures citizens, "We are still a small, safe community. Unfortunate circumstances have arisen in our town and we have expanded our department to meet these needs. The safety of our town is a concern we do not take lightly."

Wilder is being represented by Westbrook Attorneys and a court date is set for November 1st to determine bail. Any citizens with information about this case can contact the Alton Oaks Police Department.

The overwhelming guilt I felt last night crept back in as I put the newspaper down on the plastic, rooster-themed placement. Honestly and truly, all of this was happening because of me. Because I'd decided to run away from my problems and return to Alton Oaks. Every unsavory fact in that article was *my fault*. I might as well be the one in jail! I was so enraptured by the article and my self-mutilating thoughts that I forgot about the bread in the toaster until the heavily charred scent of smoke pulled me away.

Groaning loudly, I pulled the burnt bread from the toaster and dumped it into the garbage. I opened the window above the sink, hoping I wouldn't set off the fire alarm before my parents woke.

While waving a cookie sheet to clear the air, I turned to find my dad leaning against the archway. Hands folded over his cerulean work shirt, he gave me an amused smile. "You know what they say," he said, "if you can't stand the heat..." he trailed off knowing I would say, "All right! I'm getting out of the kitchen!" feigning frustration and then laugh, but humor escaped me.

That newspaper article left a sticky residue that I couldn't quite scrape away. It felt like I had been holding up a wobbly tower of bricks for so long and I couldn't hold them up anymore. My eyes stung with tears that I had put away and held back for so long. I just wanted to fall apart; let it all go.

When I looked at my father, my eyes were a desperate plea for help. Before I knew it, he scooped me up in his arms and I fell onto his shoulder, sobbing. "Oh, Charli, it's all going to be okay," he said, rubbing his hand on my back. As he soothed and shushed me, I realized he was the one person I could confide in without having to answer or evade a million questions. I wouldn't get angry or frustrated, and he wouldn't think of me as overreacting or weak, which I feared most people would do lately if I let my feelings show. He was my father and I just needed his reassurance; I needed the bout of confidence and self-assurance his hug gave me at five years old when I had the big bad wolf living in my closet and when I got my heart broken by Billy Gideon in the sixth grade.

"I don't know how to fix it," I said, sobbing over his shoulder. He smelled like his aftershave and it brought me back to my childhood. "Everything is messed up and it's all my fault," I confided, letting my tears turn his shirt a deeper blue.

"Charli," he said in the sweet deep voice that soothed my tears after a childhood nightmare. "It's not all your fault; you don't have to fix it."

Another wave of emotion knocked me over and my shoulders shook. "Charlotte May I," he said and put his hands on either side of my head and pulled my gaze off his shoulder. He looked me in the eyes—and it was hard to meet his gaze. I didn't think I deserved any reassurance. "None of this is your fault," he said.

I wiped my nose with the sleeve of my light blue alma mater hoodie. "I left my husband and now he's dead. I confided in Sadie and now she's in jail. I tried to help Sean and I think it just turned him into a murderer, and..." My sentence fell into a shuddering sob. I balled my fists beneath the sleeves of my sweater and looked at the scratched and faded linoleum floor. "I ran away instead of dealing with my problems. Now there's just more problems. It's all my fault," I admitted.

My father only pulled me into a hug again, without words. He only loosened his grip when I ceased sobbing. The only reason I stopped was because the cold morning autumn air overtook the kitchen. The smoke had escaped through the open window, but left the chilled footprints of autumn behind. "How can I help?" he asked as I pulled myself from his shoulder once more. My eyes were swollen and raw as I wiped them again with my damp sleeves.

"I don't know," I admitted. I took a deep breath that tripped over my lingering tears. I thought about asking him to talk to the police, to get them to listen, but I knew it would cause more trouble. I didn't want my father to get involved in my mess. I had to clean it up; *I* had to fix it.

Tenderly, he tucked my hair behind my ears as if it would help me see the lighter side of the world again. "How's about dinner tonight, you and me?" With the smell of burnt toast in the air and my stomach churning with self-hatred, food did not seem appealing to me at the moment. "And," my father added, "Next weekend we'll drive up to Grandpa's cabin and go hunting. How's that sound?"

I bit my lip. I couldn't think about driving away from Alton Oaks and leaving my problems behind— leaving *Sadie* behind in jail. I nodded anyway, just to make my dad feel better. He was helping just by being there at that moment. "Now," he said, with an arm around my shoulder, leading me to the kitchen table. I plopped down on the wooden chair, with the faded red-and-white padded cushion, while he closed the window above the sink. "You need a plan," he said.

Looking up from the rooster and hen themed napkin holder, I looked at him questioningly. "You, Charlotte May I," he started, pulling out the chair beside me, "will not let this rest, if I know you at all, so let's take it step-by-step."

He pushed aside the newspaper on the table so that nothing was between us. "There's nothing you can do to help Jackson right now," he said.

I shook my head, disagreeing. "I can help him by

finding out who killed him."

"Charlotte May I," he said with a hint of sternness, "that is not your responsibility. That is an unnecessary burden you're putting on yourself."

"But if I find out who killed him, then it will help Sadie," I argued.

My father used his hands when he talked next. "You have a mountain of problems you want to fix right now." He put his hand above his head, as if he was putting his hand over the mountain. "Out of everything, what it the most important issue? What is the most crucial to you?"

The tears had stopped leaking and their salty trails were encrusted around my eyes. "To help Sadie," I admitted.

"And how can you do that today?" he asked and put his hands back down on the table.

"To figure out who really killed Jackson to prove her innocence," I said, stubbornly.

My dad licked his lips. He always did that when he had to say something he knew would make someone upset. It was his version of biting his tongue, only this time he didn't hold back his words. "That is not your responsibility," he scolded, pointing a finger. "How can you help Sadie today?" he asked again. "Take small steps," he added. "Sometimes you just can't leap."

I sighed and leaned back in the chair. Frustration blinded me. How do I help Sadie without proving she's innocent? I thought back to the voicemail Jillian left and knew Sadie could really just use a friend. How could I help Sadie today? It seemed so small and insignificant, but I answered, "I can visit her."

"That's step one," Dad said with a small grin. "The rest will fall into place," he reassured. "Trust me."

I offered a small smile, not feeling any better. I wanted that *Ah-ha!* moment; the plot-twister; the revelation that made me melt with the feeling that everything would be okay. I felt none of that.

"Thanks Dad," I said anyway.

"Put together a care package for Sadie," he said. I thought back to when Sadie was really sick in eighth grade and missed two weeks of school. After three days, I began putting together small care packages for her to deliver after school. It was as simple as Mrs. Kratsky's Chicken Noodle Soup and a box of crackers that I covered in comic strips, or the newest issue of our favorite music magazine with post-its covered in my sarcastic comments on the pages. A smile almost escaped my lips when I thought back to the picture I drew in visual arts class of a photograph of us as children on the monkey bars on the playground. When I delivered it to her as part of a movie-and-Gatorade care package, she was so out of it, she told me it looked like an abstract from a serial killer.

My father threw me a five dollar bill and said, "Find a *Justy Beaver* magazine, on me."

I laughed, not only at my father's complete lack of pop culture knowledge, but also at what I imagined Sadie's reaction would be. A smile erupted on my father's face at my reaction and I stood, pushing in the kitchen chair.

"I love you, kiddo," he said and bent over to give me a hug.

"Love you too," I said as he kissed the top of my head and made his way out the door for work.

Grabbing the well-worn bill, I decided to take my father's advice and take the small steps. Once I got ready, I was going to head to Prescott's Grocers and put together a care package for Sadie. I could help her just by being there for her; to remind her that not all was lost.

CHAPTER TWENTY-ONE

I'll admit it: a hot shower felt good and I stayed under the rushing water for too long. Shivering in a towel, I pulled clothes from my closet, dressing in probably too many layers. I decided to wear my Prey for Chance tour t-shirt from 2000 when ten-year olds Sadie and I had Jillian drive us to Chicago for their concert. Singing one of their darker signature songs in my head, my heavy-soled boots exaggerated the creakiness of the staircase as I descended.

The plastic canvas was pulled aside and I noticed that Rip had dropped off lumber and power tools which sat near the entrance of the living room. Peeking past the archway, I saw that Rip had gotten a fair amount of work done yesterday without me. The wall I had torn apart was patched up, the built-in shelves were nearly all re-built, but the window seat still remained torn apart with wiring poking out.

I quickly threw on my jacket and reached for the tarnished knob on the front door. As I walked onto the porch, I paused to watch Jenna as she backed out of her driveway and across our front yard, instead of onto Oak Street. She parked beside Mrs. Kratsky's golf cart, where my mother stood in her bright green windbreaker, returning from her morning walk. The warm air from Jenna's exhaust billowed into the chilled morning, I could just imagine the heat blasting from her dashboard vents. The gossip club was in session early this weekday morning.

"Good morning, Charli," Mrs. Kratsky greeted,

raising her silver thermos mug in my direction. I could almost smell the strong black coffee in the distance between us and part of me yearned for a sip—a small caffeinated jolt to keep me going.

Though I wanted to walk straight past the Gossip Club and get to the police station at nine o'clock, I waved to Mrs. Kratsky with a smile, which was an invitation for a follow-up question. "How's Sadie doing, honey?" she asked as her gray-streaked hair blew in the autumn breeze; I had no choice but to walk towards the group of women.

My mother leaned against the golf cart looking like a sportswear model. I shivered seeing her bare ankles peeking out from beneath her nylon leggings. She subtly lifted an eyebrow, not wanting to push me for information. I wondered if this was her new tactic after getting so upset that I wouldn't share key details of my life over the past six months—especially when it involved some of the town's hottest gossip. Her feigned indifference was working, too. In order to keep her from not hovering, I wanted to share, just so she'd keep leaving me alone.

I shrugged in response to Mrs. Kratsky's question. "As well as can be expected," I offered with a sigh. "I'm on my way to see her now. Hopefully this will be over as soon when we find Sean Walters."

Mrs. Kratsky nodded as if I had done my job well. "Sean Walters?" Jenna asked from inside her car. She looked impeccable with her short, blonde, A-line bob and clean-cut white blouse popping out from behind the tinted window. The onyx necklace she wore popped against her pale features. "From Sheridan?" she asked, with a look of concern.

"Yeah," I said, confused. "You know him?" Sean was at least ten years younger than Jenna and she only became the Exceptional Students Coordinator in the district five years ago.

Jenna nodded, letting her black-and-silver earrings dangle against her cheeks. "I know his case worker." She frowned and then continued, "No one can find him. His mother's car was found in a ditch off US-16 near the Hemlock Bridge." Jenna looked down for a moment, pained, then admitted. "No one was inside but, apparently there were traces of blood."

"Did you hear about his mother?" Bailey asked, glowing with gossip. She wore a deep purple and green silk scarf as a headband, making her blue eyes seem to twinkle with the information she had to share.

Jenna and my mother nodded. The image of finding his mother at the kitchen table with maggots crawling down her neck, sent a fierce chill through my shoulders. "No," Mrs. Kratsky admitted.

"She died of a heart attack at the dinner table four days ago," Jenna added. She glanced in my direction as if to say *I know you were the one who found her.*

Before Bailey could add details that involved me, Jenna cut into the conversation with a frown. "Something this dramatic could be a huge trigger for Sean and we are all worried. No one can find him. The Sheridan police are looking all over the place. They're bringing in the dogs this morning to search the Maple Grove Preserve."

Empathy washed over me. I couldn't imagine how Sean was processing this information, though it did explain a lot about his behavior.

"Did he kill his mother?" my mother asked blatantly.

The corners of Jenna's mouth dipped and she shook her head. "No. Heart attack. She barely began eating her dinner. The table was still set."

Jenna opened her mouth to add to the conversation, but Mrs. Kratsky—bless her soul—cut her off. "Do they think the blood in the car is from Sean? Was he the one driving?" she asked. It was a well-known fact in Sheridan—and those who attend Sunday Bingo at the high school—that Sean sometimes drove his mother's car, but she was usually in the passenger seat. This fact seemed to be another puzzle piece, though we weren't sure it belonged to the puzzle in front of us.

Shrugging her shoulders, Jenna struggled to start a sentence; she really did love her job and she had the miraculous heart to love each person in her charge, and then some. "We're not sure. It's only speculation that he was driving—it might have been stolen. I imagine the police are going test it. If it is his blood, it's even more imperative that we find him."

If I had seen Sean yesterday in Sheridan, I wondered how long the car had been in the ditch, just past Blackhill Avenue, not too far out of Alton Oaks. Before I could ask Jenna, my mother chimed in with another question. "How long has he been missing?" my mother asked Jenna, tugging on the black cotton wrap that covered her ears.

Jenna shrugged. Before she could respond with fact or speculation, I opened my mouth. "Since yesterday afternoon, around lunch?" It came out more like a question than a statement.

Jenna's blue eyes looked up at me, shocked. I noticed wrinkles in her forehead that I'd never noticed before as she studied me. "He was last seen at the high school yesterday. He cleaned up the gym after the Sunday morning Bingo. How did you know that?" Jenna asked. Her eyebrows came together in confusion.

I sighed with realization. "Because I think I was the last person who saw him."

"What?" Mom asked and stopped leaning against the golf cart. She stood up straight, attentive. Her wide eyes reminded me of a doe's, though it was less due to their almond-shape, and more to their alertness.

"Where? When? What for?" Mrs. Kratsky chimed in, leaning over the steering wheel. Her black gloves gripped the faux sheep-lined covering of the wheel in suspense.

"He, um," I started and avoided eye contact. My fingers picked at the hole in the pocket of my jacket and the toe of my brown boots began to nervously kick at the dead grass stuck to the wheels of the golf cart. "I ran into him at the high school and brought him to Alton Oaks yesterday."

"Why?" Jenna asked, aghast.

I hesitated sharing the reason. Once I did, it would raise more questions and more drama, but I figured I could use whatever help and gossip I could get if it was going to help Sadie. "He said something that I thought could help Sadie's case. I was taking him to the police station."

"What did he say?" Jenna asked. Her eyes pierced through me in question.

"What happened at the police station?" Mrs. Kratsky added.

"Where is he now?" Jenna asked, leaning her head out the window of the car. All three women stared at me in anticipation. Their body language was tense, like a lioness ready to pounce on any bit of useful gossip.

My eyes brushed past my mother who seemed to be biting her tongue as her eyes studied my body language. "He kind of ran away," I admitted.

"Ran away?" Jenna asked, concerned.

"Yeah," I continued, still scraping the tires of the vehicle with my boots. "He thought he was going to get in trouble."

"Why did he think that?" Mrs. Kratsky asked. Her eyes didn't leave me as she reached for her thermos mug and took another gulp of her morning coffee.

I stammered and shifted my weight several times

from leg to leg. "I'm not entirely sure," I admitted. "I think he knows something about the night Jackson was murdered. I think he might've seen who did it."

The three women fell silent as I watched the leaves tumble across the lawn with the morning breeze. Finally, Jenna said, "I need to go." Shock covered her words and we watched silently as she put the car in gear and rolled down the Alton driveway and onto Oak Street. Not one woman objected to this theory; no one said, "Oh, not Sean!" or "I'm sure you're mistaken, Charli, there has got to be a better explanation!" and that realization made me shiver.

"Did you tell the police all of this?" my mother asked. I was taken aback when I met her gaze and concern was there instead of the yearn for gossip.

I nodded. "Alex said he would tell Mr. Westbrook and Mr. Wilder yesterday. You haven't heard anything?" I asked, shocked.

Crossing her arms over her chest, my mother pierced her lips together and shook her head. "No, I haven't," she admitted. She sounded worried and not disappointed, which concerned me. I guess the horrors that were happening in Alton Oaks lately were getting dangerously close to our family and my mother did not like it. Sighing, she extended her arm and rubbed my shoulder. "You go check on Sadie, tell her we're all here for her," she instructed genuinely. "I'll look into this."

"Okay," I said, nodding and forcing a smile. I took the cue to exit without hesitation.

"Can you believe any of this?" Mrs. Kratsky asked my mother as I began to walk away.

My mother's response was lost in the wind, but I knew she would have frowned, shaken her head, and replied, "No. None of this belongs in Alton Oaks," because this was our family's town and I felt the same exact way.

CHAPTER TWENTY-TWO

As I walked out from under the oak trees on the Alton property, I was pleasantly surprised by how warm the sun was this morning. We had had a cold front move in early this October, but I was hoping temperatures would now rise above fifty-five. The whole town could use a little sunshine.

Especially Sadie. No matter what my father told me this morning, I still tried to think about how to help on a larger scale. I just wanted her out of jail, charges dropped; a sigh of relief to melt away all the stress in our lives.

My thoughts kept coming back to Sean. He was never angry or bitter or aggressive. I remembered how he would walk through the halls on the last day before winter break wearing a Santa hat, and would pass out candy canes with a big smile on his face. Nobody ever really took the candy canes and many laughed behind his back, but he was always so happy-go-lucky. My heart broke for Sean. What happened that night? What did he see? *What did he do?* Whose bad side did Jackson get on that night? Who were the "friends" Sean referred to?

Jackson *did* have a knack for ticking people off, though. I once witnessed him pick a fight with a nun. Granted, she was an actress doing a comedy show at a Renaissance festival, but the image of a woman in holy robes flipping off my husband never left me.

On the other hand, I didn't see—or maybe I didn't want to admit—that Jackson was fooling around during our marriage. I began to bite the stub of my thumbnail as I walked down Oak Street as painful memories and excruciating truths began to press down and suffocate my soul.

I shook my head vigorously to chase away the thoughts and stuffed my hands deeper into my jacket, letting my fingers poke at the broken seam of the right pocket. I was so focused on the blizzard of unanswered questions plaguing my mind that I didn't realize I'd made a right on Main Street instead of a left.

I found myself standing outside the bright, galaxy-blue door of The Buzz Coffeeshop. Sadie would love a morning cup with a glazed bear claw, I realized. Looking at my reflection on the glass window, mixed with the gold letters of the store's name, I hesitated. This was the hub of gossip in our town. This was where all the moms went after dropping their kids off at school; where people sat and chatted about other people. As soon as I walked through that door, the customers inside would either whisper behind my back or approach me with questions I didn't want to answer. I missed the anonymity a drive-thru in a bigger city would have provided.

A young couple of Canaries exited the coffee shop and the intoxicating scent of roasted coffee beans pulled me across the threshold. "Charli! Hi honey!" I was greeted immediately by Mrs. Sullivan, the owner. She was behind the counter, wearing a scarecrow-themed apron. I don't think I could look at scarecrows in the same way, ever again.

"Hi, Mrs. Sullivan," I said, feigning a smile. I passed by the people sitting in booths and small, round, metal chairs who chatted. I breezed past the patrons in the wingback chairs, peeking behind their issues of the *Oak Leaf Press* and the ones who eavesdropped, pretending to read a bestseller.

"How are you?" I asked, putting my hands on the cold counter, beside the basket of saran-wrapped cookies.

"I'm living the dream, darlin'," she said and rearranged some of the pastries in the display case. She closed the glass door and put her full attention on me. "What can I get you?"

"Can I get two coffees and one of those bear claws?" I asked, trying not to notice the eyes boring into my back or the onlookers in my peripheral vision.

"Sure, sweetie. How's Sadie doing?" Mrs. Sullivan asked, turning to the large coffeepot. "I can't believe people actually think she did it. I don't, of course!" she explained with an eye roll, grabbing a to-go cup.

"I'm heading there right now," I explained, feeling the need to run out of there. "She's holding up as well as can be expected. There have been new developments in the case that give us all hope she'll be out soon."

"What kind of developments?" Mrs. Sullivan asked, placing the two cups on the counter and added, "Cream? Sugar?"

I shook my head; Sadie and I needed the strong stuff this morning. "No thank you." My eyes swept over the raspberry cheese Danish as Mrs. Sullivan grabbed the bear claw and my mouth watered.

"Do you think any of these *developments* will release Sadie?" she asked. I knew she was fishing for gossip, and the ears of nearby patrons were leaning towards us, eager for new information.

"The police haven't told us anything new," I said, convincing myself it wasn't a lie. "But we know that there is something they're chasing down to help Sadie."

Mrs. Sullivan put the brown paper bag on the counter and said, "Well, it's on the house, hun. You tell Sadie that The Buzz is on her side; we're rooting for her. And you come on down more often, too. You're always welcome here, Charli."

I smiled, but wondered what she meant by that. "Thanks, Mrs. Sullivan. I'll let Sadie know."

Turning to leave, I paused when an idea came to me. I threw some cash on the counter and asked, "Can I get another coffee with some assorted pastries?"

Mrs. Sullivan looked surprised. "Well, sure thing, sugar!"

The noise level in the coffee shop seemed to rise when the conversation between Mrs. Sullivan and me stopped. Maybe it was all in my head. Either way, I thanked her again and grabbed the plastic bag and cardboard cup carrier.

The chilly breeze settled around my neck and I wished I had worn a scarf, or at least zipped my jacket all the way. As Prescott's Grocers came into view, I decided against going in today. I wanted to get to Sadie before her coffee turned cold.

As I crossed Oak Street, I saw Jake round the corner, dressed in his tan uniform. He pretended not to see me and picked up his pace. "Jake!" I called, but he didn't turn around.

After the third time I called his name, he turned. "What?" he asked, exhausted. His head cocked to the left with impatience as his feet stopped in front of the heavily tinted windows of the Bank & Trust. Our reflections were clear and crisp. None of the attitude in Jake's features were reflected in the windows. The glossy, black and white versions of ourselves were simple and plain. I sighed in resignation of our reality.

"Good morning," I greeted with a smile that didn't give warmth, though I tried.

He matched the smile and turned to continue his trek to work. "I'm not sharing any details of this case with you, Charli," he said coldly when I caught up to his side and matched his stride.

The sharp knife of guilt stabbed my heart. He assumed I'd made contact with him because I wanted something. Take, take, take: that's all I do to him.

"No," I said a bit defensively. "That's not why—"

"Look," Jake said poignantly. "It's best you don't contact me."

"Anymore?" I asked, aghast at his request.

His eyes ran across the white garage doors of the firehouse, before they met mine. His brown eyes were etched in emotions I couldn't understand. A breeze sprinted down the street, ruffling his overgrown hair. He turned without a word and continued his pilgrimage to the police station, leaving me nearly speechless.

"Jake?" I called out, my voice nearly pleading.

His body seemed to struggle to turn and face me, but I was grateful that he did.

My feet rushed me forward as he stood outside Westbrook Attorneys, a good twenty yards from the police station.

"I'm sorry, Jake," I said, painfully. "I know I haven't made things easy for you, and I've hurt you more than I know I have. I could come up with a million excuses, but they'd all be empty."

Jake looked unimpressed, perhaps irritated by my words. There was definitely an eye roll he was resisting.

"I'm just a rotten friend," I admitted, feeling the weight of the plastic pastry bag in my left hand. "At least I have been to you... for longer than I care to admit." My eyes left his face and followed a yellow Volkswagen down the street as I wondered if I had always been this way.

When my eyes met his again, they were shaded beneath skeptical eyebrows. "But I'm working on it," I shared, hoping to see a spark of change in his gaze. "Really, Jake," I said again. "I'm sorry."

I held the bag of pastries and the cardboard cup holder out to him. "Peace offering," I stated. "I got you coffee, just the way you like it: one cream and a dash of cinnamon. And I know everyone at the station has been working crazy hours and I wanted to say thanks with some fat and sugar."

Jake took the bag and a cup of coffee after considering my words. He didn't say anything for a few moments. He lifted the plastic tab on the to-go cup and took a generous sip. His eyes scanned the two other cups I held and he asked, "Are you visiting Sadie?"

I nodded, fearing that words would damage the remaining link of friendship between us.

He took another gulp from his cup and his body language relaxed. "I'll bring her to the interrogation room," he informed and turned.

A smile cracked across my face in relief. "Thanks for the coffee," he said, nonchalantly, opening the door to the station. There was barely a spark of warmth in his words, but I could work with that spark.

CHAPTER TWENTY-THREE

I sat in the interrogation room with the thought that six months ago, this was the meeting room—Alton Oaks had no need for an interrogation room. Now it smelled like barbecue ribs, due to the Oakie's take-out boxes sitting in the trash. This was the room Sadie used as a window to the outside world: to her friends, family, and a tiny sense of normalcy.

The door opened and Sadie walked in, dressed in a pair of jeans and a dark blue hoodie, a size too big for her. Immediately, she enveloped me in a hug as Jake closed the door behind her. An overwhelming urge to cry came over me, and I pushed down the mountain-size lump that burned in my throat.

Releasing me from the hug, Sadie's hands held my face with concern. "How are you?" she asked, her blue eyes searching mine.

Her concern for my well-being surprised me. I wondered if all I did was take from her too, just like I had done with Jake. "Sadie," I said, brushing her concern away. "I'm fine. How are you doing? Are you hungry? I brought you a care package."

Sadie smiled endearingly at the coffee and bear claw on the table. She rubbed her stomach and replied, "Oh yes, but I feel like I've gained ten pounds. Everyone keeps feeding me. I'm beginning to think I'm being fattened for a sacrifice."

She didn't mean it to sound so negative, but it pinched my heart. "Has there been any news yet?" I asked. A small flutter of optimism ran through me when

Sadie sat down and began picking at the bear claw.

"I haven't heard much. I know everyone's out looking for Sean, but I don't know what good it'll do." She tore a piece of the pastry and popped it into her mouth. "Your mom came to see me yesterday."

"Oh?" I asked, amused by this information.

"You know your mom," she said with a smile. "Filled me in on everything I'm missing: Jane McDowell is cheating on John with Russell Lewis, Bailey's bicycle was stolen outside the playground yesterday morning." Sadie licked the icing off her fingers. "Did you hear about Sean's mom? Of course, you did." The sudden bout of energy she got from gossiping dissipated. Sadie was losing steam—hope was starting to abandon her and I wanted to fix it all, but I couldn't. "What is *that*?" Sadie asked, looking up from her hands.

I heard it too. There was a commotion inside the police station. Sadie's eyes lit up ever so slightly with the thirst for drama that wasn't her own. We both got up and opened the door an inch or two, peeking through.

"It's the University of Miami!" I heard Jessica's voice before I saw her blonde head, bobbing from in front of the partition. It was hard to tell if she was drunk or just very emotional.

She waved around a green and orange jacket in her hands. I knew it was her alma mater from often seeing her in matching t-shirts, shorts, and jerseys. "What are you going to do about it?" she asked, clearly having the attention of the station.

"First, y'all stand by and do nothin' about my husb—boyfriend's death, and now this?" she asked, waving the jacket around like a flag.

"Her husband?" Sadie whispered, looking up at me.

"In her deluded mind..." I said, not wanting to finish the sentence.

"Ma'am," Chief Gomes approached Jessica with his hand in the air as if it would stop her tirade. "What seems to be the problem?"

"This god-forsaken town!" Jessica yelled in frustration. "Look at this! My jacket is mutilated," she said, showing the tatters that once held the orange and green U in her letterman's jacket. "It was sitting in the back of our van. Who steals a god-damned letter from a jacket? This is a hate crime! What kind of Stephen King-inspired small town is this?!" she asked, hysterical. Chief Gomes nodded to a nearby officer to take care of the woman as Jessica continued, "This was *my* letterman's jacket in college. Do you know how hard I worked for this?" she asked as an officer showed her to a place they could discuss this matter.

I closed the door and knew from the light in Sadie's face that she couldn't wait to gossip about this. I, on the other hand, was caught in a train of thought. "That look! I know that look!" Sadie said, fired up. "What is it?"

"Sadie, I gotta go," I said, excited that things were beginning to click.

"You know something! You've got something!" Sadie said, nearly unable to stand still. "What is it? Never mind, you go! You got this!" she encouraged. "Come back with a full report!"

I left the interrogation room and watched Jake turn his desk chair from the dissipated scene at the front of the station, back to his desk. Seeing me approach, his voice was defeated and hesitant. "What do you need?" he asked.

It hurt that he was truly used to me taking all the time. "Nothing," I said, trying not to sound defensive. "I came over to give you something."

I noticed Jake's eyes sweep across my empty hands and a hint of confusion shaded the corners of his eyes.

"Remember that picture?" I asked. "Of the stuff you showed Bailey with her horseshoe pendant?"

It took but three seconds for Jake's eyes to light up in recognition. At the same time, we both commented, "The U!"

"Do you still have that photograph?" I asked.

As Jake sifted through reports and envelopes on his desk, Sean's ditty popped into my head and my shoulder's slumped thinking about him. Nevertheless, the tune was stuck in my head like an 80's pop song.

"Here it is," Jake said, pulling it from its manila envelope.

"I can't believe I didn't make this connection before," I commented, looking at the photograph next to Jake. "I've seen her wear that jacket. That's the U from it."

Out of the corner of my eye, I saw Jake look at me as if he had just realized how well I knew Jessica. *You, you, you, you, you, you, you.* Ugh! That tune just infested my brain!

A thought came to me then. "Jake, look!" I said, pointing to the photograph. For a moment, the random items weren't strewn on the ground at random; they had a specific purpose. "The Masterlock and the shackle bolt: both U-shapes put together look like an S. And Bailey's horseshoe together with Jessica's U—"

"—They're lined up to make an E," Jake said, tracing the curves of a capital E with his finger.

"The handle of Sadie's handsaw," I said, pointing to it, "with the cattail lying beneath it—"

"The A," Jake identified. He sat up straight, pouring over the photograph now. "The dentures and Carabineer roughly make a fluid N," he surmised.

I pointed to each "letter" in the photograph, tracing the U-shaped objects with my finger as I sang Sean's ditty, "You, you, you, you, you, you, you." Jake looked at me like I'd just performed a miracle.

"Where did you say you found this?" I asked, realizing this was a photograph of Sean's recent collection of *U*s.

"On the Miller's farm, not too far from the scarecrow," he replied. He had already grabbed the jacket that hung on his chair while I stared at the picture. Maybe we were reading too much into it, and these random stolen items were haphazardly lying on the ground.

As if Jake was reading my thoughts, he said, "It's worth a look. No one has checked the more rural parts of Alton Oaks for Sean. If he's there, maybe we'll get some answers."

I nodded, grateful that Jake and I seemed to be on the same team again. "Do you need a ride home?" he asked, passively.

'I was going to decline, that I wanted more time with Sadie, but confusion kicked in: the Miller's farm was on the opposite side of town; way out of the way for him to take me home.

"Of course," he said, pushing in his chair. "I'll have to make a stop first."

In his own way, Jake was inviting me along to investigate without inviting me along at all. "It *is* chilly out," I admitted, trying to talk myself into it.

"Low fifties today with a storm front moving in tonight," he said matter-of-factly with a thin layer of persuasion.

"Oh, okay," I gave in. I followed Jake out of the police station and I saw Sadie peeking out from the door she was held behind, and the smile she gave me was enough to know I made the right decision.

CHAPTER TWENTY-FOUR

The ride to the Miller's farm with Jake was quiet; only the creaking of the ancient station wagon made noise as we hit bumps and uneven road. While passing the streets of downtown, the people outside always stopped to watch the police car; they'd squint their eyes and shield the sun with their hand to see who was inside.

I turned to Jake, who had his window cracked slightly and the wind ruffled his hair. "Does everyone always stop and turn when you drive this thing around town?" I asked.

Jake didn't reply and kept his eyes focused on the road. I knew the citizens of Alton Oaks saw me in the passenger seat. "I wonder what they'll say about me tomorrow," I muttered, resigned.

"You once told me whatever people think of you is none of your business," he shared simply, as if he was stating the score of the Bears versus Packers game.

Naturally, I had no memory of this, but I let the words swim around my head; each word brushing against my memories.

An almost comfortable silence hung between us as we approached the stretch of cornstalks that marked the Miller's farmland. "I will admit," Jake started as we turned onto the gravel road that led into the makeshift Fall Fest parking lot, "I brought you along because I anticipate needing your help."

"For what?" I asked, taken aback.

Jake parked the station wagon on the grass, a few

yards from where the police had flattened the cornstalks to get to Jackson's body. The parking lot outside the barn was empty and some napkins and fest-related refuse had gathered in the corners of the fences. A breeze picked up, sending a stray The Buzz napkin to spin in circles between the wooden cart of pumpkins and the line of port-o-potties. It was a weekday; Fall Fest wouldn't open to the public until three o'clock, so the place was deserted.

"For reasons I don't understand, you know how to reach him," Jake shared, "and Sean's a big guy." He took the key out of the ignition, but never glanced in my direction. He scanned the field in front of him, his eyes sweeping across the rearview mirrors, too.

"Last time he just ran away from me, Jake. I'm not some Sean-whisperer," I said with a hint of sarcasm.

Jake got out of the car and I followed suit. The crows cried, flying above, and the dried cornstalks cracked under our feet as we walked into the corn maze. The eerie breeze blew silently, combing the leaves of the stalks, making my shoulders wiggle with a chill. Yellow police tape flapped in the wind at the police-made entrance of the corn maze. I noticed that it looked different than the tape outside the school parking lot in June. The idea that the department had to order more rolls, with an updated design, made me frown.

Following Jake, those pessimistic thoughts started to cloud my mind again, like a heavy fog; like a cloud of mosquitos that took turns diving down to bite me. Helplessness threatened to weigh down on me like an anchor. As I battled the demons inside, I didn't notice that we had arrived at the place I last saw Jackson.

I slowed my pace and steadied my breathing. If Jake noticed, he didn't say anything. The wooden post was empty now, though dark spots covered it and my eyes stung thinking it was the remnants of Jackson's blood. Maybe this was what I needed to see; maybe it was some kind of closure.

My eyes climbed down the post to take in the whole scene. I gasped when my eyes swept across the ground. There was Sean, his red hair mussed by the elements and dusted with dead flora. He lay on the ground, his back to us, curled up in the fetal position, hugging the discarded scarecrow. His heavy brown sweater blended in with the ground but contrasted greatly against the brightly colored scarecrow. It strangely reminded me of the Chinese yin-yang symbol.

Jake moved into action without thinking. When I found my feet, I followed Jake with a sense of urgency. Crouching on the ground, Jake delicately nudged Sean, but received no response. With two fingers, Jake checked Sean's pulse, as I noted how blue his lips were.

"He's alive," Jake informed without taking his eyes off Sean. He pulled off his jacket and laid it over Sean's large frame. "But he's not shivering. It's a bad sign: hypothermia," he said, glancing at me with unease.

Jake reached for his radio and called an ambulance. I put my hand on Sean and he stirred slightly. Through closed eyes and blue, chapped lips, with a raspy voice, he let out a long note of "Youuu," in his sing-song way before tripping over a short cough and losing consciousness.

Jake had run to the car and returned with a large first aid kit. Without a word, he took a metallic blanket from its plastic wrap and laid it out on the ground. "Charli," he said firmly. "I need your help. Do you understand?"

I nodded, trying to swallow my emotions.

On his knees, across from me, he met me eye-to-eye. "His sweater is soaked through with dew. I need to cut it off, but I need your help putting this blanket under him." Jake's voice was firm but reassuring as he cut the sweater and t-shirt off Sean.

"Now I'm going to roll him on his side," he said, bending Sean's knee closest to him and placing his hand across his chest. "I need you to come next to me," he instructed with the jerk of his head. I obeyed, kneeling beside him, the front of my jeans were damp and cold from the ground.

"When I roll him on his side, I need you to move his clothes and slip this blanket beneath him," Jake instructed.

I nodded, grabbing the metallic blanket, worrying about how slack Sean's face had become.

"Ready?" Jake asked.

"Yes," I said and nodded, feeling adrenaline kick in.

In one swift move, Jake rolled Sean's body and I worked as quickly as I could. As soon as the blanket was in place, Jake rolled Sean back in place. "You're doing wonderfully, Charli," Jake reported, his attention fully on Sean, and moving quickly.

"Now I need you to cover Sean with the other blankets," he instructed. He reached into the first aid kit beside him and squeezed a few plastic bags until they popped. "They're warm compresses," he explained, placing them on Sean's neck, chest wall, and groin.

Sirens were deafeningly close as I watched Jake take Sean's wrist and count his pulse rate, while watching his chest rise and fall. "What do we have?" one of the paramedics asked, dropping to a knee beside Sean.

"Hypothermia: weak pulse, shallow breathing, in and out of consciousness," Jake began explaining. I moved to melt into the background so I could be out of the way.

I watched Jake in awe of his response to Sean; how level-headed and confident he was in his ability; in his control of the situation. I was just beginning to understand the give and take he needed for our friendship to be healthy once again.

CHAPTER TWENTY-FIVE

"So, what exactly happened?" Alex asked, sitting on the uncomfortable wooden bench at the entrance of the police station. Mr. Westbrook and Mr. Wilder kicked Alex out of the interrogation room just before I arrived and confusion deepened the wrinkles in his forehead as he saw me enter the station with Jake. "How did you know where to find him? Did he say anything?"

I explained what I knew to my brother as the dinner crowd began commuting outside on the streets. Every time the door to the police station opened, a new blanket of chill settled upon us, despite the abundant sunshine. We sat in our coats, holding lukewarm coffees as we waited, hoping to hear a positive outcome in Sadie's fate.

"Sean's in bad shape," I admitted. "I overheard that the hypothermia was worse than it should have been."

Alex put on his metaphorical doctor's hat and nodded. "The mentally ill—" Alex started but quickly restarted his sentence. "People like Sean are more prone because they don't know how to gauge their need to find shelter; they have a hard time recognizing when to come in from the cold."

It was the first time I heard Sean referred to as "mentally ill" and not "different," or "special," or "slow," or our classmates' favorite label: retarded. I didn't like "mentally ill" either. It seemed too official, too damaging.

"It didn't help that Sean was scared and ten miles from home," I admitted and swirled my coffee. If I hadn't driven him to Alton Oaks and scared him, he wouldn't be in this position. I took a long gulp from the paper cup and my stomach rumbled in hunger.

"So Sadie's not cleared of charges until we can get a statement from Sean—that's if he knows anything," Alex admitted defeatedly and slouched a little deeper. His fingers played with the rim of his Styrofoam cup as he digested this information. I didn't want to add that because of his autism, he might not speak at all, or that the line of questioning might be different for him to understand. A frown crossed my lips too, but I had to have faith that Sean would pull through and do the right thing.

"Did they take him to St. Colette's?" Alex asked.

"I would think so. The ambulance headed west on Oak from the farm," I shared. Alex sat up straighter and I could see the wheels in his head turning. That's when it hit me that that was the hospital where both he and Sadie worked; it wouldn't be too difficult to get information on Sean's status.

Alex pulled out his cell phone and stood. "I'm going to make a few phone calls," he said enthusiastically and stepped outside. The opening of the door added another layer of cold air that settled upon the bench I occupied.

"Charli," Jake's rough voice turned my attention from the door several minutes later. I tore my eyes from the flyers of missing persons across from the bench.

"Come with me," he instructed with his hands on the hips of his belt.

Without question, I stood and followed him past the partition where the air was much warmer. Walking a little slower to warm up, I noticed Mr. Westbrook and Mr. Wilder outside the interrogation room, holding their briefcases. They seemed to be in better spirits. Even the stern and serious Mr. Wilder turned to me with an outstretched hand. "Thank you for coming, Charli.

Sadie's been asking for you," he said with optimism in his voice. "Would you like anything from Oakie's?" he asked. "We are headed there for lunch."

Dumbfounded by an amiability I'd never experienced from Sadie's father, I nodded.

"I'm getting a beef sandwich and a shake for Sadie, would the same be all right for you?" he inquired taking a step backwards.

With a brief nod from me, he turned and led Mr. Westbrook out of the police station with a light spring in his step. I had to take that as a good sign. "Ms. Wilder would like to speak with you," Jake said with professionalism. He, Sadie, and I were inseparable as kids, but Jake liked to remain professional as much as possible while in his uniform. I was used to referring to him as work-Jake or friend-Jake, so I didn't take his formalities as being cold or distant at the moment. I was thankful his demeanor was changing.

"Thanks," I said. He had opened the door and closed it after I had squeezed inside.

"Charli!" Sadie exclaimed with a smile wider than a child's on Christmas morning as she embraced me in a hug. "I don't know how you did it!" she said as she released me.

"Did what?" I asked, taken aback. "You're obviously still in jail." That fact made me feel like a failure despite the sparkle in Sadie's eyes and the color in her cheeks.

"Yeah, but I'm not the only suspect," she shared. "There's a strong case against Sean. All the cards are there: his poor mother's body, where the car was in the ditch, his timelines, your testimony." She paused and took a deep breath, elated that her proven innocence was within reach. "Charli, he had the means, the motive, and the opportunity."

I didn't mean to be a downer, but I had to point it

out: "So do you, apparently," I said. I honestly didn't think Sean was the murderer—he had so much empathy for that frog in high school—but Sadie was right: there was a lot of evidence proving otherwise.

"I know," she bit her lip momentarily. "But Mr. Westbrook went to Springfield and they had an officer go door-to-door in the neighborhood where my mother's customer lived. They asked again if anyone had seen anything at all on that block. Of course, they saw nothing, but a neighbor across the alley caught me on their security camera from their rear garage camera." She talked excitedly with her hands, full of renewed energy. "The video is grainy, but it's enough for bail. And now they're checking with other houses in the area that have surveillance cameras to see if they at least have an image of my truck. Even if Sean doesn't come to, or won't admit to what he did, I have a fighting chance at a non-guilty plea in court!" Sadie was so excited that I didn't have the heart to tell her I thought Sean was innocent.

Sadie pulled me into a hug again as she let out a small squeal of excitement. "Oh, Charli, I cannot wait to sleep in my own bed again!"

I knew the appropriate reaction was to smile and celebrate with Sadie, but no matter how hard I tried, I couldn't get my face to reflect the same optimism.

"Oh," Sadie said with realization and her smile slowly faded. She took me by the arm and had me sit in the faux-leather office chair that seemed perfect for Mr. Wilder's image as she said, "With everything that's been happening here, I haven't even thought about what you're going through."

An odd numbness slowly extended from my core and thickly covered my extremities with a mournful weight. "Everything with Jackson and—oh, Charli!" Sadie gasped. "What can I do?"

The army of demons I had been suppressing the past few days threatened to rise up again as a cold fist squeezed my heart. My eyes began to prickle behind my eyelids, and a painful lump started to grow in my throat. *Not yet.* I told myself. I was not ready to feel the first wave of crushing pain. Not until Sadie was free from Jackson. I had to make sure she made it first.

"I'll be fine," I said, meeting her concerned gaze. "We're worried about you right now," I admitted, gesturing towards her with a small smile.

"Charli," she started with a chastising tone.

"Please," I said, cutting her off. I had just locked away the demons and didn't know if I had the strength to push them away again today. "Let me worry about you," I said putting my hand on her elbow with a pleading gaze. "For now, at least. Please?"

Sadie nodded, but concern glazed over the sparkle in her eye as she bit her lip. "For now," she said, agreeing to my terms.

CHAPTER TWENTY-SIX

I know I didn't have to fear Jackson being on the other end of the phone when it vibrated on my nightstand, but my stomach still churned as I watched it in the darkness this overcast autumn evening provided. I didn't want to know who it was, but I wanted the noise to stop. Seeing that Alex was calling, I decided to answer the phone despite not wanting to talk to anyone. Ever since I'd left Sadie at the police station, a dark cloud had settled upon my shoulders and followed me home, where I went straight to bed.

"Hey, Charli, were you sleeping?" Alex asked after I answered the phone in a groggy voice.

Not wanting to answer his question, I changed the subject as I rolled onto my back and stared up at the cracks and water marks on the ceiling. "What do you need? Is it Sadie?" I asked.

"I wanted to let you know that Sean gained consciousness a little bit ago. He met with his case worker and the police." Alex paused and I knew there were words there he wasn't saying.

"What is it?" I asked, rubbing my eyes.

"Well, he's not making much sense," he supplied. "He's in with a neurologist right now to make sure there wasn't any brain damage."

"What do you mean?" I asked, confused and not quite awake.

"He's not speaking in sentences," Alex admitted with a sigh. "He's just using random letters, mostly the letter *U*. I think he's just in shock."

"What does that mean for Sadie?" I asked, remembering how Sadie calculated her freedom on Sean's capture.

"Not much," he said but didn't sound downtrodden. "However, that night Sadie drove downstate, she made a U-turn in the neighborhood, in someone's driveway. They had a motion-sensor camera. It got her license plate and a grainy picture of her behind the wheel. It gives her an alibi. They're working on her paperwork for releasing her."

"That's great, Alex," I said, but my exhaustion dragged me down from fully celebrating.

"We're going to celebrate tomorrow night at Oakie's, in the Garden Room, eight-thirty," he said. "Our whole family, Mr. Westbrook, Mr. Wilder," Alex mentioned Sadie's father with a tone mixed with hesitation and frustration.

"I'll be there," I promised. Nothing would stop me from seeing Sadie so happy. "Let me know if there's anything else I can do," I said through a yawn.

I didn't remember hanging up the phone last night or saying goodbye to Alex before ending the call. The sun was bright and high in the sky when I woke up to it trilling on the pillow beside me. I could hear Rip pounding a hammer downstairs as I saw Jenna's number flash the blue screen. "Hello?" I said, my throat needing water.

"Charli? Hey, how are you?" she asked, but didn't seem interested in an answer. "Listen, I know Alex filled you in last night, but I wanted to let you know that Sean said something other than a letter of the alphabet this morning."

I was confused as to why she was telling *me* this, but I realized that Sean didn't have any family or next-of-kin. "Oh?" I asked, sitting up in bed. My eyes scanned the surfaces in my room for a leftover glass of water.

"Yeah," she admitted. "He said your name."

I didn't say anything, hoping it would get Jenna to share more.

"Sean's caseworker, Sherry, she's wondering if you'd come down to the hospital to visit him," Jenna asked in a way that wasn't a question, but a suggestion.

"Why? Just because he said my name?" I pulled myself out of bed when I found an electric blue water bottle on my desk, peeking out from behind a pile of dirty clothes.

"Charli, you're all Sean has right now. He has some sort of connection to you. Plus," she hesitated before continuing, "the police want to question him and every time they show up in uniform, he, well, he's not handling it very well."

"So Sherry thinks that if I'm there, they might get some information out of him?" I asked, not sure how I felt about being a pawn in this situation.

"Exactly," Jenna said. "I know Sadie's charges have been dropped, but you know as well as I that Sean couldn't have done what everyone thinks he did. You have the power right now to help prove him innocent. You have to at least try," Jenna pleaded.

"All right," I admitted. "I'll head right over."

I hung up the phone and threw it on my tangled bed sheets. The sky outside my bedroom window was a bright blue. The storm that was supposed to sweep across western Illinois never arrived. My bedroom was stuffy and I opened the window an inch or two, surprised by the warmth the air provided. I watched the trees still with an absent breeze. The world seemed to hold its breath for the storm that was long overdue.

After throwing on a few layers of clothing and brushing my teeth, I popped a piece of buttered bread in my mouth and pulled my road bike out of the shed. I sighed while mounting the bike and looking down the stretch of road. Somewhere, a few miles away, stood the hospital.

There were a few days when I was working the Spook Show when I road my bike to the hospital, but mostly Sadie and I carpooled, or I stayed at her apartment and biked from there. At least it wasn't raining, or snowing, or extremely hot, or bone-chillingly cold, I told myself. It was almost the perfect day for a bike ride.

An hour later, I cursed my optimistic self as I biked up to the hospital a sweaty mess. I had stripped to the long-sleeved t-shirt layer by the time I reached downtown Alton Oaks and had to stop at Prescott's Grocer's for a drink. I parked my bike in the empty bike rack and my shoulders slumped when I realized that I had to bike all the way back to the Alton House when I was done here. I tried to fan myself as I followed the directions Jenna had texted me and rode the elevator to the eighth floor.

Sherry was a short middle-aged woman who had red cotton-like hair. She reminded me of a host on a children's show I watched growing up—she was just missing her puppets and a squeaky voice. "Thank you so much for coming, Charli. Jenna has nothing but wonderful things to say about you," she said, greeting me with an enthusiastic handshake.

Her below-the-knee khaki skirt was wrinkled and I wondered how long she had been at the hospital with Sean as we walked down the hallway. We stopped outside a room where the television was too loud. "Luckily, Sean's hypothermia wasn't severe; they were able to raise his body temperature. Tests show no neurological damage, he's probably still in shock, or perhaps witnessed something that traumatized him," Sherry shared, holding a clipboard to her chest. "You found him, isn't that right?"

I nodded. "Deputy Vega and I did, yes."

"It's lucky you found him when you did." She glanced down at her clipboard momentarily and then hugged it once more. "You've known Sean for a long time?"

"I knew him in high school," I shared, trying to peek into the room, but only being able to see a light blue curtain from my vantage point. "Before this week, I hadn't seen him in ten years."

"Ah, well," she resigned. "He's lucky to have a friend like you. Come on, I'll bring you in to see him."

She turned on her white gym shoes and walked into the entrance we stood beside. Sean was sitting up on the hospital bed; his legs were bent in a U-shape and his arms rested on his knees as he watched an animated show on television. The bed seemed too small for him, but I was relieved to see color back in his cheeks.

"Ch-Ch-Chawli," he said with difficulty, his bushy ginger eyebrows rose gleefully. I smiled though I noted how difficult it was for him with a stutter. It was as if his lips wouldn't let words pass. He smiled at me and held up his hand, making the letter C by curving his thumb and fingers.

"Hi, Sean," I greeted. I sat on the wooden chair beside the bed as Sherry sat in the corner between the radiator and television. "How are you doin'?"

"Sh-Sh-Sherry," he replied, making the letter C with both hands and putting them together to make the letter S. She looked at me impressed, and I assumed it was because he said something besides my name or a letter of the alphabet.

There was a soft knock at the door and we all turned our heads. Jake was standing at the door, dressed in jeans and a gray sweater, carrying a plastic grocery bag.

Sherry rose form her perch, "Deput—Jake," she

corrected herself, glancing at Sean. "How are you? Thank you for coming!"

I quickly realized that Jake was here to question Sean, but came in civilian clothes to put Sean at ease. "This is my friend, Jake," I said to Sean as he walked into the room. I curved my thumb and straightened out my first finger to make the letter *J*.

Sean looked confused and made a *C* with his hand. "It's like a *C*," I said and straightened out Sean's forefinger, "but one side is shorter." I noticed that Sherry returned to her corner and Jake stood at the foot of the bed.

Looking at Jake and back at me, Sean only squinted and shook his head as if I wasn't making any sense. "Actually," I started with a hushed tone, as if I was relaying a secret. "A lot of people don't know this about him," I said, pointing behind me at Jake with my thumb. "But his middle name is Jacob, but we call him Jake. Do you know what his first name is?"

Sean leaned his head towards me, eager to know the answer. "Colin," I said, holding my fist in a *C*-shape. Jake hated his first name.

A smile erupted across Sean's face as he looked from Jake to me, as if the world made sense again. The *J*-shape his fist made turned into a *C*. He went back and forth from a *C* to a *J* for a good minute, enthralled by this action, as a machine beeped intermittently in the background.

We watched as he made his *J*'s turn into *C*'s, that turned into *U*'s, and how they came together to make a big *S*. He started singing his ditty as he repeated the pattern and I couldn't help but feel as if he was trying to tell me something... but, really, he was probably just being Sean.

Sherry had turned off the television. The sudden silence seemed to rudely interrupt us as our eyes shot to the black screen. Sean flailed his hands, expressing that he did not like the television turned off. He flung himself back against the bed in protest. Sean was so big, that the bed moved slightly across the floor.

"Sean, it's okay," I said, wanting to reach out for his arm. He flailed again, nearly hitting me.

Jake stepped beside me and loudly removed the plastic bag from what it was holding. Sean stopped his fit with curiosity, though his face was still creased in displeasure.

Theatrically, Jake pulled out a board game covered in the dust of our childhood: Operation. "Buzz!" Sean exclaimed excitedly. He had quickly forgotten about the television.

I rolled over the bedside table so that Jake could set up the board. I didn't know if it was pure coincidence that he had brought that game, or if he remembered that day in science class so long ago.

I sat on the bed, beside Sean, so I could see the board, and Jake stood on the other side of the table. "Do you want to go first?" I asked Sean, handing him the tweezers. He shook his head and pointed to me. He arranged himself on the bed so that his entire body faced the game.

"Okay, I think I'll go for the bucket," I said, posing the tweezers above the illustrated man's knee. Of course the board *buzzed* when I accidentally touched the sides of the cavity, not capturing the bucket.

"Buzz!" Sean said excitedly with his hands together.

I smiled, seeing him to happy. An idea came to me then. "Once I hurt my knee," I shared, pointing the tweezers to where the bucket was located on the game board. "I banged it on the table and I got a bruise."

Jake caught onto my tactic and he added, "I accidentally kicked my friend's knee playing soccer once."

"Was she hurt?" I asked, knowing full well he was talking about me during gym class in fourth grade. My knee swelled and I had to wear a brace.

"Yeah," he admitted, trying to remove the bucket from the game board. "But I apologized," he added as the board *buzzed*.

Jake handed Sean the tweezers and he carefully perched over the board with his tongue sticking out the side of his mouth. Very carefully, he removed the bucket without the board buzzing.

"You ever hurt your knee, Sean?" I asked.

He shrugged, seeming to not pay attention to our conversation. He poised the tweezers over the caricature's stomach to retrieve the butterfly. *Buzz.* Sean handed the utensil to me without much thought.

"This one time," I started, leaning over the board. "I got so sick, my stomach felt horrible and I couldn't stop throwing up. Have you ever been that sick?" I asked, but Sean only shrugged and gave a noncommittal nod. *Buzz.*

Jake reached his hand over the board, the tweezers steady in his heads. He relayed a tale about getting punched in the stomach by a bully. Sean's eyes squinted as if he didn't want to hear about the pain. Jake had successfully picked up the butterfly and we were getting somewhere with Sean.

He eagerly took the tweezers, but studied the board for a few moments before poking the red nose that lit up when the board buzzed. "That doesn't come off," I said.

Sean shook his head but continued to focus on the nose, tapping it with the metal tipped tweezers. "Have you hurt your nose before?" Jake asked.

Sean nodded his head but didn't look up. "Have you hurt someone else's nose before, too?" Jake added and Sean replied the same way. Only, this time agony

registered in his features as he put down the tweezers
and stared at the bed sheets. I noticed his thumb and
forefinger made the letter *J* while the rest of his fingers
were clenched so that his knuckles turned white. He
began rocking back and forth slightly, as if he didn't
want to play anymore.

"I punched my sister in the face once," I said bluntly,
as if it happened every day. Both Sean and Jake looked
at me surprised. "Square in the nose. She said some
mean things to me when we were teenagers and I
punched her because she wouldn't stop," I admitted. I
hadn't thought of that in years. I still feel horrible
thinking about seventeen year old me punching my
thirteen year old sister because of the sour words of
vanity that were exchanged.

Sean picked up the tweezers and my heart swelled
with relief that we hadn't lost him yet. He tapped the
nose again and looked up at me. Ducking his head in a
clandestine way, he whispered, "Mean friend."

"Did you hurt a mean friend's nose?" I asked, adding
a touch of sympathy, matching his whisper.

Sean shook his head and pointed to me with a *J*-
shaped fist then bit his thumbnail as if it would cover
up his actions.

"You hit *my* mean friend in the nose?" I asked and
Sean nodded.

Still biting his thumb, he pointed to the wishbone on
the game board. "And his chest?" I asked, relieved we
were making progress. I could tell Sean was getting
tired and I didn't have much longer before exhaustion
made him uncooperative. He gave a slight nod and
looked at Jake as if he had just noticed he was there.

Jake excused himself to pour a glass of water near
the window, but was still within earshot. "You were
sorry, right?" I asked, our heads bent towards each
other in what Sean thought was a secret conversation.

"That's why you gave him that jersey you found cleaning up the gym, right? And let him play with your friends?"

Sean nodded slowly, looking up at me from his bushy eyebrows.

"Who are you friends?" I asked, passively. "I'd like to meet them. Are they nice?"

Horror shadowed his eyes as he shook his head vigorously. He began rocking back and forth slowly, but the speed increased when he started to moan and flap his hands. Sherry and Jake both moved to help calm him as I stood.

"Sean," I said loudly but with care. "It's okay. If they're that mean, I don't want to meet them." His feet tangled in the light blue bed sheets as an emotion I couldn't understand came over him. Still, I tried again. "They should be punished," I said adamantly. "Put in jail, right? If they did something bad they need a consequence."

With that one simple word, he stopped moaning and flapping his arms. Now he rocked back and forth, holding his elbows until his head landed heavily on his pillow. His eyes were full of stories that were too dark for his whimsical world. His eyebrows knitted together when his mind clearly wasn't as tired as his body.

With his foot, Jake nudged over the plastic bag that carried more than the board game. I took his hint without question. "Can I ask a favor, Sean?"

He didn't look at me or seem to hear me as Sherry stroked his hair. "I've been thinking about that mural you showed me and what a great job you did on it. I wanted to leave you a gift," I said and pulled the notebook and sixty-four colors of crayons out of the bag at my feet.

Jake had taken the board game from the table and I put these gifts in its place. "I was hoping you'd draw me a mural. Maybe a picture of a story only you know," I said and quickly added, "because I like the stories you tell me."

Sean sighed, still staring at the ceiling, acting as if I wasn't there. My heart sank at seeing him like this. I looked at Jake who nodded towards the hallway. "I'll let you get some sleep, Sean," I said and squeezed his hand. His response was only to shape his fist into a *C* and close his eyes.

CHAPTER TWENTY-SEVEN

"Just give him some time," Jake said as we stood in the hallway. I leaned against the wall, my eyes sweeping past his shoes and the gray running along the floor. "He's still healing and he's exhausted. We can come back later."

"No," I said though it didn't sound decisive. "You go ahead." I nodded and met Jake's gaze. "I'm going to stick around for a bit."

"Are you sure?" he asked.

"Yeah." I nodded. "You go on ahead. If you need me, you know where to find me."

His eyebrow raised slightly as if he found humor in that sentence. "Okay," he replied and glanced at his wristwatch.

I watched him get on the elevator and then turned to look out the window at the end of the hall. Even from this height I could barely make out where the cornfields ended and the urban part of Alton Oaks began. My stomach clawed and growled; I knew if I had to eventually bike back to town for Sadie's celebration, I should probably eat something more than the bread and butter I undoubtedly burned off on the bike ride here.

I knew the cafeteria well; I lived off the chocolate chip cookies that were the size of my hand when I worked the Spook Show. I thought about visiting the Children's Wing as I sat at an empty table with my turkey sandwich, but Sadie would be the one I would want to visit. On any other day I would easily catch

Alex or my best friend in these hallways, but today I was alone.

Sitting in the corner, the cafeteria was nearly empty sometime after dinner and before the cafeteria closed for the night. The bag of pretzels crinkled as I emptied its contents on my brown tray. The swarm of unrelenting thoughts began to settle upon my head and I desperately tried to shoo them away. I took a bite of the sandwich and chewed thoroughly, forcing my thoughts to go in another direction. Scenes from the past hour or so with Sean replayed in my head as the appropriate, "You, you, you, you, you, you, you," ditty became the soundtrack.

The hand motions—the letters Sean made with his fists—as he sang it intrigued me. I put down my coke and began to copy Sean as best I could: a *J* with my left, a *J* with my right. I turned them into *C*'s by curling my forefinger. Then I bent my wrist to turn the *C*'s into *U*'s. Finally, I turned them back into *C*'s to connect them as the letter *S*. I repeated the pattern to his ditty and I began to understand how Sean could find that comforting.

When I saw an elderly man and what I assumed was his daughter looking at me strangely, I stopped and put my hands beneath the table. I rolled my eyes at how awkward I was being and shoved a pretzel in my mouth. That's when I noticed that one of the pretzels on my platter was broken, and scattered away from the rest; it was shaped like a J.

Shuffling in my seat, I hovered over my pretzels and bit pieces off to form the letters I had been signaling: *J, J, C, C, U, U,* and two *C*'s shaped like a *S*. I rearranged them into words: CUJUS, JUJUS, JUSCU—No! This was silly.

Still, I couldn't stop playing as I ate my sandwich. Besides, what else was there to do but think about my sad life or terrorize the couple that probably thought I was crazy? Things didn't get exciting until I hit the tray with my coke can and one of the *J*'s spun upside down. Did you know that when placed together carefully, two *J*'s make a *C*? But what could I do with 3 *C*'s, 2 *U*'s and two *C*'s shaped like an *S*? *CUCUS*. Yes. This was *CUCU*.

I ate the pretzels around my letters thinking how I could meld together the other letters like I did to the *J*. Mirror image *C*'s kind of made an infinity sign, or a number eight. That was just me grabbing at straws. However, both *U*'s together made a *W*. Now what? *C, CC, W, S*. Maybe the *C*'s made an *O*? *COWS*? Did the Miller Farm have any cows? What if the *W* was a *M*? *COMS*? *MOCS*? *SCOM*?

Charli, I scolded myself. *You're overthinking something that doesn't mean anything. It's just Sean being Sean. Stop trying to find clues where there are none.* I sighed and drained my can of coke. There was nothing left to eat but my letters; my little game; my desperation to decipher Sean; my distraction from the reality I didn't want to face.

I spun the soda can in circles on the table between my thumb and forefinger, not yet ready to devour my letters. My thumb traced the swirly *A* in the brand name on the can. It kind of looked like two *C*'s back-to-back.

Just for fun, I laid the letters out: *C A W S*. The image of the crows picking at Jackson's face—the birds that Sean thought were his friends—hung in the forefront of my mind, giving me the chills. I realized who Sean's friends were and why he didn't want me to meet them. I rushed to the elevator, leaving my half-eaten pretzels behind.

"Sean!" I said, coming into his room, happy to see him awake. He was hunched over the table, the television on in the background. His bed was covered in pictures he had drawn.

"Look what I did!" I exclaimed, getting insight into his understanding of the world. I turned the two *J*'s I made with my hands into a *C*, then two *C*'s into an *A*, two *U*'s into a *W*, and two *C*'s into an *S*.

Sean's face lit up and nodded. He pointed to the crows in the picture he was drawing. I looked down, glowing from making sense of his world, to his vibrant and rough-lined picture.

A figure with bright red hair—I could only guess was Sean—was hiding behind the stalks of green corn along the side of the road. A man with yellowy-orange hair was on the ground, a red crayon scribbled his face. Two dark figures only drawn in black and brown stood over the man on the ground and there was a blue pick-up truck behind them.

CHAPTER TWENTY-EIGHT

"I can check the database in the entire county for a blue pick-up truck, but I don't think it'll narrow down the search," Jake shared after I hopped on my bike and flew into town, Sean's pictures tucked into my jacket. Jake was still in his civilian clothes when I slid Sean's artwork under his nose. "But it's worth a shot," he admitted, registering the worry that crinkled my eyebrows.

I sighed, thankful he was no longer being moody and unhelpful. "While you," I said, nodding at his computer. "Can I see—"

Jake shook his head, cutting off my sentence. "Sadie was released two hours ago. The charges were dropped with some new evidence," he shared matter-of-factly as he typed. His eyes didn't leave the computer screen.

There was still about an hour before Sadie's dinner at Oakie's and rather than bike back to the Alton House only to bike back into town, I decided to wait it out. While Jake ran the report, I pulled out my cell phone to check my messages. Before I could punch in my lock screen password, there seemed to be a commotion rising as officers shot up and moved quickly. I looked around for danger, finding none.

"Vega!" Chief Gomes bellowed, as he stepped out of his office. "A 10-60 was reported at the inn."

Though I didn't know what that code meant, I saw something in Jake's face that made me worry. He grabbed his coat from the back of his chair and only said, "I'll be in touch," before hastily making his way out the door.

The inn was only a short walk away: past Westbrook Attorneys, the firehouse, the bank, and across Oak Street. *No*, I told myself. I had just started to patch up my relationship with Jake and I didn't want him to think I was taking advantage of his position in the police department to satiate my Alton-born nosiness.

Still, Oakie's was on the other end of the block; I'd have to walk past the inn to get there. I noted the time on my wristwatch and thought I'd better make my way to Oakie's anyway.

I was only a few minutes behind the police officers sprinting down the street, but a crowd was already beginning to form in the heart of downtown, outside the inn. I overheard whispers about the possibilities from the onlookers:

"John McDowell found out about Jane and Russell and did 'em in! There were gunshots, didn't you hear 'em?"

"That drunk Canary was selling drugs out of her room!"

"Them Canaries are at it again! Did you hear that they found a bunch of stolen stuff in a room?"

Ambulance sirens were getting louder and I crossed the street to avoid the crowd, walking my bike past Prescott's until I reached Oakie's at the end of the block. My mind reeled, wondering about what had happened—I had to take what I overheard with a grain of salt. It was only the smell of Oscar's deep fried onion rings that brought my mind back to reality when I opened the doors to the restaurant.

"Charlotte May I!" My father was crouching below the hostess stand, replenishing the children's' menus and crayons when I walked in. His face lit up and he bounced up without a sign that his knees were fifty-two years old.

He enveloped me in a hug; he was always so happy to see me and I hoped that never changed. "Hi, Dad," I greeted. I let my cheek rest against his shoulder for a moment and noticed that his shirt smelled faintly of hollandaise sauce.

"You're here early," he said and released me. His hand rested on the wooden podium and his necktie swayed with the movement.

"I was nearby," I admitted, relieved he wouldn't question me further like the women in my life would have. "Besides, I get to spend time with my favorite guy!" I said, elbowing him lightly in the stomach.

He looked at me with a smile, but there was sadness there as well. "Let's not waste a moment then," he said, quickly brushing away the emotion. "Pie?" he asked and moved to the glass display.

"Banana cream?" I asked as he rounded to the other side.

"Not pumpkin?" he asked, holding up a can of whipped cream.

I shook my head. "Nah, but I'll take the extra whipped cream!"

My dad smiled, his wrinkles more pronounced, but in a debonair fashion. "That's my girl!" he said and pulled out two plates.

It was a rare treat to get my father's full attention, by myself, at Oakie's. Usually he was popping out of his seat; he couldn't quite keep still at work. Tonight, however, we sat in a table near the fireplace and I had my father's complete attention. It was probably due to all the events going on in my life at that moment and he was worried about me, but I didn't want to think about that.

"Pie without me?" Eli asked as he bounded up to his grandpa. His bottom lip pouted slightly as he held a superhero action figure. I looked over as Bailey and

Carter rounded the corner. There was one bit of pumpkin pie left on my dad's plate and he popped it into Eli's mouth.

"Hey, Charli," Carter greeted, bending over and giving me a hug.

"Mom's outside with Sadie and Alex," Bailey reported. "There's something going on at the inn and they're trying to get some answers."

"Well, that shouldn't stop us from appetizers and drinks in the Garden Room," my father said, standing up with Eli in his arms.

We followed him down the hall, past the bathrooms, and into the room many citizens rented for birthday parties, anniversaries, graduations, and celebrating a variety of life's milestones. The last time I was in the Garden Room was for my grandma's reception after her funeral, about fifteen years ago. Back then the walls had white wallpaper with a green vine print. It had been renovated some time during my absence from Illinois. Now the walls were white and panels of mirrors were placed intermittently between sconces of beautiful plastic flowers, their ivy cascading down the walls. Lights meant to look like candles were mounted to illuminate them and add glamor to the reflections in the mirrors.

There was a small bar in the corner where an employee I knew as Sam was waiting to fill drink requests. Two round tables were set up beautifully in blue linen for our party and soft music played in the background. Plates of appetizers were on the tables: onion rings, bacon-wrapped asparagus, potato skins, and garlic fries—some of Sadie's favorites.

"Mr. Parker!" I heard Sadie's voice and turned towards the entrance. "This is much too much! It's beautiful!" she exclaimed, giving him a hug.

My dad never blushed, but I saw a bit of pink rise to

his cheeks. My mother and Alex followed suit and exchanged hugs with him.

Sadie and I made a beeline for each other when our eyes met. Our embrace said more than words could have and I tried not to completely lose my emotions. How did I live so long being away from her encouragement and friendship? Sure, we had watched television shows together while on the phone and left each other numerous messages each day, but I couldn't handle all this without her.

"You okay?" I asked as she wiped away a tear.

"I'm golden!" she exclaimed, exuberant.

Alex crept up behind me with a hug and I noticed my mother and sister deep in conversation, undoubtedly about what was happening down the block. Sadie's father and attorney filed in moments later.

"Eat! Eat!" my dad encouraged, pulling out a chair for the guest of honor. Alex and Mr. Wilder sat on either side of Sadie as Mr. Westbrook and I filled in the two empty seats at their table.

The conservations ranged from Mr. Wilder's retired life to Sadie returning to work on Monday. I happily munched on my onion rings, watching Alex's body language. There was definitely some tension between him and Mr. Wilder but my brother was being mature and giving enough distance to Sadie, but not ignoring her completely. Sadie lightly touched his arm and exchanged glances with him that made Mr. Wilder's lip twitch.

When dinner was brought out—the smell of pecan encrusted chicken and Oscar's herbed three-cheese macaroni hung enticingly in the air—my cell phone buzzed. I should have ignored it, but I pulled it out of my pocket instead. It was Jake.

I looked up and Sadie caught my eye right away. With a look that begged forgiveness, I stepped into the hallway and answered.

"Hi, Jake," I greeted, the empty hallway filtered in noises from the main part of the restaurant.

"Charli, what is your location?" he asked, getting to the point quickly.

My eyebrows pulled together in worry. "Oakie's, why?"

"I need you to answer some questions," he said then added in a softer tone, "I need your help."

"Sure. What is it?" I asked.

"I'll pick you up outside. I need you to come to the hospital with me," he said. The background noise was distracting and I couldn't tell if he was at the station or at the inn. "Your," Jake paused trying to find the appropriate word, "*neighbor,* Jessica. She tried to commit suicide."

The words hit me like dodgeballs in gym class. "I'll be right out," I said, already walking towards the entrance.

CHAPTER TWENTY-NINE

"She's conscious," Jake said as we walked into the hospital. "The staff at the inn said they heard arguing—some say loud noises—and the manager entered the room seconds after she wrapped her neck in a belt and jumped off a chair."

"Arguing? Noises? Was anyone else in the room?" I asked, trying to keep up with his stride.

"No. The manager said she was the only one in the room," Jake informed as we walked towards the emergency room. "You might be able to get some information out of her. She can't speak, her throat is going to need some time to heal. But you're the only one for miles who knows her. You might have some luck—if nothing else, knowing how to contact her family."

I honestly didn't know what good I'd do since she hated me simply because I was married to Jackson. "I can't promise anything," I admitted, rounding the corner and going through a set of official-looking doors. "But I'll see what I can do."

"Remember, most hanging victims sometimes have a ringing in their ears, so she might not hear you very well," Jake said and handed me a Steno pad that had never been used. "You might need this."

We walked down a hallway and Jake stopped outside a room at the end. "You go ahead," he nodded towards the open door. I guessed his hesitation had more to do with a professional decision than a personal one.

The room was different than Sean's. The walls were

still blue and the bed Jessica was lying in was similar, but it was smaller and there were many more machines. Each one beeped or blinked. There was no television or any other noise than the machinery and voices of the staff from outside the room.

Her eyes were closed when I neared the bed. I didn't see how me being here would help—when she opened her eyes she would only freak out seeing me and it could make things worse. I had to trust Jake knew what he was doing.

An oxygen mask covered her mouth and she wore a neck brace that didn't completely hide the fresh bruises that were bound to get darker and more obvious. I studied her knotted blonde hair and the bruises beneath her eyes. What would have caused her to do such a thing? If losing Jackson caused her this much grief, what was wrong with me—his *wife*?

There was a series of beeps and then the blood pressure cuff around her arm inflated. The pressure stirred her to consciousness and her eyes fluttered open momentarily. "Don't freak out," I said, noting how her heart rate jumped on the monitor.

Her eyes were bloodshot and there was terror in them.

She squirmed and I backed away, hoping my presence wouldn't kill her. She lifted the oxygen mask and tried to say something—probably sharp words that wanted me to leave her alone. What did Jake expect me to do here?

"Don't speak," I said. "The doctors say you need to heal. I'll leave if that's what you want."

Her eyes swept across the room frantically and she reached her hand out towards me. *She probably wants to strangle me*, I thought, but took a step closer anyway; I didn't think she could do much damage in her current state.

To my surprise, she grabbed my hand. Her eyes were trying to tell me something that I didn't think translated to cuss words. She reached for the Steno pad in my other hand and slipped the pencil out from the spiral.

I noticed that she couldn't lift her head and she lifted the pad of paper above her head as she wrote. The pale skin on her forehead wrinkled as she ripped the paper from the pad and slipped it in my hand. She tucked it into my fist with a determined and desperate look that would haunt me the rest of my life. I unfolded the crinkled paper in my hand. In shaky writing, she only wrote two words: *Find Jesse.*

Moments later I rounded the corner outside Jessica's room. Jake was leaning against the wall, looking down at his phone. "What is it?" he asked, seeing me.

I handed him the note. "Jesse?" he asked. I wasn't sure if it was out of confusion or if he didn't remember who Jesse was.

"Jackson's best friend," I shared. "Though the last I knew, they weren't speaking to each other. He came to Alton Oaks with Jackson and Jessica. He was the one you said the Carabineer in the photograph might have belonged to."

A memory of this earlier conversation sparked recognition in his eyes. He slowly began walking back to the main entrance and I followed. "I'm sorry I've been such a pain," he admitted.

Emotion began to swell in me once again today. I fought back the tears that were long overdue. "Me too," I said, but quickly added, "It's water under the bridge."

Jake pulled his Steno pad—with it's bent edges and coffee stained cover—out of his brown deputy's jacket. "Tell me what you know about Jesse," he said as we approached the lobby. We stood in a corner out of the way, near the empty couches and chairs used by visitors.

I spent a good fifteen minutes telling Jake about how I first met Jesse when Jackson and I came back from the Peace Corp and how Jesse never held down a job. I explained in as much detail as I could remember about the fist fight I witnessed at Jackson's family reunion. I shared short stories about how Jackson and Jesse were bad influences on each other. I shared every detail about my conversation with Jesse on the Canal Trail and by the time I finished, Jake couldn't hide the look of surprise on his face. As I heard myself tell tales of Jackson and Jesse, I couldn't help but think along the same lines: why did I put up with it for so long?

Jake turned a few pages in his pad and said, "You described Jesse as about six feet tall, dark brown hair, brown eyes, with a scar on his right forearm, correct?"

I nodded, remembering the conversation we had on my parent's front porch. "Do you know where he would be?" Jake asked, flipping back to the page he had been writing on in his Steno pad.

I shook my head. "No. No idea," I admitted. "He could be in China by now."

Deflated, I shifted my weight and leaned against the back of a dark blue chair. It was long past visiting hours and the night staff was significantly fewer than the day staff. Not much was happening at the main entrance except for the one woman going through files behind the desk, which is why my attention went to the man in a baseball cap and oversized jacket exiting the stairwell.

Jake had positioned himself to have a vantage point of the entrance, as all police do, whether or not they're on the clock. He noticed my intense gaze and turned. Just as the man passed ten feet beside us, I saw his face. For a moment we locked eyes and Jesse looked startled. "That's him," I said to Jake. "That's Jesse."

When Jake called after Jesse, he took off out the

glass doors. "Stay here," Jake called without looking back at me, and chased after Jesse. I tried to catch a glimpse of anything through the wide open windows, but I couldn't see anything past the bright lights of the entrance besides the shadows of the trees blowing wildly in the wind. I really wanted to chase after, but knew I had to stay put for the sake of mending our friendship.

Not five minutes later a security guard ran through the main hall and I figured I would see police lights coming up the drive at any moment. I sat in one of the dark blue chairs and strained to see something out the window, but only studied how the wind picked up. The storm front was moving in quickly as I bit my nails in anticipation.

After what seemed like hours, I got an answer. "Charli Parker to the emergency room nurse's station," a voice announced over the speakers that usually alerted doctors and nurses. The announcement repeated once more and dread spread though me as I thought that something had happened to Jake.

Quickly, my pace turned into a sprint as I made my way down the hallway and back through the official-looking doors, thinking the worst. My heart pounded and I didn't think I could bear seeing another one of my loved ones tortured by Jackson's decisions. As I rounded the corner, elation and relief overcame me as I saw Jake at the nurse's station, looking down at a clipboard.

Without knowing what I was doing, I embraced him in a hug. "I thought you were hurt!" I exclaimed when I felt him go rigid with surprise.

"No," he said, relaxing a little. "I'm fine."

When my arms let go of him, chagrin burned my face with how childish I had been. "What is it then?" I asked, knowing from Jake's body language that something was amiss: his eyebrows didn't move and his hand touched his belt. There was something he didn't want to tell me. That's when I saw the body bag being wheeled out of Jessica's room.

I looked up at Jake. "Jessica?" I asked, feeling Jackson's poison seep further into my life. "What happened?"

"She died," Jake said, his elbow on the ledge of the nurse's station. "She was smothered with her pillow. With her injuries, it didn't take long and it didn't take much." I watched the gurney roll down the hallway in shock: I had *just* spoken to her. Was I the last person she communicated with? Then a chilling thought crossed my mind. "Was it Jesse?" I asked.

Jake rubbed the scraggly facial hair on his chin. "I don't know. There is a heavy suspicion."

"What happened when you chased after him? Did he get away?" I asked.

Jake nodded. He turned his head to meet my gaze. "In a blue pick-up truck," he said in a tone that gave me the chills.

CHAPTER THIRTY

"I'm headed to the station now," Jake said and glanced at his watch. "Do you want a ride?"

We walked down the long hallway I had emerged from only minutes earlier. I shook my head at his answer. "No," I said. "I want to visit Sean. I want to make sure he's okay."

Jake squinted his eyes in thought and then nodded. "Promise me one thing, Charli?" he asked.

"What?"

He ran a hand through his bushy hair. "Don't bike home tonight. Don't walk home from here tonight. Promise me?" He glanced over at me and his request was as serious as this murder case.

I nodded; I knew I had to keep this promise in the name of rebuilding our friendship. I had to keep it no matter what happened; even if I had to spend the night in the waiting room.

As if Jake read my thoughts, he added, "Call me if you have to and I'll send Seth or Pete with the station wagon. Or call Alex. Just don't walk home tonight."

"Okay, Jake. I promise," I said as I stopped at the elevator.

Jake hesitated for a moment then added, "Thanks for your help today, Charli," as he continued his path towards the parking lot.

I only sent him a smile that he didn't catch.

The events of this incredibly long day played in bits across my memory as I rode the elevator up to the eighth floor. Jake had made arrangements with the hospital to allow me to visit Sean so long after visiting hours had ended. The two nurses behind the desk were gossiping about a reality television show when I showed them my identification. It was almost refreshing to hear about gossip so far away from my tiny little world.

When I walked into Sean's room, I saw the light jumping from some anime show on television, sending fast shadows racing across the darkness. He held the blanket up to his chin as he watched the show. My heart broke with the fact that he didn't have his mother—or anyone really—to tell him it was time to go to bed.

"Hi, Sean," I whispered as I tip-toed into his room. I didn't want to startle him after everything he had been through.

"Chawli," he greeted without stuttering. I took it as a sign that his recovery was going well. He padded the back of the chair that I had occupied several hours earlier, inviting me to sit with him.

And that was all I did. Sean leaned back, still gripping the blanket to his chin, as the illuminated colors of the animated show tortured the shadows throughout the room. Perhaps I was hiding from reality in a small corner of the world, or maybe I sought solace. Either way, Sean let me sit beside him without having to say anything.

I let myself think about the events that had just occurred, no matter what emotions appeared. I wondered if my Alton-born nosiness was a survival technique because instead of mourning, I began to wonder if Jessica really tried to commit suicide in the first place. She wanted me to *find Jesse*; did he know something, or was it an accusation?

"Chawli?" I looked up from my gaze on the enervating beige floor tiles to Sean. His television show had ended and an infomercial boasted a one-of-a-kind, can't-live-without kitchen utensil. Sean's eyebrows were raised in a questioning gaze.

"I'm okay, Sean. Just came to check on you," I reiterated, more for my benefit than his, I think.

"Fwends," he said it more as a passing statement than as a question. He picked up the remote and began channel surfing.

Friends. Like Sadie and me. Or Jesse and Jackson. An idea struck me. It might lead to nothing, but I still had to try. I pulled out my cell phone and ignored the five texts from Sadie, the missed call from my sister, and the voicemail from my mother's cell phone. I searched my social media until I found what I was looking for.

"Sean?" I asked and leaned over with my phone.

Sean's head moved towards me, but his eyes were locked on the television screen. "Have you seen my friend Jesse?" I asked, pointing to the picture of Jesse and Jackson standing on a boulder that overlooked a lake. They were dressed in cargo shorts with flannel shirts wrapped around their waists. It was a trip I wasn't invited on, or one that happened after my departure.

He peeled his eyes from the screen and glanced at my phone. He shook his head and continued to channel surf. "Are you sure?" I asked.

The small pang of disappointment I felt must have shown on my face. When Sean looked over again, he shook his head but said, "Him," and pointed to Jackson. "I saw him."

Of course, he saw Jackson. How could I have been so insensitive? From what I gathered, he had punched Jackson in the nose and in the stomach for saying some mean things. What else had he witnessed? When I looked up at Sean, he didn't seem traumatized or scared. He looked far away, staring at a spot a few inches above my phone, as if he was lost in thought.

"You can tell me about it, if you want. You don't have to," I encouraged. Part of me hoped he would divulge everything at once, but I knew that wouldn't happen with Sean.

Moments passed as if each one was an eternity and Sean's face remained unchanged. "Do you remember anything else that happened that night? Did you hear them say anything?" I asked, trying not to be pushy. The two dark figures Sean had drawn marched to the forefront of my thoughts.

Sean shrugged. "I didn't undastand," he said simply.

"Did they talk too fast?" I asked.

"No," Sean said and flipped through the channels. I knew I was losing his attention and focus and was too exhausted to fight it. I leaned back in the chair, resigned. "They used diffwent wo'ds like channel sixty-six," Sean shared, pointing the television. "Spanish," he informed.

A wave of adrenaline kicked in with this information. "The two people with Jackson spoke Spanish?" I asked, studying Sean's face carefully as he watched the dramatic soap opera, his features distorted in confusion.

"They all did," he corrected and changed the channel until he came to an old 1950's, black-and-white show.

"Did they hurt each other?" I asked, tentatively.

Whether or not Sean heard me, I couldn't say. He either ignored the question or avoided it. "I'm going to sleep now," he said and nestled his large body under the thin blankets. He reminded me of a large bear settling in for the winter.

I sighed. "Good-night, Sean," I said, noting that it was nearly midnight. I would come back tomorrow and try again with an ice cream taco.

As I walked out of the room, into the brightly lit hallway, a steam engine of chills raced down my back and Sean said loud enough for me to hear, "Be safe, Chawli."

CHAPTER THIRTY-ONE

As I rode the elevator down to the main floor, I wanted nothing more than to walk home and burn off some energy to think clearly. Or, at least, melt away the chills that still clung to my shoulder blades. I knew I had to keep my promise to Jake though. He was either still busy doing paperwork at the station or had retired for the night. The Alton Oaks police station had one—maybe two—officers on duty overnight, and I really didn't want to waste their resources for a simple ride home. I scrolled past Jake's number in my contacts and settled on Rip.

I knew he'd be awake and (most likely) available, but having to drive all the way to the hospital would irritate him. After realizing that most of the things I did irritated him, I called him without feeling guilty.

His black pick-up truck pulled up under the brightly lit U-shaped driveway of the visitor's entrance. A light rain began, worsening the chill I couldn't shake. The blatant disregard for the posted speed limit got Rip here in no time. The look he gave me as I walked to the truck was a juxtaposition of emotions: confusion, exhaustion, elation, frustration, worry. He said nothing, though.

As I climbed into the passenger seat, the heat that billowed from the radiator vents erased the goose bumps. "Thanks for the ride," I said as he peeled out of the drive.

"Why are you at the hospital?" he asked with some abrasiveness. We left the bright lights of the building and pulled onto the rural roads of Oak Street.

"Long story," I said and leaned my head against the window. His truck smelled of new car and saw dust, it was a soothing combination.

Rip applied pressure to the brake suddenly, and in moments we were moving at a snail's pace. "Good thing we've got time," he jeered. "Long ride home and all."

"If withholding information made you drive safely, I would have started doing that a long time ago," I shot back with a lot less sarcasm than his statement.

Rip didn't hit the brake pedal or the accelerator. He only propped his elbow on the door with one hand on the wheel, like he was enjoying this.

I guess I owed him some type of explanation for picking me up in the middle of the night. "Remember Jessica, who came to town with Jackson?" I asked without waiting for a response. "She tried to commit suicide so Jake had me talk to her, and then somebody killed her while she was in the hospital. While Jake went back to the station, I went to visit Sean. Now here I am," I shared as quickly and as cleanly as possible.

Without a word, Rip accelerated in response. Apparently that was enough information to satisfy him or, like me, he needed time to digest it.

I figured the ride back to the east side of town would be silent and I suddenly grew sleepy, watching the lines on the road pass by in a rhythmic lullaby. "Is that a deer?" I asked, pointing to a figure in the road. At first I thought it was a figment of my exhaustion, but it definitely did not look like it belonged in the road.

Rip had hit the brake pedal and the red tail lights glowed into the dark cabin. "It's a person," he said dismissively as the car pulled closer. The headlights illuminated a figure running in the middle of the road, waving their hands. Rip swerved to pass them and hit the gas.

"Stop!" I shouted, aghast that he would do such a thing. "It's past midnight in the middle of nowhere." I neglected to mention that we were eerily close to where Jackson's body was found. I shuddered as cornstalks on either side of the road bent unwillingly in a strong breeze. "And there's a storm coming in. They probably need help or are lost," I added for good measure as the rain drops grew steadier on the windshield. The sudden thought of Sean roaming these fields in the middle of the night broke my heart.

I felt the momentum of the truck slow down as my body leaned forward with Rip's decision. He sighed as he pulled alongside the man who was waving his hands.

The truck's headlights gave the man an eerie illumination. "Please help," he pleaded, holding onto Rip's door.

My stomach sunk with a gut feeling that things were not okay. The man's eye was swollen, as was his lip and—was that blood on his shirt?

Rip moved to pry the man's hands from his door when a realization struck me as cold as ice water. "Jesse?" I asked as stone cold shock shook my voice. His one good eye looked past Rip, to me. "Charlotte," he pleaded, using the only name he knew for me. "Please help. Please! They're coming!" he said, glancing over his shoulder, before running in front of the truck to my side of the cabin.

"Who's coming?" I asked.

Jesse pulled open my door and threw himself inside so that I could feel Rip's frustration radiating from him in uncomfortable waves. "Drive!" he pleaded, hitting the dashboard repeatedly, looking out the back window. Rip hit the gas pedal in frustration of his lack of control, rather than from Jesse's command.

"Who is coming? What happened to you?" I asked,

noticing the missing teeth in Jesse's mouth.

"It's a long story," he evaded.

I felt the frustration Rip must've felt when I pulled this line on him not ten minutes ago. "I deserve some kind of explanation," I started. I mean, was he running from the police or a rabid dog, or someone he ticked off?

Jesse took his eyes off the road behind us and sighed, realizing I was right. He hesitated; he knew what he was about to tell me would change my perspective on all that I thought I knew. In the end, I guessed he decided to spill everything because it all poured out of his mouth. "Jackson started making contacts in Latin America when he was waiting for you to finish the Peace Corp," he began.

With a fleeting look behind us, he continued, "He *is* an artist," he said with conviction but then corrected himself: "He *was* an artist. But he quickly realized how he could make more money. His studio was a front. He sent hollow sculptures to Mexico—they used them to move drugs. He was happy knowing that people paid big bucks for his work, not completely realizing that most of the money went towards what was inside."

Jesse's bruised knuckles gripped the dashboard and he radiated anxiety. The muscles in Rip's arm tensed behind me, against my back, and I dismissed it. I'd worry about him after I got some answers from Jesse because so far, none of what he said was making sense. Nevertheless, I let him continue as he kept running his tongue over his busted lip.

"Then he got worse," Jesse admitted, his eyes constantly moving to the road behind us. "He began transporting drugs in his sculptures across the border himself, and then hid cocaine between the layers of canvas in his paintings. He was gone so often—yes, he was with Jessica, but most of the time they were driving across the border. Jessica became his *curator*," Jesse said the word as if he didn't agree with the term. "Jackson has a tidy sum of cash in offshore accounts. It's why we fought that day in El Paso. He became careless. He dug himself deeper into trouble. He trusted me—and lord knows why—he began to pay me to protect Jessica. We weren't on our way to Boston, Charlotte. He wanted a divorce not only for his own selfish reasons, but to keep you safe. We were going to get you to sign the papers and then hop on the next flight to the Cayman Islands."

This all sounded like a scene from a television show, not from my real life. Denial hit me unexpectedly. There was no way *my* Jackson was into any of that! I would have known! I would have seen something! This is Jesse's dumb way of getting back at me. No, he was delirious with grief from Jackson and Jessica's death.

Then again, I never expected Jackson and Jessica were sneaking around for so long. How did I miss something so blatantly obvious now that I look back? "How did I not know this?" I asked aloud, more to myself than to Jesse.

Rip seemed to growl, but I ignored it. Jesse seemed to relax from his paranoia as he asked without tact, "How did you not see he had been cheating on you since before you guys got married?"

Anger rose up in me. Jackson's unfaithfulness had been going on longer than I initially thought? "Listen," Rip started, aggressively.

I elbowed him, probably with too much anger, cutting him off. "Why the hell did he marry me then?" I asked Jesse, rage bubbling.

Jesse shrugged, his attention moved from Rip, to me, to the back window. "Image?" he asked with the same amount of sass. "Maybe you were a reminder of wholesomeness—an uncorrupted reminder of who he used to be. Maybe he just liked the control, the secrets, the way he secretly tortured you. Your guess is as good as mine. All I know is that once you left Albuquerque, everything began to snowball. It took you long enough to wake up," he shared with a snort that made my blood boil.

Rip's entire body seemed to tense as I leaned into him slightly when the road curved. If we weren't driving—if I wasn't in between the both of them—I was sure Jesse would have added to his collection of injuries. I gave Rip some credit for controlling himself and his lack of retort.

"So I was just a cover for him?" I asked, growing increasingly upset. Did Jackson ever feel *one ounce* of what I felt for him during our marriage?

"I don't know, Charlotte," he admitted with gusto. "Jackson changed after the Peace Corps." Jesse took a moment to sigh dramatically, as if my questions were unimportant. "If it's worth anything, he ran everything out of his studio and kept you and that apartment out of the thick of it. You can think of it as keeping you safe."

"Or him being selfish!" I know it wasn't good manners to talk about the dead in such a way, but if he had all this money, why didn't he have any to pay the bills each month? Why did he let me save my pennies in order to afford plane tickets to Illinois? Why didn't he ever buy groceries or only leave me scratch-off lottery tickets in my stocking at Christmas? Then again, his studio and art supplies were the only things I never paid for. It was no wonder he was never evicted! This idea that Jackson was self-serving—and I *never* saw it before now—really frosted my cookies.

My fist clenched and I gritted my teeth. "So, you had a falling out with Jackson because you found out about his, *lifestyle*?" I asked incredulously. I never saw Jesse as a chivalrous person with many values.

Jesse shrugged indifferently. His shoulders seemed to relax a little and he didn't glance out the back window as often.

"So why did you come back?" I asked.

"Money," he said unabashedly. "You know holding down a job was never my thing. It was an easy out. Plus," he added without a shade of remorse, "Jessica was cute. I was going to be the knight in shining armor once it all caught up to Jackson."

I couldn't suppress an eye roll. *That* was the Jesse I knew. "You have to go to the police," I urged.

"No," he said firmly, throwing a relieved glance out the back window.

"Jesse, they think you killed Jessica," I informed. Rip sighed and grumbled, but I ignored it quickly.

"Jessica's dead?" he asked. His jittery movements and paranoia seemed to cease for a few moments as he moved in slow-motion with the realization.

I nodded. "She was smothered with a pillow while she was in recovery."

"No," Jesse said, shaking his head. "I was just there. That's impossible."

A thought occurred to me and it came tumbling out of my mouth. "The night Jackson died, did you—"

Jesse shook his head—not so much to answer my question, but to cut me off. He put the realization that Jessica was dead to the side for a moment. "We went to the bar, like I said. Jackson saw someone and his paranoia was scary. He made me stay with Jessica; protect her if they came after her. He went off that night, almost sober with the situation. I told you the truth." He said the last sentence as if he deserved a badge of honor and I tried not to blatantly roll my eyes at him.

"I get why they were after Jessica, but why are they after you?" Jessica, after all, crossed the border with

Jackson all the time, it sounded like. She had to have seen things, heard things.

Jesse shrugged. "I think they think I know too much since I was traveling with them." I held my tongue as to not say, "Well, you do!"

"Wait a minute," I exclaimed, talking with my hands. "Jake said you got away from him in the hospital parking lot in the blue pick up truck."

Jesse looked at me confused. "Charlotte, they *took* me in the pick-up truck," he said almost convincingly. "They took me to the old pull-barn on the Miller's property. I think it's where they've been hiding out. Do you think I did this to myself?" he asked, pointing to his distorted face.

Rip snorted and his wordless commentary was irritating me. Whether or not Jesse's injuries were self-inflicted, I began to doubt his story. Jesse was never one to tell the truth—at least not the *complete* truth. Without a doubt, I held Jake's story in a much higher regard than his.

"Why did you run when we saw you in the hospital then?" I asked, skeptical.

Jesse was offended. "I saw a random man start to chase after me and—after what happened to Jackson— of course I'm going to run. I don't know who to trust anymore."

"You think you can trust me?" I asked.

Despite the tone of the conversation, Jesse broke out into laughter. I felt heat rush up to my face out of anger. "Of course, I trust you, Charlotte. You've always been a girl scout."

I sighed heavily out of frustration and crossed my arms over my chest. It would have been the perfect time for Rip to start a sentence because I wouldn't have stopped him. Out of the corner of my eye, I only saw his white knuckles gripping the steering wheel, though.

Street lamps began to appear on either side of the road as we entered the neighborhood on the west side of downtown Alton Oaks. Rip slowed the truck, but still exceeded the speed limit by fifteen miles per hour. As we passed Main Street, with a few windows still lit at the inn on the corner, a truck with bright headlights caught up to us quickly.

Rip swore under his breath, turning his rearview mirror down so the light didn't shine directly on his face.

Terror erased the momentarily light humor around Jesse's injuries. "Oh god," he exclaimed, turning to look out the back window. "They found us."

CHAPTER THIRTY-TWO

Leaning slightly into Rip, I turned my body to follow Jesse's gaze to see a blue pick up truck behind us. Just past the bright headlights I made out the figure of a man hanging halfway out the passenger door, pointing at us. No, not pointing.

Rip noticed the gun the same time I did as he hit the gas and swerved back and forth on the road when the gun fired. It was a sound so fearsome and hungry that it ruptured my soul. The framed picture of my childhood hometown rattled on the walls of my heart. "Hang on," Rip said through gritted teeth and we gained speed.

I was thankful that no one was regularly out this late in Alton Oaks. We sped past the east side of town in seconds and I did not want to glance at the speedometer to gauge why. Rip made a hard turn onto US-16 so that our bodies leaned towards Jesse. A sharp intake of breath on his part made me wonder if his injuries were worse than I thought.

Any doubt I had about Jackson's story dissolved as the safety of the Alton House was quickly getting further from my grasp. "This can't be real," I muttered to myself. This stuff only happens on television; in movies. This was sleepy Alton Oaks, not Chicago, not New York City.

"It's all too real," Jackson said, his right hand on the dashboard and left hand on the headrest. His eyes watched the truck behind us as our bodies swayed with the movement of the swerving vehicle. I held my breath as I saw the bright headlights get closer with gained speed, and how I'd let out the breath when the headlights grew fainter with the turns and twists of the five miles of road we were on before we hit Sheridan.

Coming down the road on Blackhill, the blue pick-up truck gained enough speed to fire the gun again and I tucked my head below the dashboard as they hit the mirror on Jesse's side of the car.

Anger or adrenaline—or maybe both—fueled Rip to go faster. "Charli," he said. "You might want to call Deputy Do-Right."

My hands shook as I slipped the phone from my back pocket, keeping my head below the dashboard. Jesse had moved so that he leaned over me—low enough to be safe, but still keeping an eye on his enemies.

"Hey, Charli," Jake greeted. "You need a ride? I can call Alex. We have a situation right now."

My voice shook nearly as bad as my hands. "Jake," I started. "I am the situation."

A moment of silence seemed too long as the facts of that sentence permeated the world. Another gun shot hit the back of the truck and a small fearsome squeal escaped my lips. "Where are you?" Urgency and tact coated his voice and it comforted me, if only somewhat.

"Rip's pick-up truck, US-16, headed towards Sheridan," I shared, trying to be emotionless and to-the-point but knew I was failing.

There was no sigh, no retort, no panic from Jake; only a type of reassurance in his voice. "Charli, listen, stay on the phone with me." I heard the crackling of his radio in the background. "Is anyone hurt?" he asked.

"Not terribly," I said, thinking of Jesse's distorted face.

"Is someone chasing you?" I had guessed Jake already deduced this as correct, but wanted my confirmation.

"Yes," I said, feeling like a rag doll as Rip swerved across the road. "The blue pickup truck. They have a gun."

I heard the crackling of the radio again. "All units respond," he said, sounding far away. "Gun shots fired. US-16 outside Alton Oaks. Two vehicles headed North."

My phone dropped the call before I could hear anything else. A small bout of panic came over me; I didn't get service for about a mile on this road. I squeezed my knees, waiting an eternity until I had service again. I found myself closing my eyes and praying for help; this was all too real. I wanted to wake up from this nightmare.

Rip and Jesse's voices were distant as they threw insults and not well-thought out plans to each other. Relief flooded through me as the sound of sirens grew closer. My phone trilled in my hand and my eyes popped open to Jake's phone number on the screen.

Before I could say anything, Jake's voice came across the line. "Charli?" he asked without waiting for confirmation, "you should have a police vehicle in pursuit."

"Yes," I confirmed, my voice quavering.

"Charli, you're doing great," he said in a calm, measured tone. "The Sheridan Police Department has been dispatched. I'm on my way. Keep your head down, you hear me?"

"Yes," I said, feeling the pressure of Jesse's body on my back, which made it hard to breathe.

Jesse threw in a few explicits as he told Rip to go faster. Rip replied in his own colorful retort. I heard the sirens get louder and blue and white lights filled the cabin.

"Now who's in the vehicle with you?" Jake asked. I wasn't sure if it was vital information or if he was trying to keep me focused.

"Rip and Jesse," I said. When a reply from Jake didn't immediately come, I felt the need to explain and anxiety rushed out. "You were right not to walk home," I began to explain. "I thought you'd be busy and I knew Rip would be awake, so he picked me up and we found Jesse all beat up, running away from something on the road by the Miller's Farm." Tears started pouring out with my consent. "Jackson was into drug trafficking— he and Jessica. He screwed someone who came after him. How they're after Jesse—after us."

"Charli, you're doing great," Jake said without skipping a beat. "I'm almost there. No matter what happens, you keep your head down, okay?"

I nodded, though he couldn't see the gesture. "Jake?" I asked. The truest words I ever spoke fell out of my mouth next.

"Yes, Charli?" I heard the crackling of the radio and sirens in the background of the phone call.

"I'm a small town girl. I'm not meant for this; I can't—"

Jake cut me off. His voice was firm but reassuring; enough to give me a boost of confidence I needed. "Charlotte May Parker, you are absolutely the heartbeat of this town. You will get through this. I will not hang up on you. *We* will get through this."

Before I could respond, the car swerved sharply to the right and I felt Rip lean into me as he gripped the steering wheel to keep control. My phone toppled to the floor, skidding into the corner where Jesse's muddied shoes were covered in shadows.

When the car came to a stop, it leaned forward and I could only guess we were facing downwards in a drainage ditch on the side of the road. My heart beat wildly, unsure what would happen next. I followed Jake's instructions and kept my head down, though

Jesse sat up straight, relieving pressure from my back.

"It's okay, Charli," Rip said, trying to help me up. "The Sheridan police and two Illinois State Troopers stopped the car. It's like a scene from a cop show."

I shook my head. "Nope," I said firmly, not letting him sway me. Out of the corner of my eye, I saw the police lights scanning the maple and fir trees on the side of the road and heard men yelling to gain control of the situation.

A man's voice approached our vehicle not too long after. "I need you both to get out of the car slowly," he instructed to Rip and Jesse from the tailgate. "I need to see your hands."

As both doors opened and the chilling breeze entered with the smell of cold rain, I squeezed my knees together and wished for this night to be over. I found myself whispering Sean's ditty under my breath.

The sirens had ceased, but another one was approaching fast and I wasn't sure from which direction, but I knew it was from that trusty old Alton Oaks station wagon. I could hear the officer instructing Rip and Jesse to put their hands on either side of the truck. Foreign voices asked the men questions and the thirty seconds that passed seemed like an eternity. Goosebumps erupted down my back and the rain poured harder—lightning flashed so bright I could see it from behind my eyelids.

"Charli? You okay?" The sound of Jake's voice three feet away willed me to open my eyes again. He stood at the opened driver's door in a dark raincoat.

"It's over?" I asked with desperation, still hugging my knees.

"Yeah, it's over," he said, reaching out his hand.

I grabbed it and let him pull me out of the vehicle and into the rain. I didn't care that it was Jake and that we'd had a rocky patch or that he was on duty. The only thing I cared about was this nightmare being over. That I was safe; that he was safe. I wrapped my arms around him, thankful that he was around. Thankful that it was over. Thankful that he understood and didn't dismiss my phone call this time.

And it might have been that he was still dressed in civilian clothes, but for once, friend-Jake appeared alongside work-Jake and he hugged me back. "You did great, Charli," he said reassuringly as the thunder struck and the cold bullets of rain shot down around us.

CHAPTER THIRTY-THREE

"So what happened to Sean?" Mrs. Kratsky asked from her perch on the rocking chair. Everyone was interested in hearing my account of last night's events.

The storm western Illinois had been waiting for had started when I'd left the hospital last night, hitting its peak around three in the morning—when my parents showed up at the police station in Bailey's car. It had been steadily raining ever since. I shared the porch swing with Sadie and my mother. I had a quilt pulled up to my chin as Sadie leaned on my shoulder.

"The therapist has made progress with him," Jenna informed, sharing what she'd heard through the grapevine. Her straight blonde hair curled a bit at the end with the humidity.

"Did he have anything to do with..." Bailey trailed off, glancing in my direction.

"Not that we know," Jenna shared. "From what I can gather, anyway. His mother had a heart attack which triggered Sean to act differently—he didn't quite comprehend what happened. Since his mother couldn't say no, he took her car to Alton Oaks. Somehow he came across Jackson." She paused and many of the women on the porch looked at me from the corner of their eyes.

Jake had already filled me in on all of this. I was merely trying to keep a grasp on normalcy, being present for their Gossip Club this morning. I watched the rain drops splash in the puddles of muddy patches of the front yard.

"Jackson hadn't been nice to him and Sean punched him in the chest and in the nose—best we can guess—and knocked him out cold. Sean said he felt bad and wanted to make things right—you know how he thinks," Jenna continued. She paused to drink from her blue and white monogrammed chevron-patterned travel mug. Her engagement ring sparkled in the muted sunlight with the movement. "He loves the high school and the animals—all of them: the pigeons, mice, crows. He put Jackson in Sadie's jersey—he apparently found it cleaning the gym after the volleyball game—and took him to play with his crows."

"I remember seeing him playing and chasing the pigeons on the football field after bingo," Mrs. Kratsky said. The old rocking chair creaked with her weight, mixing with the steady beat of raindrops. "His laughter was contagious," she reminisced.

"From there, it gets a bit hazy," Jenna admitted. "There are some blanks that have yet to be filled in, but Jackson came to when the car stopped. Jackson chased Sean down the road. Some strangers in a blue truck appeared and Sean ran through the cornfield, Jackson chased after him.

"Somehow Sean saw what the strangers did to Jackson after they caught up with him. Sean still won't talk about it. He was so shook up from what he saw that he drove off the road outside Alton Oaks. Best we can guess, he walked the five miles back to Sheridan because he was back the next morning to set up the gym for bingo."

"And these guys in a blue truck?" my mom questioned.

Jenna shrugged.

"They were from Mexico," I shared flatly. "Jackson had been instrumental to them in trafficking items." I would like to say my voice held no emotion, but there was a hard edge to my words. "He'd been doing it for years, apparently. He and Jessica. He ticked someone off and now..." I didn't have to finish my sentence for the women on the porch to nod their heads while gasping or tisking under their breath.

"And Jesse?" Bailey asked.

"He's fine," I said almost grudgingly. "Jake said there's talk about the witness protection program. The men in the blue truck were just henchmen for something bigger."

"All in Alton Oaks," Mrs. Kratsky replied, shaking her head. "This beats the bathtub gin my grandpa got caught making in the 20's," she said in a way that lightened up the mood. Bless her heart.

"No!" my mother exclaimed, shocked. We knew the Kratskys were one of the first families in our town; that our families went way back together. This, however, was news to us.

"Oh, yes," she said with a smile. "My family were the first troublemakers in this town," she boasted and a small smile tugged on the corner of my lips.

"Well, I need to get to work," Jenna interrupted the conversation, looking at her silver wristwatch.

"And I need to get Eli to school," Bailey admitted, standing from her place on the bench below the living room window.

As Bailey and Jenna opened their umbrellas and descended the stairs, Mrs. Kratsky added, "We should go too, Rose, if you want to catch that sale at Prescott's."

My mother looked at me as if she was seeking permission to leave. I envied how easily these women slipped back into their normal lives; I don't think I ever could again. "I'm fine," I lied. Hesitantly, my mother rose from the creaking porch swing and followed Mrs. Kratsky to her golf cart, looking back at me at least three times.

After the hum of the cart disappeared into the rain and and whistling wind, Sadie and I sat in comfortable silence. The rain was the only sound until Rip began hammering away at eight o'clock.

I was surprised he showed up, despite the night we'd had, but he trudged up the porch stairs without a word as I filled my mother in on everything with Sadie by my side; before the Gossip Club showed up.

"Thank you," Sadie said as a breeze ruffled the remaining leaves on the oak tree nearby.

I didn't say anything; I didn't have to. "Thanks for not giving up even when I was about to," she added.

After several moments of me biting my thumbnail, Sadie kicked off the quilt and sat up. "I have to drive my dad to the airport," she shared, stretching. "Do you want to come with?"

I shook my head. The idea of squeezing between Sadie and her dad the whole way to Davenport did not appeal to me. Also, I was exhausted. I wanted nothing more than to be alone. There was a heavy weight darkening my world and I honestly didn't mind it. I didn't want to talk to people, or be social, or put on a mask of happiness. I wanted to be alone and to be left alone.

"I'll be back after, okay?" she said, squeezing me in a hug. We almost lost each other because of Jackson and it still hadn't completely hit me.

I watched her red pick-up truck disappear down Oak Street as I pulled the quilt up around me. I don't remember climbing the stairs or tossing the quilt from my shoulders on the journey, but I stood with my back to the closed door of my bedroom. The sound of rain hit my window and the roof leaked into a bucket on my desk with the tempo of a tango.

Just like the storm this morning, a downpour of the

crap I pushed away began to pummel my resolve. I had spent so much time and effort making sure Sadie was okay, that I ignored the emotions that I was supposed to feel with the death of Jackson: Anger, for coming into town with Jessica. Frustration, for leaving a mess I had to clean up after his death. Fear and shock about the world I had lived in without knowing how dangerous it was. Sadness, that I never got closure; a real conversation with him about what had happened. Guilt, for bringing so much danger to my loved ones. Sorrow, for how Jackson's life had ended; how our marriage had ended. Scared, because now I was truly alone—we were never going to be together again; no matter what, there would be no chance for reconciliation. Mourning, because he was, after all, my husband. I had loved him. We had had happy memories and memories were all they would ever be now.

As I sat on the old bamboo papasan chair in the dark corner of my room, on top of a pile of dirty clothes, I let the tears fall as I wrapped a still-damp bathrobe around me. The autumn breeze whistled through the drafty windows as if it was wailing along with me. I was suddenly grateful that both of my parents were out of the house and that Rip couldn't hear me over the pounding of his hammer.

After Jackson and I had exchanged vows in that clichéd Elvis-themed chapel in Las Vegas, we'd sat in the back of his van, with the doors wide open, and soaking in the sun. Jesse had snapped a picture of us with a disposable camera: our feet hanging over the bumper, hitting the dusty New Mexico license plate. We were so happy at that moment. Though the venue seemed odd and the ceremony spontaneous, it felt right. *He* felt right. Mournful tears poured down my face for that memory.

And then, nine months later, I was up late grading

papers, watching old episodes of *Frasier* on Netflix. The light from the TV made shadows dance across the walls of our tiny apartment as I checked my phone for the hundredth time. At ten o'clock I finally got a text back from Jackson saying that he was staying late at his studio—that he had finally found his muse! That was the first night he didn't come home. Now I wonder if his muse was actually another woman. Hot angry tears washed over my face for the unanswered questions.

"Charli?" His voice was meek and so tender, I barely recognized it was Rip as he knocked on my door.

Feeling as though I was caught doing something Jackson had probably done, guilt soaked me to the bone as I jumped up from the papasan and stumbled to the door, hoping Rip wouldn't open it. "Yeah?" I asked, feigning an upbeat tone. I let the palm of my sweaty, tear-drenched hands push against the wooden door, just in case.

"There's someone at the door for you," he reported without a hint of sass in his voice. I expected him to follow it up with an, "I'm not your butler," or "I'm going to start charging for extra services," but neither came.

The sleeves of my flannel shirt were drenched in tears, but I still tried to wipe my eyes as I planted my foot firmly against the door, still hoping he wouldn't try opening the door. "Thanks," I said, ignoring the cracks in my voice. "I'll be right down," I informed.

I held my breath as I listened intently. A few long moments later, I heard his heavy work boots descend across the old carpeting in the hallway. After I was sure he had gone downstairs, I left my room and scurried to the bathroom down the hall like a mouse in the daylight.

Meeting my gaze in the mirror was a chore. My whole face was swollen and red. I filled the sink with cold water and continually splashed my face with the frigid liquid, hoping that I'd see the old Charli each time I glanced up at the mirror.

When the front of my shirt was soaking and I was shivering in my bare feet on the cold tile, I defeatedly made my way back into my bedroom. I had borrowed a black sweater the last time I was at Alex's house and I saw it lying on the floor by the closet. I threw it on and turned up the hood, not daring to glance at my reflection before leaving my bedroom.

I noticed Rip had on a white face mask and was putting up new drywall over some brightly colored insulation. He only glanced at me and then dismissed me as if I wasn't there at all. After squeezing a bottle of adhesive to the studs, he began carefully putting the drywall in place.

Through the window I saw dark clouds that blotted out the weak morning sun. Every once in a while the shadows seemed to grow deeper and the air became cooler.

"Hey, Charli." I fully expected to see Sadie on the front porch before heading to the airport, or Alex, ready to take me to breakfast at Oakie's, which I would try my best to decline. I did not expect to see Jake standing at my front door, especially since he'd either be buried in paperwork or sent home for a well-deserved rest.

Nevertheless, he forced a smile as I opened the screen door and walked outside. He was dressed in wrinkled jeans, that were spotted in dark blue raindrops and a blue Cubs sweater that was stretched out around the neck. A large black umbrella sat open on the floorboards beside him, fresh with rain. For a few moments the rain poured harder and the noise it made on the tin roof of the shed traveled to the front porch like a loud garage band.

Jake stood under the porch light clean-shaven, which

was a pleasant shock. His hair had been cut and tamed as well. No longer was there that curl in his hair that frizzed up when he ran his hand through it with anxiety or frustration.

"Hi, Jake," I said, feigning a smile. Exhaustion was evident in my tone.

"How are you doin'?" he asked. His eyes swept across the ground as a slight breeze played with the leaves dancing in the corner. I dug my hands deep into the pockets of the large sweater as I looked from his feet to his shoulders. I still couldn't quite look him in the eye—I was hoping he wouldn't notice how horrible I looked in this altered morning sunlight.

"I'm okay, Jake," I said, looking down at my bare toes. "Thanks for being there last night." Guilt coated me like a weighted blanket. I had brought danger to this town—to my loved ones—through Jackson. It would take a long time to forgive myself for that, if ever.

"It's my job," he said modestly.

I curled my toes and felt the rough weathered wood on my soles. I was losing feeling in them. My gaze avoided his, not knowing what to say; what more could be said?

Rip interrupted the awkward moment by stepping outside, carrying his toolbox and wearing his black baseball cap backwards. "Hey, I'm heading out for an hour or two to meet with an associate about the chimney," he informed. He glanced at his cell phone as he squeezed past us.

Before hopping down the stairs, he turned with hesitation and added quickly, "Call if you need anything, Charli." He then darted across the lawn to his truck, without looking like he was in a hurry.

Jake hesitated when I turned back to his attention. "Charli, you know I'm here for you, no matter what, right?" he asked.

I nodded and shrugged at the same time, sending a mixed message.

"I know I haven't been..." he said, struggling to find the right word, "*available* to you lately. I cannot tell you how sorry I am." He reached and put a warm hand on my shoulder. "I know I betrayed a trust, but we go way back, don't we?"

I nodded again, staring at his black boots that were wet and splashed with mud.

"I'll always be there whenever you need me. I promise you that," he said and squeezed my shoulder lightly, then dropped his hand so it returned to his side. His body language shifted and he admitted, "Hearing that gunshot when you were on the phone last night scared the—well, it scared me. More than anything. Just—" He cut himself off with a sigh.

Emotion overcame me once again and I wanted to give him a hug, for him to understand that we were okay, but I knew I couldn't handle it.

"Jake, we're okay," I said, finally meeting his gaze, if only for a second. I wish I could've said more, or cracked a joke to lighten the mood, but I couldn't.

"You still have my six?" he asked, good-natured. I thought back to when I saved his life right after he saved mine this spring.

I nodded with a small, yet genuine smile.

Satisfied, he opened his umbrella and turned to leave. "Bye, Charli," he said simply and it reminded me of when we were kids. His mother would call him home for dinner and he'd turn on the same spot, wave a hand in my direction, and yell those two words.

"Jake?" I called after him. He turned around on the bottom step. "Thanks," I said before turning to retreat inside.

I didn't wait to see his reaction or wait for a response. I pulled open the door, letting the screeching hinges protest, and closed the storm door behind me with a thud. For a few moments I stood there with my back against the door, staring at the house around me.

I was lucky to be able to come home to my childhood home, not many people my age had that opportunity. Memories of flying down the stairs in a laundry basket, or colorful "Happy Birthday" banners hanging in the dinning room flew around me. I was even more lucky to live in a house that four generations before me lived in as well. If these walls could talk...

My feet wandered into the living room and I looked around at how oddly bright the room was compared to its history of darkness. Most of the furniture had been moved to the shed. Rip had put new insulation in the outer walls and it looked like new wiring had been installed, based on the gaping hole that used to be the window seat. The green paisley-like wallpaper that covered the interior walls had been entirely scraped off and an electric sander sat on the floor nearby. There were going to be so many more memories made in this room.

The wind wheezed through the fireplace and a draft crept throughout the room. The drastic temperature change was probably due to the lack of furniture, but I wanted to make sure the damper was shut so that the chill didn't creep upstairs in the middle of the night.

Rip had stacked some lumber and a piece of drywall against the fireplace. For a moment I was going to ditch this task due to the amount of effort it would take, but I watched as my body decided against my brain.

Putting the drywall aside, I accidentally knocked down a two-by-four. I winced as it hit the stone fireplace and fell to the floor with a clatter. To my horror, part of the brick fireplace knocked loose and fell to the ground as well. Of course, I would make more work and a bigger mess by trying to help. That's how my life seems to work out!

Sighing in frustration, I turned on a nearby clamp light to make sure I could fix the damage before Rip could give me a hard time about it. I placed the two-by-four carefully against the wall and bent down to inspect the pieces of brick that fell.

It was probably the original brick from when my great-great grandfather built the house and it was crumbling due to age. No doubt it was beyond preservation, but that wasn't up to me. It was probably up to the person Rip was meeting with right now. I picked up the biggest piece of brick and wondered if I could set it into place without too much attention being brought to it.

My eyebrows furrowed in confusion as I looked at where the brick had come from; the space behind it was hallow. Unsure if that was normal, I carefully placed my hand inside in case I did more damage than I thought. To my surprise, a small thin leather bound book fell onto the floor when I pulled my hand out of the cavity.

For a moment, I looked down at the ground, through the dust that filled the air, confused. When the book collapsed onto the wooden floorboards, it opened to the first page. In long sweeping letters, faded black ink spelled out: *The Journal of Andrew Alton.*

THE END

ABOUT THE AUTHOR

 Megan Rivers is a former world adventurer and life-long writer who graduated from Northern Michigan University with a degree in writing and literature. She recently returned to live in her hometown of Evergreen Park, Illinois, with her spoiled pup Gracie. Megan teaches both outdoor and environmental education. When not writing, she loves to visit thrift stores, bask in the outdoors, get lost in a good book, or cook delectable vegan dishes.

The Scarecrow's Secret is the third in her Alton Oaks Mystery series. The first two books are *Murder in Aisle Three* and *School's Out for Murder.*